D0496200

BORKMANN'S POINT

THE INSPECTOR AND SILENCE

Also by Håkan Nesser

BORKMANN'S POINT
THE RETURN
THE MIND'S EYE
WOMAN WITH BIRTHMARK

HÅKAN NESSER

THE INSPECTOR AND SILENCE

AN INSPECTOR VAN VEETEREN MYSTERY

Translated from the Swedish by
Laurie Thompson

PAN BOOKS

First published in Great Britain 2010 by Mantle

This edition published 2011 by Pan Books
an imprint of Pan Macmillan, a division of Macmillan Publishers Limited
Pan Macmillan, 20 New Wharf Road, London N1 9RR
Basingstoke and Oxford
Associated companies throughout the world
www.panmacmillan.com

ISBN 978-1-4472-5704-2

Copyright © Håkan Nesser 1997
English translation copyright © Laurie Thompson 2010

The right of Håkan Nesser to be identified as the
author of this work has been asserted by him in accordance
with the Copyright, Designs and Patents Act 1988.

Originally published in 1997 as *Kommissarien och tystnaden* by
Albert Bonniers förlag, Stockholm

1 3 5 7 9 8 6 4 2

A CIP catalogue record for this book is available from
the British Library.

Typeset by Intype Libra Ltd
Printed and bound by CPI Group (UK) Ltd, Croydon, CR0 4YY

Visit **www.panmacmillan.com** to read more about all our books
and to buy them. You will also find features, author interviews and
news of any author events, and you can sign up for e-newsletters
so that you're always first to hear about our new releases.

Imagine a twelve-year-old-girl.
Imagine her being attacked, raped and murdered.
Take your time.
Then imagine God.

M. Barin, poet

ONE

15 JULY

1

The girl in bed number twelve woke up early.

A summer morning. The gentle light of dawn sneaked in through the inadequate curtains. Started thawing out the night, a bit at a time. Levering up the darkness out of corners, prying into the other girls' innocent dreams. Their contented sniffling. She lay there for a while, listening to them. Trying to identify them. Kathrine was lying on her back as usual, snoring gently through her open mouth. Belle was hissing like a snake. To her right, Marieke was puffing away; one arm was dangling down by the side of the bed, and her mop of red hair was spread like a fan over her pillow. A drop of saliva trembled in the corner of her mouth – perhaps she should creep over to her and use a corner of the sheet to wipe it away? But she desisted.

She would have liked to tell Marieke what she was going to do. Marieke if nobody else. Say something; leave a message, anything. But she still hadn't made up her mind the previous evening. She'd been humming and hawing. It wasn't an easy decision to take. She'd lain there, brooding over it; tossing and turning and making the iron-framed bed groan and creak until well into the night – both Marieke and Ruth had wondered if she was ill, and Belle had begged her several times to stop making such a row.

Belle was a bit of a pain, but her dad was a close friend of Yellinek's so it was advisable to keep well in with her. That's what they said, at least. But then, they said all kinds of things at the Waldingen camp.

Anyway, she'd been tossing and turning. She'd no idea when she'd eventually fallen asleep, nor did she know what time it was now – but her body was telling her that she hadn't had all that much sleep. In any case, now the moment had arrived – and . . . ah well, she'd better get up. Her internal alarm clock had worked as it always did; but of course there was no reason why it should continue to keep her awake. No reason at all.

She carefully folded back the heavy duvet and sat up. Dug out her jeans, T-shirt and trainers from the bedside cupboard and dressed quickly. Noticed that the pain in her stomach had returned, but brushed it to one side with the aid of her anger.

Her anger and sense of justice.

Scraped together the rest of her belongings in con-trolled haste: not easy to find room for everything, but she managed it. Fastened her rucksack and crept out. The door creaked as usual as she opened it, and some of the steps sighed unhappily when she trod on them, but in less than half a minute she was outside.

Scampered over the dew-laden grass and up towards the edge of the forest, stopping only when she had crossed over the little ridge and descended into the first of the hollows. Out of sight from the buildings, and out of reach.

She paused for a while among the blueberry sprigs, shivering in what remained of the chilly night air while she worked out points of the compass and directions. Noticed that her teeth were chattering. If she kept going straight ahead through the trees, she must sooner or later come to the road, she knew that. But it was a long way. Even if she managed to stick to a more or less straight line it would take half an hour at the very least, and of course she couldn't be certain that she'd be able to avoid going round in circles. By no means certain. She had lived in cities all her life: being close to nature among all these trees was not the environment she was used to.

She was playing away from home, you might say.

In normal circumstances she could have said a prayer, of course. Prayed to God and asked Him to stand by her and help her along her way; but it didn't seem right this morning.

Not right, and somehow not really honest.

God had started to look different recently. Yes, that's roughly what it seemed like. Become big; difficult and unapproachable, and – even if she didn't like to accept the thought – a bit frightening. The gentle, bearded, grandad-figure of her childhood was swathed in shadows.

In darkness.

And now that she came to think about it, she realized that it was because of that very darkness that she was standing here in among the blueberry sprigs, wondering what to do next.

Hesitating and fighting against her fear and her anger. And her sense of justice, as already mentioned.

Yes, that was why.

The terrain sloped down to the right. Towards the lake and the winding dirt road leading to Fingher's farm, where they used to take it in turns to go every evening, to fetch the milk. And potatoes and vegetables and eggs.

Always two groups of four, each with one of the rickety carts, and with Yellinek in the lead. Nobody could really understand why it was necessary for Yellinek always to be there when they went to the farm. Surely one of the sisters could have done it? Although it could have been to protect them from danger. That's probably why. Fingher's farm was the only contact they had with the Other World, as Yellinek used to call it in his talks, the ones he held both in the mornings and every evening.

The Other World?

Now I'm standing in the Other World, she thought. I've only ventured a couple of hundred metres into it, and already I'm not sure which way to go. Perhaps everything really was like Yellinek said it was, after all? Perhaps it really was Yellinek's God who was the real God, and not her own – her kind and forgiving and almost a little bit child-like God, full of joy?

The hell it is, she muttered to herself with another shudder, this time mainly to reinforce her thoughts. What's the point of a God who isn't gentle and kind?

But what she would do if she did eventually manage to get to the main road – well, that was something neither she nor either of the Gods could answer.

Something will turn up, as her grandma used to say. I'll think of something. She cast one more glance back over the ridge, towards the buildings; all she could see sticking up over the trees was the very top of the pointed roof of the dining room.

And the big, black cross, of course, the one they'd nailed together the very first day they arrived. She took a deep breath, turned her back on all that and began to make her way down towards the lake. Best to stick to the familiar dirt road after all.

★

She emerged from the trees close to the enormous birch that she and Marieke had discussed carving their names into before they left.

Always assuming they could find a way of slipping out unnoticed, that was the problem. They would have to steal twenty minutes from the Pure Life, sneak out and then back in without being seen. They didn't really fancy their chances of actually doing it, it was just one of those things people said; but here she was now, in fact, rubbing her hand over the smooth, white bark.

The Pure Life? she thought. The Good Shepherd?

The Other World?

A lot of crap.

The word came into her mind just as quickly as it had done yesterday. Crap. She hadn't been able to hold it back then, it had flown out of her mouth like an angry and hot-headed little swallow, and in a flash it had changed into a big cloud.

Yes, that's exactly what it was like. A dark and threatening cloud hanging over the heads of everybody in the Hall of Life. It made the girls hold their breath, and Yellinek's pale eyes slowly turn to stare at her for several seconds that felt like days.

'I want to have a word with you afterwards,' he'd said eventually, then turned his eyes away again and continued talking in his usual low voice. About Purity and Whiteness and Nakedness and all that stuff.

Then later on in the White Room.

But not even there did he waste many words on her. Merely stated the fact.

'The Devil, my girl. You have the Devil inside you. Tomorrow we'll drive it out.'

Then he'd sent her off to bed with a weary gesture.

She had heard about driving out devils, but had no idea how they went about it. She'd thought it was something that only grown-ups did, but evidently not. Anybody could be possessed by the Devil, even a little child; that was something she'd learned last night.

And now it was going to be driven out. That was bound to be an unpleasant experience. Much worse than the caning to drive out sin – and although she had been here for two weeks now, she still hadn't grown accustomed to that. After every session she needed to cry a bit in private, but she hadn't noticed any of the other girls needing to do that.

And now the need to cry had struck her again. Without any warning, she felt a burning sensation in her throat and then the tears started to flow and she had to sit down by the side of the road. Just for a few moments to let it run its course and go away. It was silly, wandering around in the middle of the road and sobbing. Even if it couldn't have been later than six or half past – and even though there was virtually no risk of meeting another soul – it was silly.

She found a handkerchief in her rucksack and blew her nose. Remained sitting there for a few minutes, to be on the safe side, and it was just as she was about to stand up and continue on her way that she heard a twig snap close by, and she quickly realized that she was by no means as alone as she had imagined.

TWO

17–18 JULY

2

'And who's saying that?' wondered Jung as he opened a can of Coca-Cola. 'That he's intending to pack it in, I mean?'

Ewa Moreno shrugged.

'I don't know who started it,' she said. 'But Rooth and Krause were talking about it in the canteen yesterday . . . I'm not surprised, if it's true.'

'By what?' asked Jung. 'What doesn't surprise you?' He took a few large swigs and tried not to belch.

'That he's had enough, of course. He must have been at it for thirty-five years, at least. How long are you intending to keep going for?'

Jung considered the question while discreetly breathing out some carbon dioxide fumes through his nose.

'There's always a chance of getting shot before your time's up, that's for sure,' he said. 'If you're lucky. No, I try to keep fit and healthy by not thinking about such matters. Have some of this.'

He handed over the can and Moreno emptied it in one go.

'It's incredibly hot,' she said. 'I must have drunk three litres since this morning. You could always ask Münster – if anybody knows, he will.'

Jung nodded.

'How old is he?'

'Who? Münster?'

'The chief inspector, of course. He can't be sixty yet, surely?'

'No idea,' said Moreno. 'How much longer are we going to have to hang around here? Nothing's happening. Apart from the fact that my brain's starting to boil.'

Jung checked his watch.

'Another hour, according to our instructions.'

'Drive round one more time,' said Moreno. 'At least that'll start a bit of air flowing. There's not much point in sitting here and getting sunstroke. Or what do you say, Inspector?'

'One has to be prepared to die while doing one's duty,' said Jung, starting the car. 'That's what it says in the rule book. I think it would be a damned shame if he were to leave . . . He can be a pain at times, but so what? Where do you want me to drive to?'

'To the snack bar, so we can buy some more Coke,' said Moreno.

'Your word is my command,' said Jung. 'But I think we should get something non-fizzy this time. Look at that, for Christ's sake! Mind you, it's been in full sunlight . . .'

He pointed at the gigantic thermometer on the gable end of the swimming baths.

'Thirty-seven degrees,' said Moreno.

'Exactly! Body temperature, more or less.'

'I'm thirsty,' said Moreno.

Chief Inspector Van Veeteren clambered into his car and closed his eyes.

'Thát woman!' he muttered. 'I've given that woman my life.'

He groaned. The car had been parked in the square for over an hour in roasting hot sunshine, and when he touched the steering wheel he smelt a whiff of burned flesh. Gehenna, he thought. That's where we all end up.

Sweat was pouring off him. Down his face, the back of his neck, under his arms. He wound down the windows and carefully wiped his brow with a less than immaculate handkerchief.

He contemplated the soaking wet rag. There were traces of cold sweat there as well.

'Twenty-five years of my life!' he said to himself,

correcting his earlier claim. Started the car and swung out from his parking space. 'A quarter of a century!'

And now she had tried to steal two more weeks. He began to recall the conversation in detail.

A holiday cottage out at Maalvoort. Well, that's great . . . Plenty of space. Four rooms plus kitchen. Dunes and beach and the sea . . . Renate and him. Jess and the twins . . .

He wondered how carefully she had planned it all. They had been talking for quite some time; everything had been going fine, from his point of view, it seemed – and then the questions and the proposal had come out of the blue . . . He ought to have known. For Christ's sake, he ought to have known by now! He would also be on holiday in August, wouldn't he? Just when Jess would be coming home at last for a few weeks. The grandchildren and Grandma and Grandad all together, one big family, what good fortune . . . ! (Huh, misfortune more like! Very unfortunate, and he couldn't help smiling at the unfortunate fortune, despite everything.) The cottage was on the big side; she'd been late in making a booking and most places were already taken. If he wanted to have time to himself, that wouldn't be a problem, there was plenty of room for him to be alone. Both indoors and outdoors . . .

Oh yes, this had been planned all right. It was a trap, he

thought. A typical carefully laid trap by his ex-wife, a spider luring the unwary into her web. Hell and damnation!

He switched on the stereo, then switched it off again.

Jess and the kids . . .

'I'm afraid not,' he'd said.

And Erich had promised to come as well, for a few days at least.

'I'm afraid not, my dear,' he'd said. 'You're too late. I'm already booked up.'

'Booked up?' Her eyebrows had been raised in chastened despair. 'You, booked up already?'

'Crete!' He blurted out the first place that came into his head. 'Two weeks, from the first onwards.'

She didn't believe him. He could see that right away; one eyebrow sunk back to scratch position, but the other remained dangling from her forehead like a silent reprimand.

'Crete,' he said again, quite unnecessarily. 'Rethymnon, but I'm thinking of going down to the south coast as well . . . and, well—'

'Are you going on your own?'

'On my own? Dammit all, of course I'm going on my own! How the hell could you think otherwise?'

He bumped against the kerb of a traffic island with his left front wheel, and cursed to himself.

A quarter of a century. Then five years of freedom, but

still she was there, setting her traps. What was she really after? He shuddered, despite the summer heat. Wiped the back of his neck with the handkerchief as well. Turned into Rejmer Plejn and was fortunate enough to find an empty parking space under one of the elms.

Crete? he thought as he got out of the car. Why not?

Yes indeed, *why not*? If you could redeem your sins by doing penance, it should be child's play to conjure up a retroactive truth from a white lie.

I'm on good form linguistically today, he thought. Unfortunate fortune! Retroactive truth! . . . I ought to start writing my memoirs PDQ.

He crossed over the square. Inserted a toothpick into his mouth and marched into the travel agent's on the corner.

The woman standing at the counter had her back turned towards him, and it was a few seconds before he realized who she was. Her chestnut-brown hair had become slightly more chestnutty since he'd seen her last, and her voice more resonant.

I should damned well think so.

Ulrike Fremdli. When he met her the previous – and only – time, her husband had just been murdered. He made a rapid calculation and concluded it must have been in February. Last February – that chilly, godforsaken month.

The blessed time of hopelessness, as Mahler used to call it. They had been sitting in an ordinary, cosy living room in an ordinary, cosy terrace house in Loewingen. He and Ulrike Fremdli, newly widowed. He had asked her the usual, clinically disconsolate questions and he had been impressed by the way in which she handled them.

Handled both the questions and the grief and shock she must have been feeling.

When he left her, he had realized that she was a woman he could easily have fallen in love with. Thirty years ago. At the time when he was still capable of falling in love. He had thought about it quite a lot afterwards. Yes, it certainly would have been possible.

If he hadn't already given away his life to somebody else, that is.

And now she was standing here, booking a holiday. Ulrike Fremdli. Fifty and a bit, he would have thought. With her hair recently dyed even more chestnut brown.

There were certain patterns . . .

He took a queue ticket and sat down on the narrow tubular-steel armchair behind her, without greeting her. Of course, there was no reason to think that she would remember him as clearly as he remembered her. Or would even remember him at all, come to that. He waited. Shifted the toothpick to the right side of his mouth and tried to look as if he wasn't listening.

As if he were just a very ordinary customer wanting to book a package holiday. Or an unusually sweaty part of the furniture.

But he certainly was listening. Ears cocked. At the same time he could feel a worrying sensation beginning to nag at him. Both in his gut and behind his larynx, where he had long been convinced that the soul was situated. In his case, at least.

Because Crete was what was being discussed. As plain as a pikestaff, he'd realized that right away. The attractively sun-tanned travel agent was talking about Theseus and Ariadne and the Village of Widows. About Spili and Matala and the Samaria Gorge.

And now about Rethymnon.

Chief Inspector Van Veeteren gulped. Took out his handkerchief and wiped the back of his neck again. Despite the slow-moving fans whisking the air under the ceiling, it was as hot as a baking oven.

'You mustn't underestimate the currents,' stressed the bronzed young man.

Certainly not, Van Veeteren thought.

'The Christos Hotel,' suggested the young Adonis. 'Simple, but well run. Situated in the middle of the old town . . . Only a minute's walk to the Venetian harbour.'

Ulrike Fremdli nodded. The demigod smiled.

'Leaving on the first, then? Two weeks?'

Van Veeteren felt an attack of giddiness rising up inside him. An almost pubertal feeling of dizziness. He put down the magazine and stood up quickly. I must get a breath of fresh air, he thought. Hell's bells! I can feel a heart attack coming on.

Out in the street he paused under a lime tree. Spat out the toothpick and bit his bottom lip hard. Confirmed that this did not wake him up, and hence he had not been dreaming.

For Christ's sake, he thought. I'm too old for this sort of thing.

He bought a bottle of mineral water at the newspaper stall and drank it all in one gulp. Then paused for another minute, thinking things over. It would be silly to get carried away, he told himself.

But it would be even sillier to ignore all the signs that are dangled in front of me. By the way, seeing as I'm here . . .

He emerged into the sunshine again. Walked quickly and jauntily over the square and turned into Kellnerstraat. Passed by a few second-hand bookshops before stopping at the corner of Kupinski's Alley. Wiped the sweat from his brow and looked hard at the over-full display window.

Carefully, as if studying a poker hand.

Yes, the notice was still there.

Assistant required.
Partnership a possibility.
F. Krantze

It must have been hanging there now for – he worked it out – six weeks. He breathed a sigh of relief. Yes, half the summer must have passed since he first saw it.

He hesitated again before slowly walking back towards the square. Chewed at a toothpick and contemplated the Art Nouveau facades dating from the turn of the century. Weather-beaten, but still looking good. The leafy lime trees casting shade over the pavements. Yorrick's pavement cafe on the corner. Winderblatt's directly opposite. A large, panting St Bernard dog under one of the tables, its tongue reaching out as far as the kerb.

Oh yes, he thought. I sure as hell could see myself living here.

And by the time he got into his car, he had made up his mind.

If that notice is still there in August . . . well, I'll go ahead and do it.

It was as easy as that.

It was then even easier to drive hell for leather back home to Klagenburg, pick up the telephone and order a two-week package holiday to Rethymnon, Crete . . . the Christos Hotel, which had been recommended to him by a good friend. Single room. Departing 1 August, returning on the 15th.

When he hung up, he glanced at his watch. It was 11.40, 17 July.

Not much point going to the police station before lunch, he decided, and tried to feel a little regret. Didn't succeed very well. He wandered around his flat, fanning himself with yesterday's *Allgemejne*. Not that it did much good. He sighed. Pulled off his sticky shirt, fetched a beer from the fridge and inserted a Pergolesi CD into the hi-fi.

Life? he wondered.

Arbitrary or well-planned?

3

'The heat makes people less inclined to commit crimes,' said deBries.

'Don't talk crap,' said Reinhart. 'The facts are the precise opposite, of course.'

'Meaning what?' wondered Rooth, with a yawn.

'They just don't have the strength,' said deBries.

'Of course they do,' said Reinhart. 'The hotter it gets, the lower the defences – and human beings are criminal animals at heart. Read *The Stranger*. Read Schopenhauer.'

'I haven't the strength to read anything,' said Rooth. 'Not when it's as hot as this, for fuck's sake.'

'And people's urges become more urgent,' said Reinhart, lighting his pipe. 'No wonder. Just look at all those women running around town half-naked – it's not surprising that frustrated studs throw their inhibitions aside.'

'Frustrated studs?' said Rooth. 'What the hell . . . ?'

'Hmm,' muttered deBries. 'Sex murderers will obviously

be inspired to act in weather like this – but at least we haven't had any such cases yet.'

'Just wait a bit,' said Reinhart. 'The ridge of high pressure is only four days old. Where the hell's the chief inspector, by the way? I thought we were supposed to have a meeting after lunch. It's nearly half past one.'

DeBries shrugged.

'He's probably playing badminton with Münster.'

'No,' said Rooth, tucking into an apple. 'Münster was in my office a few minutes ago.'

'Don't speak with your mouth full,' said Reinhart.

'He'd say next to nothing if he didn't,' said deBries.

'Shut your trap,' said Rooth.

'Exactly,' said Reinhart.

The door opened and Van Veeteren entered, followed by Münster.

'Good morning, Chief Inspector. Slept well?'

'I was somewhat delayed by the heat,' Van Veeteren explained as he flopped down onto his desk chair. 'Well?'

There was a moment's silence.

'What do you mean by "Well?"?' asked Rooth and took another bite.

Van Veeteren sighed.

'Report!' he said. 'What the hell are you all planning to do? Reinhart first. The Vallaste pyromaniac, I assume?'

Reinhart knitted his brow and sucked at his pipe.

Nodded rather vaguely. The arson attack in Vallaste had been occupying the police for two and a half years now, and the investigation had been put on ice several times; but when there was nothing else of a serious nature going on, he usually unfroze it again. He had been the officer in charge, and it was his reputation that suffered as long as the culprit remained at large.

There were not many officers left in the force who thought along those lines, as Van Veeteren knew only too well; but he knew that Reinhart did.

'I have a few loose ends,' he admitted. 'I thought it might be worthwhile looking a bit more closely at them. Unless there's something else that craves the attention of a somewhat bigger brain than the average . . .'

'Hmm,' said Münster.

'Certain parts of the body swell in hot weather,' said deBries.

'No doubt,' muttered Van Veeteren. 'Okay, start rummaging around among the loose ends.'

He leaned back and contemplated his subordinates with a resigned expression. They were a bit of a motley crew, in outward appearance at least. DeBries had got divorced a month ago, and had made use of his first few weeks of freedom to renew his wardrobe in an attempt to make himself look younger – the result had been something reminiscent of an ageing and depraved yuppie from the eighties. Or a resuscitated and semi-detoxicated rock artist from the sixties, as Reinhart had suggested. The Woodstock Mummy. As for Rooth, possibly as a reaction to the heatwave, he had finally got round to shaving off his straggly beard, and the lower part of his face, now as smooth as a baby's bottom, stood out in sharp contrast to the tanned cheeks, forehead and whisky-fuelled wrinkles.

He looks like the missing link, Van Veeteren thought.

As for Münster – well, he looked like Münster, albeit with sweaty patches under his arms; and Reinhart had always reminded the chief inspector of what he no doubt really was, deep down: an intellectual docker.

Van Veeteren himself was hardly a thing of beauty. But luckily one has an inner self, he consoled himself, and yawned.

'And when do you gentlemen intend going on holiday?' he asked. 'Take it in turns.' He might get more sense out of them than asking them to report on their work plans.

'The fifth,' said Reinhart.

'Next week,' said deBries. 'I'd be grateful if you don't put me on some case or other.'

'Same here,' said Münster. 'But no doubt Jung and Heinemann will be able to run the show in August, if something crops up. And Rooth and Moreno, of course.'

'*Natürlich*,' said Rooth.

'Can you speak French?' deBries wondered. 'Maybe you've done a correspondence course?'

Rooth scratched at his phantom beard.

'Fuck off,' he said. 'That's a German proverb. Shall we continue with this hotel burglary, or do you have something else lined up for us?'

'Be off with you,' said Van Veeteren. 'But make sure you arrest Pompers and Lutherson. Everybody knows they did it.'

'Thank you for the tip,' said deBries.

He and Rooth left the room.

'People get irritable in this weather,' commented Münster when the door had closed behind them. 'It's not surprising, really.'

'That's exactly what I've been saying,' said Reinhart. 'Is there anything else, or can I leave? You can always phone if anything crops up.'

'Be off with you,' said Van Veeteren again, and Reinhart trudged off.

Münster walked over to the window and looked out. Over the town, and the heat trembling over the rooftops.

'Let's hope we don't suddenly find ourselves with a murder on our hands now, or something of the sort,' he said, leaning his forehead against the glass. 'Just before the holiday. I remember what it was like two years ago—'

'Shush!' The chief inspector interrupted him. 'Don't

wake up the evil spirits. Incidentally, I'm booked up for the first half of August. Impossible to change it. I shall delegate every corpse that turns up during the next few weeks to you and Reinhart.'

Perhaps for ever in fact, he thought. He kicked off his shoes and began leafing listlessly through the piles of paper on his desk.

'Fair enough,' said Münster. 'I'll be incommunicado from Monday onwards anyway.'

The chief inspector inserted a new toothpick and clasped his hands behind his head.

'It would be good if a nice little two-week case were to crop up now,' he said. 'Preferably away from town, something I could sort out on my own.'

'I bet it would,' said Münster.

'Eh?'

'I bet it would be nice,' said Münster.

'And what exactly do you mean by that?'

'Nothing special,' said Münster. 'Something by the seaside, perhaps?'

Van Veeteren thought it over.

'Hmm,' he said. 'No. I'll be damned if somewhere by a little lake wouldn't be preferable. I'll be off to the Med after that anyway . . . Do you happen to have your racket handy?'

Münster sighed.

'Of course. But isn't it a bit on the hot side for that?'

'Hot?' snorted Van Veeteren. 'On Crete the average temperature at this time of year is forty degrees. At least. So, shall we get going?'

'All right, since you asked me so nicely.' Münster sighed again, leaving the window.

'I'll treat you to a beer afterwards,' Van Veeteren assured him generously. He stood up and made a couple of practice shots. 'If you win, that is,' he added.

'I think I can say thank you for the beer in advance,' said Münster.

He's in an unusually good mood, he thought as they took the lift down to the garage. Almost human. Something absolutely extraordinary must have happened to him today.

Spili, the chief inspector was thinking at the same time. The source of youth . . . half an hour up the mountain in a hired car from Rethymnon . . . the wind blowing through her hair, and all that.

Why not?

And then Krantze's antiquarian bookshop.

4

From a purely physical point of view, the morning of 18 July was perfect.

The sky was cloudless, the air clear and still cool; the dark water of the lake was mirror-like, and Sergeant Merwin Kluuge completed his run round the alder-lined shore, nearly seven kilometres, in a new record time: 26 minutes and 55 seconds.

He paused to get his breath back down by the marina, did a few stretching exercises then jogged gently up to the terraced house, where he took a shower, and woke up his blonde-haired wife by carefully and lovingly caressing her stomach, inside which she had been carrying the fruit and aspirations of his life for the past six months.

The terraced house was even more recent. Barely eight weeks had passed since they had moved in – with the kind assistance of his parents-in-law's savings; and he was still overcome by feelings of innocent wonder when he woke up in the mornings. When he put his feet on the wine-red wall-to-wall carpet in the bedroom. When he tiptoed from room to room and stroked the embossed wallpaper and pine panelling, which still exuded a whiff of newly sawn timber hinting at unimaginable possibilities and well-deserved success. And whenever he watered the flower beds or mowed the little lawn flanked by the trees, he could not help but feel warm and genuine gratitude to life itself.

Without warning, everything had suddenly fallen into place. They had been shunted onto a bright and sun-soaked new track, with himself and Deborah as the only carriages of any significance in a solidly built and smooth-running train heading into the future. All loose ends had been tied together when it became clear that Deborah was pregnant – or rather when that fact became public knowledge. They had married two weeks later, and now, on this lovely summer morning, when Merwin Kluuge toyed gently with the soft – and to the naked eye almost invisible – hairs on his wife's rounded stomach, he was filled with a sensation bordering on the religious.

'Tea or coffee?' he asked softly.

'Tea,' she replied without opening her eyes. 'You know I haven't touched a drop of coffee for three months now. Why do you ask?'

Oh yes, of course, Kluuge thought, and went into the kitchen to prepare the breakfast tray.

They had breakfast together in bed, watching the early

morning programme on their new 27-inch television set, and once again Kluuge ran his fingers gently over the tense skin, feeling for kicks and any other sign of life from Merwin junior. At precisely 07.45 he left his home and his married bliss.

He wheeled his twelve-gear bicycle out of the garage, clipped back his trousers, fixed his briefcase on the luggage carrier, and set off.

Exactly eleven minutes later he came to a halt in Kleinmarckt. The square was still more or less deserted; three or four market traders were busy opening up their stalls next to the town hall, arranging displays of fruit and vegetables. A few fat pigeons were strutting around the fountain, for want of anything else to do. Kluuge parked his bicycle in the stand outside the police station, secured it with a couple of stout locks, and wiped a drop of sweat from his brow. Then he walked through the semi-transparent glass doors, greeted Miss Miller in reception, and took possession of the chief of police's office.

He sat down behind the impressively large desk, removed his bicycle clips and turned to the first page of the notepad beside the telephone.

Missing girl??? it said.

He looked out of the window, which Miss Miller had opened slightly, and gazed at the blossoming elder. The chief of police had informed him that it was an elder, but anybody could see that it was blossoming.

From a purely physical point of view it was still a perfect morning; but as far as Merwin Kluuge's duties as acting chief of police were concerned, there was beyond doubt a cloud on the horizon.

At least one.

Precisely one.

'Holiday,' Chief of Police Malijsen had said, tapping him on the collarbone with two fingers. 'I hope to God you're fully aware of what the word holiday means. Peace and quiet. Being alone and left to yourself. Coniferous forests, mountain air and new waters to fish in. I've invested my hard-earned wages in hiring this damned cottage, and I have every intention of staying there for three weeks, provided the Japs don't attack us. Is that clear, Sergeant Kluuge?'

For the last thirty years Chief of Police Malijsen's credo had been that sooner or later the Japanese would inflict upon the world a new – but much better executed – Pearl Harbor, and he rarely missed an opportunity to mention it.

'You'll be in charge of the shop. It's time for you to stand on your own two feet and become more than a mere paper shuffler and a thorn in the side of Edward Marckx.'

Gathering together and sending off the monthly reports

from the Sorbinowo police district really did comprise the major part of Kluuge's regular duties; that had been the case ever since he first took up his post just over three years ago, and would no doubt continue to be until the day – still ten years or more away – when Malijsen reached an age enabling him to resign his job and devote all his time to pleasure, sitting in front of the television. Or tying fishing flies. Or building defences to foil the increasingly inevitable attack from the slant-eyed yellow hordes from the east.

According to Kluuge's view of the world and its inhabitants, Chief of Police Malijsen had a screw loose, an opinion probably shared by a few other Sorbinowo residents, but by no means all. Despite being a bit of a one-off character, Malijsen had the reputation of being the right man for his job, and for keeping the gap between right and wrong, between upright local citizens and crooks, open and wide. Even such a dodgy character as Edward Marckx – arsonist, jailbird, hot-tempered drug addict and violent brawler – had once, presumably in connection with one of his many brushes with the law, expressed his grudging admiration of the chief of police:

'A particularly obnoxious bastard, but with a heart in his body and a hole in his arse!'

Perhaps Kluuge could sign up to the second part of that assessment.

On his way out of the door, Malijsen had paused and

been serious for a few moments. Checked the torrent of words and raised an eyebrow.

'Are you sure you can cope with this?'

Kluuge had snorted quietly. Not rudely. Not nervously.

'Yes, of course.'

Nevertheless Malijsen had looked a bit doubtful and taken a card out of his wallet.

'For Christ's sake don't disturb me unless you really have to! There's a public telephone in the village, of course, but I need these weeks to get over Lilian.'

Lilian was Malijsen's wife, stricken by cancer; after many years of more or less unbearable suffering she had finally given up the ghost and departed from this world. Drugged up to the eyeballs, and a shadow of a shadow . . . That was in the middle of March. Kluuge had attended the funeral with Deborah, who had noted that the chief of police had shed the occasional tear, but not excessively.

'If the shit hits the fan, you can always get in touch with VV instead,' Malijsen explained. 'He's an old colleague of mine, and he owes me a favour.'

He handed over the card and Kluuge put it in his breast pocket without so much as glancing at it. A quarter of an hour later, he sat down behind the imposingly large desk, leaned back and looked forward to three weeks of calm and prestigious professional activity.

That was six days ago. Last Friday. Today was Thursday. The first call had come last Tuesday.

The second one yesterday.

Oh hell, Kluuge thought and stared at the card with the very familiar name. He drummed on it with his finger, thinking back to what happened two days ago.

'There's a woman who'd like to speak to you.'

He noted that Miss Miller avoided addressing him as 'Chief of Police'. She'd been doing that right from the start; at first it had annoyed him somewhat, but now he just ignored it.

'A telephone call?'

'Yes.'

'Okay, put her through.'

He lifted the receiver and pressed the white button.

'Is that the police?'

'Yes.'

'A little girl has disappeared.'

The voice was so faint that he had to strain his ears to catch what she was saying.

'A little girl? Who am I speaking to?'

'I can't tell you that. But a little girl has disappeared from Waldingen.'

'Waldingen? Can you speak a bit louder?'

'The Pure Life Camp at Waldingen.'

'You mean that sect?'

'Yes. A little girl has disappeared from their confirmation camp in Waldingen. I can't say any more. You must look into it.'

'Hang on a minute. Who are you? Where are you calling from?'

'I must stop now.'

'Just a minute . . .'

She had hung up. Kluuge had thought the matter over for twenty minutes. Then he asked Miss Miller to look up the number for Waldingen – after all, there was nothing there apart from an old building used as a centre for summer camps. After a while he had given them a call.

A soft female voice answered the phone. He explained that he'd been informed that one of the confirmands had disappeared. The woman at the other end of the line sounded genuinely surprised, and said that nobody had been missing at lunch two hours previously.

Kluuge thanked her, and hung up.

The second call had come yesterday. Half an hour before the end of office hours. Miss Miller had already gone home, and the phone had been switched through to the chief of police's office.

'Hello. Chief of Police Kluuge here.'

'You haven't done anything.'

The voice sounded a little louder this time. But it was the same woman, no doubt about it. The same tense, forced composure. Somewhere between forty and fifty, although Kluuge acknowledged that he was bad when it came to guessing age.

'Who am I speaking to?'

'I rang yesterday and reported that a little girl had disappeared. You've done nothing about it. I assume she's been murdered. If you don't do something, I'll be forced to turn to the newspapers.'

That was the point at which Kluuge felt the first pang of panic. He gulped, and his mind was racing.

'How do you know that a girl has disappeared? I've investigated the matter. Nobody is missing from the camp at Waldingen.'

'You mean you've called them and asked? Of course they'll deny it.'

'We've carried out certain checks.'

He thought that was quite a good line, but the woman wouldn't be fobbed off.

'If you don't do something, they'll kill some more.'

There was a click as she hung up. Kluuge sat there for a while with the receiver in his hand, before replacing it and diverting his attention to the portrait of Lilian Malijsen in her bridal gown, in a gilded frame at the far end of the desk.

My God, he thought. What if she's telling the truth?

He had heard quite a bit about the Pure Life. And read a lot. As he understood it, they got up to all kinds of things.

Speaking in tongues.

Exorcizing devils.

Sexual rituals.

Mind you, the latter was probably just a malevolent rumour. Wagging tongues and the usual upright envy. Rubbish! Kluuge thought, and returned to contemplating the blossoming elders. But somewhere deep down – perhaps at the very core of his emotions, to borrow one of Deborah's latest pet expressions – he recognized that this was serious.

Serious. There was something about that woman's voice. There was also something about the situation in itself: his own disgracefully well-organized existence – Deborah, the terraced house, his stand-in duties as chief of police, the perfect mornings . . . It was only fair and just that something like this should crop up.

There has to be a balance, as his father used to say. Between plus and minus. Between successes and failures. Otherwise, you're not alive.

He stuck a pencil in his mouth. Began chewing it as he tried to imagine Malijsen's reactions if it turned out that a little girl had been found murdered on his patch, and the police had been tipped off but ignored it. Then he imagined the consequences of disturbing the divine peace that ruled over the heavenly fishing grounds. Neither of these options produced especially cheerful visions in Merwin Kluuge's mind's eye. Nor especially useful ones with regard to his possible future career prospects.

The Pure Life? he thought. A little girl missing?

It wouldn't surprise him.

Not at all, dammit.

He'd made up his mind. Picked up the telephone and dialled the number of the police station in Maardam.

5

'A hand grenade?' said the chief of police.

'No doubt about it,' said Reinhart. 'A seven-forty-five. He chucked it in through an open window, it rolled along the floor and exploded under the stage. Incredibly lucky, only eight injured and they'll all pull through. If it had gone off on the dance floor we'd have had a dozen corpses.'

'At least,' said deBries, adjusting his wine-red silken cravat that had become slightly awry.

'Do you need any help with your scarf?' Rooth wondered.

'And then what happened?' Münster was quick to intervene.

'He peppered some parked cars with an automatic weapon,' Reinhart continued. 'A nice chap, no inhibitions to speak of.'

'My God,' said Ewa Moreno. 'And he's still on the loose?'

'Getting ready for this evening, no doubt,' suggested Rooth. 'We ought to go after him.'

'Professional soldier?' wondered Jung.

'Very possibly,' said Reinhart.

'Excuse me,' said Heinemann, who had arrived late. 'Could we start from the beginning again? I've only heard about it on the radio.'

Chief of Police Hiller cleared his throat and wiped his temples with a tissue.

'Yes, that's probably best,' he said. 'Reinhart, you've been there, so I think you ought to give us the full story. Then we'll have to decide how to allocate available resources.'

Reinhart nodded.

'Kirwan Disco,' he began. 'Down at Zwille, alongside Grote Square. Full of people. Shortly after half past two this morning – they close at three – an unknown person threw a hand grenade in through an open window. The explosion was audible all over the centre of town, but as I said, the damage was limited because it went off under the stage. The band that had been playing there ten minutes previously were still there, but they're not feeling too good.'

The door opened and Van Veeteren came in.

'Carry on,' he said, flopping down onto a chair. The

chief of police looked at the clock. Reinhart raised an eyebrow before continuing.

'Eight people injured, but none of the injuries life-threatening. Twenty or so with minor wounds were admitted to the Rumford and Gemejnte hospitals, but most of them will be allowed home today. There are a few witnesses who saw a man running away from the scene.'

'Not a lot to go on,' said Jung. 'It was dark, and they only saw him from quite a long way off. But all were sure that it was a male person though.'

'Women don't behave like that,' said Rooth. 'Not the ones I know, at least.'

'Typical male behaviour,' said Moreno. 'I agree.'

Chief of Police Hiller tapped his desk with his Ballograf in irritation.

'And then what?' asked Münster. 'You mentioned cars.'

Reinhart sighed.

'About half an hour later, somebody – let's hope it was the same idiot, or we're dealing with two of them – started shooting at parked cars outside the Keymer church. Probably from somewhere in Weivers Park. That could be heard all over town as well. It only lasted for about fifteen to twenty seconds, and nobody saw a damned thing. An automatic weapon. Two to three salvoes. About thirty shots, at a guess.'

'Klempje, Stauff and Joensuu are busy crawling around

among the cars,' Jung explained. 'And Krause is taking care
of the car owners.'

'A fun job,' said deBries.

'No doubt,' said Reinhart. 'Krause could probably do
with some help. There are twelve owners concerned, including two German families in transit.'

'White Mercs,' elaborated Jung.

Van Veeteren stood up.

'Excuse me,' he said. 'I've forgotten my toothpicks
downstairs in my office. I won't be long.'

He left the room, and silence reigned.

'Ah well,' said Hiller after a while. 'This is most annoying. What with it being the holiday period and all that.'

Nobody present reacted at all. Jung held his breath.

'Ah well,' repeated Hiller. 'We obviously need to set
a few officers to work on this. All available resources.
It's clearly a lunatic who could well strike again. At any
moment. Well? Who's available?'

Reinhart closed his eyes and Münster studied his fingernails. DeBries left for the lavatory.

'Satan's shit,' said Rooth.

'Okay,' said Reinhart twenty minutes later, stirring his
coffee gloomily. 'I'll take care of it. I'll have Jung and Rooth
to help me in any case. And Münster, to start with at least.'

'Good,' said Van Veeteren. 'You'll soon sort it all out.'

Reinhart snorted.

'What did the gardener have for you? I heard a rumour.'

Van Veeteren shrugged.

'Dunno.'

'Dunno?'

'No. I thought I'd have lunch before confronting him.'

'Lunch?' said Reinhart. 'What's that?'

Van Veeteren examined a chewed-up toothpick and dropped it into the empty plastic mug.

'Do you know Major Greubner?'

Reinhart thought that one over.

'No. Should I?'

'I play him at chess occasionally. Sensible fellow. It might be an idea to pick his brains.'

'About this madman, you mean?'

Van Veeteren nodded.

'There's only one regiment based in this town, after all. I don't think they've started selling hand grenades in the supermarkets yet.'

Reinhart stared at the dregs in his coffee mug for a while.

'But perhaps I've got that wrong?'

'You never know,' said Reinhart. 'Do you have his number?'

Van Veeteren looked it up and wrote it down on a scrap of paper.

'Thank you,' said Reinhart. 'Anyway, duty calls. Do have a pleasant lunch.'

'Thank you,' said Van Veeteren.

'Come in,' said Hiller.

'I'm in already,' said Van Veeteren, sitting down.

'Please take a seat. I take it it's generally agreed that Reinhart looks after this lunatic?'

'Yes, of course.'

'Hmm. You're going on holiday at the end of this month, aren't you?'

Van Veeteren nodded. Hiller fanned himself with a memorandum from the Interior Ministry.

'And then what? You can't really be serious?'

Van Veeteren said nothing.

'You've had your doubts before. Why should I believe you'll actually do it this time?'

'We shall see,' said Van Veeteren. 'You'll get my final decision in August, but it looks like coming off this time. I just thought I'd better inform you. You like being informed, after all.'

'Hmm,' said the chief of police.

'What did you want me for?' asked Van Veeteren.

'Ah yes, there was something.'

'That's what Reinhart said.'

'A chief of police called from Sorbinowo.'

'Sorbinowo?'

'Yes.'

'Malijsen?'

'No, I think it's his stand-in while he's on holiday . . .'
Hiller took a sheet of paper from a folder.

'. . . Kluuge. He sounded a bit inexperienced, and he's
evidently been saddled with a disappearance.'

'A disappearance?'

'Yes.'

'But surely there must be help available closer to home?'
Hiller leaned over his desk and tried to frown.

'No doubt. But this Kluuge chappie has evidently been
instructed to turn to us if anything should crop up. By
the real chief of police, that is. Before he went on holiday.
A Wilfred Malijsen. Is he somebody you know?'

Van Veeteren hesitated.

'I have come across him, yes.'

'I thought as much,' said Hiller, leaning back in his chair.
'Because he mentioned you specifically as the man he
wants to go there and help out. To be honest . . . to tell you
the truth, I have the feeling there's something fishy behind
this, but as you've evidently talked Reinhart into taking
on the other business, you might just as well go there.'

Van Veeteren said nothing. Snapped a toothpick in two and stared at his superior.

'Just to find out what's going on, of course,' said Hiller. 'One day, or two at most.'

'A disappearance?' muttered the chief inspector.

'Yes,' said Hiller. 'A little girl, if I've understood it rightly. Come on now, what more can you ask for, dammit all? There can't be a more idyllic place to be in than Sorbinowo at this time of year . . .'

'What did you mean by something fishy behind this?'

For a brief moment it looked as if the chief of police blushed.

But it's probably just his daily cerebral haemorrhage, Van Veeteren thought, then realized that was an expression he'd borrowed from Reinhart. He stood up.

'All right,' he said. 'I suppose I'd better go there and see what's happening.'

Hiller handed over the sheet of paper with the details. Van Veeteren glanced at it for two seconds, then put it in his pocket.

'That hortensia's looking a bit miserable,' he said.

The chief of police sighed.

'It's not a hortensia,' he explained. 'It's an aspidistra. It ought to be coping well with the heat, but it obviously isn't.'

'Then there must be something else it can't cope with,' said Van Veeteren, turning his back on the chief of police.

6

Among the information on the sheet Hiller had given him was Sergeant Kluuge's private telephone number. The chief inspector waited until he'd got home before ringing it. A young woman answered promptly, and announced that the acting chief of police was in the shower at the moment, but perhaps the caller could try again a little later. Van Veeteren explained who he was, and suggested that instead the sergeant should call him as soon as possible, if he really did have something of importance to discuss.

Kluuge called three minutes later and they had a short conversation. Van Veeteren had always been allergic to telephones, and once he had established that there might be a grain of truth in the story, they arranged to meet the following day.

If nothing else, it might be an idea to check out the alleged idyllic nature of the location.

'I'll come by car,' he said. 'Arriving about noon. You can fill me in over lunch.'

'That's fine by me,' said Kluuge. 'Thank you for agreeing to help.'

'No problem,' said Van Veeteren, and hung up.

Then he sat for a while, wondering what to do next. Decided eventually to stay at home rather than eat out; took out bread, beer, sausages, cheese and olives and sat down on the balcony under the awning. Stood up again after the first swig of beer and went back inside. Hesitated again before picking out an Erik Satie CD. Put on the *Gymnopédies* and went back outside into the summer evening.

Wilfred Malijsen, he thought. That damned crackpot.

As he sat there enjoying the scent of the blossoming lime trees drifting in over the balcony railings and watching the sun set over the tiled roof of the Kroelsch Brewery, his mind wandered back to the only occasion he had met this colleague he hardly knew.

He reckoned it must have been nearly twenty years ago now, but it might be worth fishing up the details from the muddy waters of his memory.

1978, he thought. Or possibly 1979.

Anyway, a one-week course for high-ranking police officers and detectives. Time: late autumn, October or November. Place: a tourist hotel, one or two stars, by the sea in Lejnice. Purpose: lost in the murky depths of time.

The incident, the thing that made this week more

memorable than similar lugubrious jamborees, had taken place – if his memory served him correctly – on the Wednesday, after three or four days of lectures by bearded psychologists in sandals, and pointless group sessions, and later and later evenings in bars and pubs. A young desperado who was staying at the same hotel as the police contingent barricaded himself into his room with a young woman he had abducted at gunpoint.

It soon transpired that this weapon was a Kalashnikov, and the young man's demand was that the police should bring his ex-girlfriend to his room together with a million guilders, otherwise he would turn his blonde hostage (who was three weeks pregnant, to make matters worse) and anybody else who was foolhardy enough to come anywhere near him into minced meat.

The timescale did not leave the police much room for manoeuvre: two hours, not a second more.

As the terms were more or less impossible – apart from anything else the ex-girlfriend was on holiday somewhere in Italy, and in all probability not especially interested in cooperating in any case – the local police leaders in consultation with the top-ranking officers attending the conference decided to attempt a rescue operation. Tactics were drawn up in great haste despite a mass of contrary opinions, Van Veeteren was judged suitable to play a leading role, and after a fairly successful ploy he suddenly found himself in the barricaded room with the desperado and his hostage. The intention was that he should trick the youth to move towards the window and start negotiating for at least ten seconds – long enough for one of the sharp-shooters on the roof opposite to take aim and liquidate him by means of two or three well-directed bullets in the head and chest.

The gunman, that is, not Van Veeteren.

However, the young man turned out to be less than enthusiastic about this scenario. Instead of standing by the window, he bundled Van Veeteren into the far corner of the room and urged him to close his eyes and offer up a final prayer to his creator, assuming he thought he had one.

Van Veeteren was unable to hit upon a suitable deity on the spur of the moment, and instead started counting from one to ten. When he got as far as seven there was a commotion on the balcony and Malijsen barged into the room – in accordance with plans that nobody else had had a hand in devising, nor even had any idea about. Van Veeteren opened his eyes just in time to hear Malijsen fire and see the young man's head transformed into something beyond description, but a sight that for many years after-wards was not infrequently in his head when he woke after a bad dream.

'You can thank your lucky stars I happened to be pass-ing,' were Malijsen's first words.

They had spent several hours together on subsequent evenings, and the lasting impression Van Veeteren had of his rescuer was that he was a rather untalented crackpot holding a series of – more or less seriously meant – ideas and principles about practically everything. Unfortunately. A middle-aged boy scout, as Reinhart would no doubt have called him: weird, overweening, and a warmonger. Van Veeteren was sick and fed up of his company after only half an hour, but as the fact was that this podgy policeman had saved his life, he had no alternative but to treat him to an occasional beer.

During the rest of the conference there had been a great deal of discussion about competence and the scope for individual initiatives in advanced police work, and only a few months after the incident in Lejnice Van Veeteren had read in the police journal that Inspector Wilfred Malijsen had just been appointed chief of police in Sorbinowo.

It was not outside the bounds of possibility that there could be a connection.

Malijsen? Van Veeteren thought as he took two olives. Time to pay off an old debt?

Then he turned his mind to other things. First to Crete, and then to a variation of the Scandinavian Defence he had read about, and that might be worth trying in his next match.

★

The club's premises in Styckargränd were almost deserted, as they often were in summer, and the air felt pleasantly cool under the domed ceiling when the chief inspector walked through the door. As usual, Mahler was sitting right at the back, under the Dürer print. For once he was looking gloomy, and Van Veeteren recalled that he had just returned from Chadów where he had attended the funeral of an aunt.

'Do you miss her?' he asked in surprise. 'I thought you said she had a personality like a verruca.'

'They're squabbling about her inheritance,' Mahler explained. 'A depressing business. If those are the bastards I'm related to, there's not much hope for me either.'

'I've never held out much hope for you,' said the chief inspector, sitting down. 'But I'll get the first beer in if you set up the pieces. I'm intending to murder you tonight with a new opening gambit.'

Mahler brightened up slightly.

'He who murders last murders best,' he said, adjusting the board.

The first game took an hour and a half, and they agreed on a draw after nearly eighty moves.

'That early bishop was a good move,' said Mahler, scratching at his beard. 'Very nearly caught me on the hop.'

'You were lucky,' said the chief inspector. 'I regard myself as the moral victor. Speaking of morals, what do you know about the Pure Life?'

'The Pure Life?' Mahler looked bewildered for a few seconds. 'Oh, you don't mean that blasted sect, do you?'

'Yes, I think so,' said Van Veeteren.

Mahler thought for a moment.

'Why do you ask? In the name of duty, I hope? Or are you thinking of joining?'

Van Veeteren didn't respond.

'Nasty,' said Mahler after another moment's thought. 'Not that I know all that much about them, but I wouldn't want to pick my friends from that lot. A smart leader, sucks in emotionally unstable and scared people, turns them into robots, and presumably gets up to no good. Mind you, to the casual observer they're meek and mild, as soft as sugary angel-drops, needless to say. Especially after what happened.'

'Hmm,' said Van Veeteren. 'You're taking the words from my lips.'

'What's it all about?'

The chief inspector shrugged.

'I don't know yet. It might be just a false alarm. I'll be leaving town for a few days, in any case. Off to Sorbinowo.'

'Aha,' said Mahler. 'That could be very pleasant at this time of year. All those lakes and so on.'

'I'll be there on duty, of course,' Van Veeteren pointed out.

'Of course you will,' said Mahler with a smile. 'But I expect you'll have half an hour off now and then . . . I remember a very good writer from those parts, by the way.'

'Really?'

'He wrote about my first poetry collections. Positive and intelligent. Seems to have a good grasp of what this damned life is all about. He's still editor-in-chief there, I think.'

Van Veeteren nodded.

'What's his name? In case I need to talk to somebody with a clear head.'

'Przebuda. Andrej Przebuda. He must be getting on for seventy by now, but I'm sure he'll be continuing to man the cultural barricades until they scatter his ashes in the winds.'

Van Veeteren made a note of the name and emptied his glass.

'Ah well,' he said. 'I suppose it might be fun to get away for a bit.'

'Of course,' said Mahler. 'But steer well clear of funerals.'

'I'll do my best,' Van Veeteren promised. 'Have we time for another one?'

Mahler checked his watch.

'I think we can fit another one in,' he said. 'Aren't you due for a holiday soon, by the way? Or have they withdrawn perks like that?'

'First of August,' the chief inspector said, turning the board round. 'I'm off to Crete, and I have a few hopes of that.'

'Well I'll be damned!' Mahler exclaimed. 'What hopes?'

But the chief inspector simply contemplated his black queen, an inscrutable expression on his face.

'Mind you, I have misgivings,' he admitted after a while.

'About Crete?'

'No, about Sorbinowo. There seems to be a child missing. I don't like that sort of stuff.'

Mahler emptied his glass.

'No,' he said. 'Children ought not to go missing. Especially if they die. As long as Our Good Lord can't take care of that detail, I shall refuse to believe in him.'

'Same here,' said Van Veeteren. 'Anyway, it's your move.'

THREE

19–23 JULY

7

Elgar's cello concerto came to an end a hundred metres before the road sign at the entrance to the town. He switched off the CD and drove into a parking area with a tourist information board and an excellent view over the countryside below. Groped around in the glove pocket and produced the half-full pack of West he had been thinking about for the last half-hour. Lit a cigarette and got out of the car.

He stretched his back and performed a few cautious physical jerks while taking in the panorama spread out before him. The water course – basically the River Meusel that three or four times expanded to form long and narrow dark lakes – flowed towards the south-west through a flat, cultivated valley. The town of Sorbinowo was scattered around and between lakes number two and three from where he was standing, and he counted half a dozen bridges before the river disappeared from sight among wooded hills some six kilometres or so further on. Yachts, canoes and every kind of boat you could think of were bobbing up and down in the water, rocked by the gentle breeze. Directly below him several anglers were fishing from an old stone bridge, and about three kilometres to the west hordes of children were laughing and shouting and splashing around in an area designated a bathing beach.

This really was an idyll; Hiller and Mahler had been right. Dark, glittering waters. Fields of ripe corn. A scattering of deciduous woods and occasional villages in a half-open landscape. The whole area encircled by silent coniferous forests. The armies of silence.

A quivering summer heat made the rippling water enticing, even for a bather as hesitant as Chief Inspector Van Veeteren.

An idyll – yes, okay, he thought and drew deeply on his cigarette. Seen from a distance, before you've had a chance to scrape the surface, most things could seem pretty and well-organized. That was a reliable old truth.

As he stood there listening to the usual signals from the small of his back after a long car journey, a many-threaded skein of thoughts came to life inside him – about age and distance. For when he eventually (August? Krantze's antiquarian bookshop?) asserted the undoubted rights that came with his age and retired . . . when he gave up once and for all rooting around in the rubbish heaps of his environment, what he intended to seek out and lay claim to was distance – to occupy the elevated position afforded by keeping things at a distance. The observer's perspective. At long last to allow himself to be satisfied with the surface – glittering or not – and to interpret all the signs in a positive way. Or better still, not at all. To allow a pattern to be just that, a pattern. To leave the world and himself in peace.

In other words, just to sit there gaping at what went on. With a beer and a chessboard at Yorrick's or Winderblatt's. The wages of virtue after a life spent on the shadowy side?

Some bloody hope, he thought, stubbing out his cigarette. There are so many snags. Always these goddamned snags.

Anyway, time to lift the lid of summer-slumbering Sorbinowo.

A little girl missing?

The Pure Life?

Pure drivel, more like! he thought, drinking the last few lukewarm drops of mineral water that had been lying and sloshing about for far too long on the passenger seat. The paranoid imaginings of a nervous summer stand-in, nothing more . . . But if he could drag things out for a few days and at the same time repay his debt to that crackpot Malijsen, he had no real reason to complain.

There were worse times than wasted time – perhaps

that was precisely what constituted the observer's position? One of the things, at least.

Or so the chief inspector thought in the back of his mind as he wiped the sweat off his brow. Then he clambered back into the car and started to freewheel slowly down towards the village.

It only took five minutes to walk from the police station at Kleinmarckt to Florian's Inn, and it was immediately obvious to Van Veeteren that this was not one of the places where Sergeant Kluuge normally had his lunch. Crisp white tablecloths, discreet waiters dressed like penguins and an air-conditioning system that seemed to work even on the open terrace where Kluuge had reserved a table.

And the establishment was deserted.

'My God, what a place!' said the chief inspector in a friendly tone, and sat down.

'It's our treat,' explained Kluuge, somewhat embarrassed and completely unnecessarily. 'Choose whatever you like!'

Van Veeteren gazed out over the water, potentially threatening and still glittering some twenty metres below, and thought about that business of surfaces again. Then he applied himself to a study of the menu brought to him discreetly by one of the penguins.

*

'Perhaps we should talk a little about . . . about those telephone calls,' said Kluuge when they had made inroads into their salmon roulade. 'That's why you've come here, after all.'

'Hmm,' agreed Van Veeteren. 'Tell me about them. I can eat and listen at the same time, it's a skill I've developed over the years.'

Kluuge laughed politely and put down his knife and fork.

'Yes, well, it's just those two phone calls, but I got the feeling . . . the feeling . . .'

Van Veeteren nodded encouragingly.

'I reckon it could be serious. There was something about her voice. I don't think she sounded like a loony, or anything like that.'

And you have a long experience of loonies, do you? Van Veeteren thought; but he didn't say anything.

'Obviously, I called that camp to check up, but they didn't seem to know what I was talking about. Then I tried to find out a bit about what they get up to, but I didn't get very far. Waldingen is owned by a foundation that's been going for a long time, and they rent the place out to sizeable groups, mostly during the summer of course. The Pure Life were there last year, and they've booked themselves in for more or less the whole of this summer. From the middle of June until September the first, if I've understood it rightly.'

'Hmm,' said Van Veeteren, taking a swig of beer.

'I drove out there yesterday afternoon to take a look. It's about thirty kilometres from here. I just drove past, without stopping. It's pretty remote, I must say: nothing but the lake and the forest, and it must be at least a kilometre to the nearest neighbour. I suppose it's pretty ideal if you want to be on your own. I seem to remember that my old school organized camps there, but I never attended any of them.'

'That woman,' said Van Veeteren. 'The one who called. Who do you think she was?'

Kluuge looked blank.

'I've no idea.'

'Have a guess.'

Kluuge shrugged.

'If she's telling the truth,' said the chief inspector, wiping his mouth with his serviette, 'we have to assume that she must know about what's happened somehow or other. Don't you think?'

Kluuge nodded thoughtfully.

'Er, yes, I suppose so.'

'I assume you don't have one of those telephones that tell you the number of the person who's called you?'

Kluuge shook his head and looked embarrassed again.

'We'll get one after the summer holiday. Malijsen has ordered one, but there have been delivery delays.'

Van Veeteren changed track.

'Do you know how many people there are at the camp?'

'Not exactly. It's some kind of Confirmation jamboree. Only girls, I think. And I suppose they'll have a few leaders, and then there's that priest.'

'Priest?'

'Oscar Yellinek. He's the one who started the sect, if I've got it right. I spent some time yesterday looking into it. Set it up ten or twelve years ago, based mainly in Stamberg – well, more or less only there, apparently. There was a branch in Kaalbringen, but it didn't last long and has closed down. There have been quite a few articles and suchlike written about it, and there was a scandal a year or so ago. Yellinek was in jail for a few months, but it's been all quiet lately . . .'

Van Veeteren washed down the remains of his salmon with half a glass of beer. Kaalbringen? he recalled. Chief Inspector Brausen? The axe murderer . . .

He suppressed the memory. Gazed out over the lake, and the clusters of children romping around on the beaches. Summer camps, he thought instead. The whole area is infested with summer camps, of course. A few unpleasant memories from his own childhood began to stir, but he managed to bite their heads off.

'But you didn't go in and take a closer look?' he asked. 'When you were driving past anyway?'

'No,' said Kluuge. 'I didn't.'

'Why not?'

'I thought I'd better wait until you arrived. I'd called them earlier, and they said there was nobody missing.'

Great, Van Veeteren thought. That's what I call socking it to 'em.

'I see,' he said. 'Perhaps we ought to drive out there and take a look even so. The lion's den and all that.'

Kluuge nodded enthusiastically. Sat up straight and gave the impression of being ready to set off without delay.

'Calm down,' said the chief inspector. 'All in good time. We must first see if we can get a decent dessert at this place.'

'I suppose you're snowed under with work, are you?' the chief inspector asked when they got back to the chief of police's apricot-coloured office. (Apricot? Van Veeteren thought. I bet the bugger painted it himself!)

'Well,' said Kluuge. 'I've got loads of reports and such-like to see to.'

Van Veeteren dropped a toothpick behind the radiator.

'Okay, I suggest you try to find out a bit more about that sect. Call the police in Stamberg and hear what they have to say, that's probably easiest. I'll take care of Waldingen myself, if you don't mind. Do you have their number, so that I can give them a ring first?'

Kluuge wrote it down on a scrap of paper.

'I think I'll book myself a room for the night as well, to make sure that we can get to the bottom of this. Can you recommend anywhere?'

Kluuge hesitated.

'The City Arms or Grimm's,' he said eventually. 'The City Arms is probably a bit higher class, but Grimm's is located by the edge of the lake. A hundred metres or so from Florian's, where we had lunch. Not quite as good, but still . . .'

'Grimm's will be fine,' said the chief inspector, standing up. 'You can give me a buzz if anything crops up, otherwise I'll see you here tomorrow morning.'

Kluuge stood up and shook hands.

'Thank you,' he said. 'I'm grateful to you for taking this on.'

'No problem,' said Van Veeteren, leaving Sergeant Kluuge to his fate.

The room was a most unfortunate mixture of old and new, but there was an ample bath and a balcony with a pleasant view over the lake and the village climbing up the slope towards the edge of the forest on the far shore. Van Veeteren moved in, put his suitcase in the rickety wardrobe and dialled the number to Waldingen.

Still no answer after ten rings, so he replaced the receiver. Turned his attention instead to the map that Kluuge had provided him with. Waldingen wasn't a village even, the sergeant had explained, it was really only the name of that old summer camp for children – built sometime in the twenties – but nevertheless it was named on the map. A little black square next to a road branching off from a bigger road that ran round two little lakes before joining up with the main road again.

Forty or fifty kilometres into the forest, in other words. Hmm. He folded up the map and tried the number again.

Still no answer. He checked his watch. Five past three. The sun was still blazing down over the lake. His room was in the shade, but even so the temperature was approaching thirty-five degrees. He sat there for a while, in two minds about what to do next.

What the hell should he do?

Then he remembered that he'd noticed some sort of outdoor dining area under capacious parasols facing the lake. He dug out Klimke's *Neutral Observations* from his case, collected his pack of cigarettes and left the room.

*

Two dark beers and four cigarettes later he made another attempt to call Waldingen, with the same negative result.

What the hell are they up to? he wondered. If they are taking care of a gang of teenage girls, surely the least they can do is to man the telephone.

Or had Kluuge been so shit-scared that he'd supplied the wrong number?

Van Veeteren rang directory enquiries: the number was correct.

He checked his watch.

Half past four. Now what?

A shower, and then a slow stroll through Sorbinowo, he decided. Preferably along a few shady alleys, if there were any. In order to work up an appetite for dinner, if for no other reason. That visit to God's chosen flock would have to wait until tomorrow, no matter what. He didn't fancy the idea of heading off into the forest without having established contact first.

But never mind that. If he was hoping for a case that would keep him occupied for the next two weeks, the last thing he wanted was to rush things.

He undressed and marched into the yellow-and-blue bathroom.

For Christ's sake, he thought.

Then he showered in complete darkness for the next ten minutes.

8

The drive to Waldingen took thirty-five minutes. The last six or seven kilometres involved a narrow and decidedly bumpy dirt track that seemed to be about as infrequently used as his own sexual urges. The forest was dense and aromatic, settlements were few and far between. When he emerged from the trees and drove out to the lake and the buildings used for children's camps, he noted that since he'd left the main road he couldn't have passed more than four farms, and he hadn't met a single vehicle driving in the opposite direction. He drove into a space marked out by a few sunlit pine trunks, and parked his car.

A woman dressed in a grey and white sari came to greet him, before he'd had the chance even to get out of the car. Or rather, it looked like a sari, but when he looked more closely he could see that she was wearing a length of thick, unbleached cotton cloth. Her skin, hair, lips and eyes were about the same colour, and Van Veeteren had a fleeting vision of a bowl of porridge left out of the fridge overnight.

Forty-five, he decided. A bit dotty. Man-hater.

'Chief Inspector Veeteren?' she said, proffering a some-what limp hand.

'Van Veeteren. Yes, I phoned you last night. I wanted to speak to Mr Yellinek.'

'Come with me.'

She led the way to the horseshoe-shaped building that embraced an overgrown grassy patch with islands of blueberry sprigs and wild raspberries. The dark brown, substantial wooden buildings with newly fitted tin roofs comprised a main house that was quite large, with two storeys, a veranda and chimneys, and a smaller one on each side – simple, rectangular boxes from a much later date. The lake was on the other side of the road, only fifty metres or so away, and when he glanced in that direction he became aware of the naked bodies on the shore.

A dozen or so girls, paddling in the shallow water or sitting in the sun on towels, chatting away to one another.

But no splashing about. No noise, no giggling and shout-ing, no carefree laughter. In their midst he noticed two other women, dressed in exactly the same way as the one in front of him. He paused in mid-stride, and observed the painting – that's what it was, no other word would suffice – while associations raced in torrents through his mind.

But nothing stuck. Only a feeling of somewhat worrying admiration. And when the man on the veranda cleared his throat, Van Veeteren turned his back on the scene and wiped it from his memory.

'Welcome to our abode.'

'Thank you.'

'We are not happy about your visit, but we offer you our hospitality and will answer your questions.'

'Excellent,' said Van Veeteren. 'I take it you are Mr Yellinek?'

The man said nothing but bowed his head. He was older than Van Veeteren had expected, presumably round about his own age. Not many years younger, in any case. Thin and somewhat lopsided. His hair was mousey and shoulder-length, tied in a sort of ponytail. His beard hung down over his chest in tufts, and his clothes had evidently been made from the same material as those of the three women. Wide-fitting, greyish white shirt and voluminous trousers ending halfway up his shin. Sandals.

A prophet, no doubt about that, Van Veeteren thought, following him into the house. They sat down opposite each other at a large, round wooden table surrounded by ten simple chairs. Yellinek put on a pair of glasses with taped frames, and looked the chief inspector in the eye.

'You have fifteen minutes,' he said. 'We have prayers at eleven o'clock.'

Van Veeteren raised an eyebrow and left it up there for a few seconds.

'The fact of the matter is,' he explained, 'that I am here on behalf of the police investigating a crime, and I shall spend as much time on it as I consider to be appropriate. But if you are cooperative, I see no reason why it should take more than a quarter of an hour.'

Oscar Yellinek said nothing.

'How would you describe your association?'

Yellinek took off his glasses and put them in a brown leather case.

'I don't suppose for one moment that you intend to become a member of our church, Chief Inspector. Might I suggest that we devote our time to discussing the reason you have come here instead?'

'I gather you have had previous contact with the police?'

'I'm afraid so.'

'So you accept our authority?'

'As long as what you want doesn't conflict with the will of God. Might I ask you to come to the point?'

Van Veeteren shrugged.

'You know what this is all about. We have been informed that a little girl has disappeared from your camp. I'm just looking into the matter.'

'Nobody is missing.'

'How many young people do you have here?'

'Twelve.'

'Exclusively girls?'

'We don't believe in unregulated relations between the sexes at a young age.'

'So I have gathered,' said Van Veeteren. 'So you have a dozen girls here. How old are they, and what's the point of their stay?'

Yellinek clasped his hands on the table in front of him.

'Between twelve and fourteen,' he said. 'The purpose is to prepare them for reception into the Pure Life.'

'A sort of confirmation?'

'You could say that.'

'How long do they stay here?'

'Seven weeks.'

'So you hire this place for the whole of the summer?'

'Yes. We have two devotional weeks for adults in August as well. Our girls have about half their time left now.'

'Twelve, you said?'

'Yes, twelve.'

'And what do you spend the time doing?'

'Prayers, self-denial, purity. Those are the pillars of our faith – but I don't think you are interested in that kind of spirituality, Chief Inspector.'

Don't say that, Van Veeteren thought. It's more a question of what the hell it means, and how a normal thirteen-year-old could possibly be interested in it.

'How many adults?'

'Four. Me, and three assistants who help with practical things.'

'Women?'

'Yes.'

Van Veeteren thought for a moment.

'Can you give me a list of the girls you have here now?'

Yellinek shook his head.

'Why not?'

'It's not in our interest. Neither the girls' nor their parents'.'

'Meaning what?'

'We have had some experience of the police. As you said yourself.'

'You realize that I can compel you to tell me if needs be?'

Yellinek didn't turn a hair. Merely paused, while contemplating his crossed thumbs.

'Of course. But I'm not going to give you any names unless you force me to by violent means.'

'So you think you are above the law?'

'There's more than one law, Chief Inspector.'

'Rubbish.'

Van Veeteren leaned back in his chair and fumbled in his breast pocket for a toothpick. Found one, held it up to the light and inspected it for a moment, then inserted it into his lower teeth. Yellinek observed his shenanigans with undisguised scepticism.

'So you are suggesting that I should accept your word?'

There was a glint of something yellow in the depths of the prophet's beard. Possibly a smile.

'Yes. That's what I'm suggesting.'

'I want to speak to one of the girls. Several of them, in fact.'

Yellinek raised a finger and shook his head.

'We don't allow them to do anything that isn't in their programme. It's important that they are left alone during this time.'

Van Veeteren took out the toothpick.

'Are you saying that you keep them incommunicado for seven weeks?'

'You don't understand what this is all about, Chief Inspector. It's sometimes necessary to protect the spiritual. Not to expose it to the bumps and bashes of everyday life. It's absolutely essential at this stage of their education.'

'So you are refusing to let me speak to any of them? Just for a couple of minutes?'

'It's so easy to undermine what has been built up over a long period. I know this might sound harsh, Chief Inspector, but you have to understand that we mean well. We believe in what we are doing. We are practising our religion – it's easy to mock and pour scorn upon us, but we have a legal right. Since you seem to be so obsessed by rights and the law . . .'

He looked at the clock. Van Veeteren replaced the toothpick. Five seconds passed.

'And those telephone calls?' he wondered. 'That anonymous woman who insists that one of the girls has been murdered – what do you have to say about that?'

'Malevolence,' said Yellinek without hesitation. 'This isn't the first time we've been accused, Chief Inspector. We've been through this before, as I've said.'

Van Veeteren thought that over.

'What about the women?' he said. 'Your assistants. If I were to grab one of them and chat to her for a while – would that reduce your spiritual palace to ruins?'

'Of course not,' said Yellinek. 'I have to leave you now. It's time for prayers. If you stay put here, I'll send one of them in to you.'

He left the room. Van Veeteren closed his eyes and clenched his fists. After a while he clasped his hands instead.

What a load of crap, he thought. Oh lord, give me strength!

He made up his mind on the drive back.

Not to start more intensive investigations and not to shoot and sink Yellinek's spiritual longboat, but to stay in Sorbinowo for another day.

Perhaps just one. Perhaps several.

For there was something. It wasn't clear what, but hidden away somewhere in this story – which presumably wasn't a story at all – was something that reminded him of . . . Hmm, what did it remind him of?

He didn't know. The underhand and unmotivated sacrifice of a peasant? A monster concealed inside stupidity? Why not?

Or was it just his imagination? The woman he had spoken to for ten minutes was the one who had come to escort him from his car. She introduced herself as Sister Madeleine, and didn't have much to say over and above what Yellinek had told him already.

Except that she had been a member of the Pure Life from the very start. Unlike Sisters Ulriche and Mathilde, who had joined rather later.

That the group was a collective, but that Yellinek was their spiritual leader.

That her life had changed eleven years ago, and since then she had lived in enlightenment and purity.

That the three sisters shared all the chores at the camp; that the girls – all twelve of them – were still wandering around in the dark, but were on their way towards the light, and everything was in the hands of God.

And in Oscar Yellinek's.

Also that all these things were beyond the chief inspector's comprehension, because he was not initiated.

Van Veeteren spat out an ill-treated toothpick through the driver's window and chanted a long sequence of curses to himself. Tried to identify the dark suspicion that had been lurking deep down inside him ever since he backed out from between the pine trees.

All the time, in fact. While he was talking to Yellinek. While he'd been sitting waiting, and watched the girls walking in neat formation back from their bathing expedition. While he'd been listening to Sister Madeleine's pious outpourings.

He eventually realized that it was probably a question of being unable to do anything about it. Impotence.

Pure, unadulterated impotence.

He made a supreme effort to suppress it, and lit a cigarette instead.

There are too many ingredients in this soup, he decided. Far too many. I don't even know if it is a soup.

Anyway, time to stop thinking, he decided a few moments later. I'm just rambling on. Like some damned television personality.

'Word for word?' asked Kluuge, puckering up his brow. The chief inspector noted that it was quite a high brow with room for rather a lot of creases, and decided that he must not underestimate what was behind it.

'Preferably,' he said. 'As accurately as you can remember, in any case.'

'The first time she just said that a girl had disappeared,' Kluuge explained. 'And that we must do something about it. The second time she added a bit more detail.'

'What?'

'Well, she maintained that we hadn't done anything. Said she might bring in the press, and that they might murder somebody else . . .'

'Murder?'

'Yes.'

'You're sure she used that word?'

'Absolutely.'

Kluuge nodded several times, to remove any possible doubt.

'Anything else?' asked the chief inspector.

'I don't think so.'

'Age?'

'Hard to say. Somewhere between forty and fifty, but I'm not sure . . . Could be older. Voices are not my strong point.'

'What did she sound like?'

'Like I said. She spoke quietly, especially the first time . . . Sounded very serious anyway, as if she really meant what she was saying. That's why I concluded that I ought to call the chief inspector.'

'Hmm,' said Van Veeteren. 'Have you got any more information about that sect?'

Kluuge scratched nervously at his neck.

'I've spoken to colleagues in Stamberg. They promised to gather together a bit of information and fax it over, but nothing's come yet.'

Van Veeteren nodded.

'All right,' he said. 'I'll go back to my hotel – you can let me know if anything turns up. I'll be staying on here for a few more days, no matter what.'

'Good,' said Kluuge, looking a bit self-conscious. 'I'm grateful, as I said.'

'You don't need to keep on being grateful all the time,' said the chief inspector, rising to his feet. 'I suspect there's something rotten going on here – I've paid, by the way.'

'I understand,' said Kluuge.

By the time Van Veeteren had returned to his room at Grimm's, it was half past two in the afternoon and the sun was shining diagonally through the open window. He closed the curtains and took a long, cool shower, this time not paying any attention to the colour scheme.

When he had cooled down sufficiently, he stretched himself out on the bed and called the police station in Maardam. He eventually got hold of Münster.

'How's it going?' Van Veeteren asked.

'How's what going?' Münster wondered.

'How the hell do I know? The trigger-happy lunatic, for instance.'

'We caught him this morning. Don't you listen to the radio?'

'I've been a bit busy,' Van Veeteren explained.

'Oh dear,' said Münster.

'So I might be able to get a bit of help?' asked Van Veeteren rhetorically. 'Now that you've got your man.'

Münster coughed and sounded worried – and the chief inspector recalled that Münster was about to go on holiday. He explained what he wanted, and Münster promised to do whatever he could – to find out all there was to know about the Pure Life, and to fax it without delay to Grimm's Hotel in Sorbinowo.

'The quicker, the better,' said Van Veeteren, and hung up.

No harm in casting out a few more lines, he thought, and started to get dressed.

In case Kluuge might have rung the wrong number, or something.

A quarter of an hour later he was back in the car, armed with a new pack of cigarettes and a few fugues. He wasn't heading anywhere in particular – unless an hour's unhurried drive round the lakes and through the aromatic forests could be defined as somewhere in particular.

And a trip through Bach's unfailingly logical variations.

He was back by five o'clock. Took another shower, and before going out to choose a suitable eating place, he enquired at reception if there were any messages for him.

There were not.

Nothing from Kluuge.

Nothing from Münster.

Ah well, he thought. Sufficient unto the day is the evil thereof.

And as he wandered towards the town centre, he wondered what on earth he meant by that.

9

Despite the massive influx of tourists seeking fresh air and good walking country – at this time of year the town probably housed twice as many people as during the winter, Van Veeteren would have thought – Sorbinowo had it limits. The number of respectable eating places (to qualify as such in his opinion you needed to be able to sit down and eat at a proper table, and be spared having to listen to canned music at more or less unbearable sound levels) was precisely five. Including Florian's, where he had taken lunch with Kluuge, and Grimm's Hotel, where he was staying.

This second evening the chief inspector chose number four: a simple, quasi-Italian establishment in one of the little alleys leading from Kleinmarckt up the hill to the church and the railway station. The pasta turned out to be a bit sticky and the beer lukewarm, but it was peaceful and quiet, and he could sit there alone with his thoughts.

Something which rarely happened, in fact.

Prayers? he thought.

Self-denial? Purity?

He had been thinking about such things in the car as well, while listening to the fugues.

And the image of the tranquil bodies of the little girls at the water's edge came back to him. And the pale women wrapped in their lengths of bleached cotton cloth.

What the devil was going on?

A justified question, no doubt about that. There were voices inside him – loud voices – stubbornly demanding that he should sort them out. Return to Waldingen without a second's delay – preferably together with Kluuge in his uniform – and bring the lot of them to book.

Give Oscar Yellinek a good dressing-down and set about all that sanctimoniousness with a sledgehammer. Find out the name of every single girl and send them off home at the first opportunity.

Very loud voices.

But there was something else as well. He took another swig of beer and tried to pin it down.

Something to do with freedom and rights, presumably.

With the right to practise one's religion in peace and without interference. Not to have the police lurking round every corner, ready to come storming in the moment anything happened that didn't conform with convention.

With defending, or at least not squashing, a minority.

Yes, something of that sort. Definitely.

Despite his instinctive dislike of Yellinek, he couldn't help agreeing with him when it came down to basics. What right had he, the unbeliever, to stand in judgement over these members of a drop-out sect?

Two anonymous telephone calls. Little girl missing? Was that sufficient reason?

It could no doubt be argued that one should have rather firmer ground on which to stand. Somewhere a bit drier for one's feet.

The fair-haired waitress came with his coffee and cognac. He lit a cigarette.

Not to mention the inconvenience!

He took a sip of cognac. Perhaps that was what put him off the most. The inconvenience. In the other half of the scales, comfort and warmth – for if he really did make up his mind to move in now, wasn't it likely that Yellinek and the female troika would make him take the consequences as well? Force him to take responsibility for the whole group of girls and make sure each of them got back home safely?

And there was no reason to think that the girls' parents would have a more benevolent attitude towards the police than their spiritual leader had displayed. After all, they had sent their offspring to this camp, and whether or not they were completely naive, they were hardly likely to be pleased to receive their half-confirmed teenagers three weeks earlier than expected. Anybody would be able to understand that. Even Kluuge. Even an agnostic detective chief inspector on his last legs.

Hell and damnation, Van Veeteren thought as he gestured for the bill. I'm sitting here like a donkey in two minds, thinking rubbish.

About a case that doesn't even exist!

Or at least, probably doesn't, he added. It must be the weather.

He paid, and left El Pino. It occurred to him that perhaps a decent glass of wine might help to get his mind back on track. White, of course, in view of the temperature; it was a few minutes short of half past eight, and the heat of the day was still lingering around Kleinmarckt, where the occasional tourist (and perhaps one or two locals) were strolling around in the gathering dusk.

Mersault, perhaps? Or just a simple glass of Riesling? That would probably be easier to find.

He could feel his mood improving already.

After all, the only reason he'd come here in the first place was to fill in time until Crete. Christos Hotel, the source of youth and that chestnut brown hair.

No other reason at all.

The cinema was called Rymont, and the mere existence of such an establishment in Sorbinowo was just as surprising as the films it was showing. Evidently something called a 'Quality Film Festival' was on offer during the summer, and when he discovered that a showing of the Taviani brothers' *Kaos* was due to start in about two minutes, there was not a lot of time to hesitate.

He entered the auditorium just as the lights were being dimmed, but that gave him ample time to greet the rest of the evening's audience. It comprised five people comfortably spread over the back few rows: four gentlemen and a lady – all of them past the first flush of youth, but with the kind of features characteristic of genuine cinema enthusiasts, Van Veeteren was pleased to note.

With a satisfied sigh he slumped down a few rows further forward – his satisfaction being intensified when it transpired that there would be no advertisements, and that the main film would begin at the exact time stated on the billboards.

So there is still a grain of quality left in this world of ours, he thought. Even a blind chicken can sometimes discover that fact occasionally.

Afterwards none of the audience was in much of a hurry to leave the premises. Two of the gentlemen launched into an animated discussion of the film. Comparisons were suggested with Pirandello's texts and with other films by the Italian brothers, and it was clear to Van Veeteren that this was no ordinary group of people he'd found himself a part of. When he eventually stood up, another member of the audience came up to greet him – a short grey-haired gentleman exuding an aura of energy.

'A new face! It's a pleasure to welcome you!'

He held out his hand, and Van Veeteren shook it.

'Przebuda. Andrej Przebuda. Chairman of the Sorbinowo Film Society.'

'Van Veeteren. I just happen to be passing through . . .'

He searched his memory.

'Life is a series of coincidences.'

'Yes indeed,' said the chief inspector. 'Very true. Hmm . . . I'm delighted to see that the cinematographic arts are still alive and kicking even outside the metropolitan centres.'

'Well,' said Przebuda, 'we do our best – but as you can see, there aren't all that many of us.'

He gestured towards the others.

'And we're not exactly spring chickens either.'

He smiled broadly and ran his hand apologetically over his almost bald head.

'Andrej Przebuda?' said the chief inspector – the penny had dropped at last.

'Yes.'

'I think we have a mutual friend.'

'You don't say? Who?'

'W.F. Mahler.'

'The poet?'

Van Veeteren nodded.

'He claimed that you appreciated his poems.'

Przebuda burst out laughing and nodded enthusiastically. He was certainly closer to seventy than anything else, Van Veeteren thought. But the intensity in those eyes of his suggested the timeless twenties; and when the chief inspector looked more closely, it seemed to him that the man's face was distinctly Jewish. He realized – or suspected at least – that he was talking to one of those rare people who had been ennobled by suffering. Who had passed through fire and brimstone and been hardened rather than cracked.

But that was only a guess, of course. One of those sudden surges of speculation that demanded to be considered, and he was old enough to do so.

'A damned fine poet, that Mahler,' said Przebuda. 'Fastidious, and as clear as a mountain tarn. I think I've reviewed every collection he's published, right from the start. But how . . .'

It was another ten minutes before Van Veeteren was able to leave the Rymont cinema, armed with an insistent invitation from Andrej Przebuda to meet again and get to know each other better in the very near future – either in the editorial offices of his magazine, or at his home, which was nearby.

If the fact of the matter was that the chief inspector had come to Sorbinowo on official business, rather than as a tourist, then it could well be – not to overstate the matter – that he, Andrej Przebuda, might well be able to supply appropriate information.

If that should prove to be necessary. He'd been living here for forty-four years, after all.

If nothing else, perhaps they could exchange a few words about films and poetry.

Why not? Van Veeteren thought, having eventually taken leave of Przebuda and the other members of the Sorbinowo Film Society. It could be rewarding, from various points of view.

On the whole, not a wasted evening by any means, he decided as he made his way back to Grimm's. But even so, once he had gone to bed what dominated his consciousness were the images from the morning. They kept him awake until the small hours.

Those young, naked little girls.

Those pale women.

The prophet's beard.

10

The information about Oscar Yellinek and his spiritual activities had arrived on the Sunday morning. Both from Münster and from Stamberg. After a substantial breakfast in his room with two daily newspapers, Van Veeteren devoted an hour of the morning to sitting at Sorbinowo's police station and going through the material.

And wondering what to do next.

Always assuming there ought to be anything to do next. Kluuge had been sent home to look after his pregnant wife, who had evidently been unwell during the night. The chief inspector was sweating. The sun had turned a corner, and was now slowly warming up Chief of Police Malijsen's office to a state that would soon be just as unbearable as a fried apricot. There was no way of preventing that, despite all the blinds and curtains.

To what extent the Pure Life was an even more unbearable business was a matter of opinion.

Oscar Yellinek was born in 1942 in Groenstadt. Studied

theology and took the cloth in Aarlach in 1971. Was active as a curate and spiritual guide in half a dozen places until he broke loose in the autumn of 1984 and started the free-church community (alternative synod) of the Pure Life. The main centre of recruitment was Stamberg, where he had also lived and worked since the beginning of the eighties.

In its early years the Pure Life had evidently led a quite anonymous existence. Nobody had a word to say against it; the number of proselytes seemed to be upwards of thirty souls (there were no reliable figures), most of them women – a characteristic that continued into the future. Meetings and services were held in various different locations, which often seemed to be rented for just a week or so, and sometimes for only one occasion.

As time went by, however, the movement began to develop a more populist profile. Together with a former fellow student, Werner Wassmann (who later left the movement after an internal schism), Yellinek began to arrange open-air meetings and to appear in more or less public places.

The message was simple, the tone attractive:

Leave the sinful, materialistic world! Come to us! Live in purity and harmony in contact with the only true God!

Membership increased, quite a lot of money was donated, and in 1988 the Pure Life's first church was opened. It was later extended to accommodate various school activities, and eventually became competent enough to teach years one to six in accordance with official education regulations.

From the start there had been rumours circulating about Yellinek's movement, and letters were sent to the editors of local newspapers and calls made to local radio programmes. Accusations varied from brainwashing and fascism to contempt for women and sexism, and in 1989 the mother of a member who had left the sect – a seventeen-year-old girl – brought an action against Yellinek for indecent assault and sexual abuse.

The case attracted a lot of attention, and had undeniable appeal for the mass media. Speaking in tongues. Compulsory mortification of the flesh. Big meetings at which all participants were naked, and Yellinek exorcized the devil collectively from the whole congregation. Girls being spanked on their bare bottoms. And a number of other activities with marked sexual undertones. Or overtones. The Pure Life was sometimes described in newspapers as the sex-sect, sometimes as devil-worshippers, and the eventual outcome was that Yellinek was sentenced to six months in prison for mild indecency and illegal compulsion.

Mild indecency? the chief inspector thought, fanning himself with an old newspaper. Was there really such an offence? He couldn't remember ever having come across it before, that was for sure.

Paradoxically, the sentence and Yellinek's time behind bars seemed to result in a slight change in public opinion, according to Münster's documents. The imprisoned priest achieved a certain martyrdom, and the reputation of the Pure Life seemed – temporarily at least – to rise out of the dirt. While waiting for their spiritual leader's return, most members went to ground; but the sect was not wound up, and surprisingly few left.

After half a year of diaspora, the shepherd returned to his flock, and as far as one could tell, activities began again on the same basis as before. There were no obvious changes, except perhaps a more marked tendency to remain aloof from the everyday world and discourage interest from outside, be it from journalists or anybody else. Even so the membership continued to expand slowly but surely, and by the middle of the nineties it appeared to be about a thousand souls. Oscar Yellinek's position as the sole spiritual leader had probably never been stronger.

The view of other communions when it came to the Pure Life was more or less one hundred per cent critical; there had never been room for any interest in fellowship and ecumenical matters in Yellinek's teachings, and serious commentators obviously regarded the sect as a rather promiscuous and generally dodgy phenomenon.

Among Kluuge's information from the police in Stamberg were also several indications of the so-called defector syndrome, which meant that former members had been harassed in various ways after leaving the sect. Such incidents were by no means unknown in similar circumstances, but as far as the Pure Life was concerned it seemed to be mainly rumours and occasional notices in the local press. There had been no cases leading to police intervention or any other kind of reaction from the authorities.

But there was no doubt at all that there were a lot of critical voices complaining about Oscar Yellinek and his flock. Nevertheless, the general opinion seemed to be that they were pretty harmless – a collection of vulnerable and confused melancholics who could be left to get on with whatever kept them happy, so long as they left ordinary honest people in peace.

Which is what they had evidently been doing since Yellinek's release from prison. No public meetings. No ads in newspapers or anywhere else. No missionary activities. Any recruitment was obviously carried out by members on a private basis.

It could hardly be said that there was any reliable information available regarding the Pure Life's activities and ideas, however.

Neither Münster's nor Kluuge's informants could provide any such thing.

So that was that. Van Veeteren slid the papers to one side and mopped his brow. Looked to see if there was anything drinkable around, but it was clear that it was not part of Chief of Police Malijsen's routine to offer unexpected visitors a drink. Or perhaps he had locked the stuff away in some secure hiding place, safe from the grasp of stand-ins or any other possible spongers.

'All very fishy,' muttered the chief inspector.

He wasn't sure if that comment was aimed at Yellinek or Malijsen. Probably at both of them. He sighed. Lifted the telephone receiver and started to ring Kluuge's home number, but then stopped. Better to let him devote his energy to his family, he decided.

Better – moreover – to give himself the opportunity of discussing the situation with himself over a cold beer in the garden of the City Arms Hotel.

In so far as a run-through was called for now, that is.

And – in so far as it was called for now – two beers. The City Arms Hotel's garden wasn't a bad place to be on a day like this; he'd gathered that when he passed it on his way to the police station earlier in the day. Not bad at all.

He stood up. Purity? he thought – for the fiftieth time since he had taken his leave of Yellinek out at Waldingen. It didn't inspire any good associations this morning either.

I suppose I've been living among the dregs for too long, Chief Inspector Van Veeteren thought.

★

The two men were busy clearing brushwood from the edge of the road. The chief inspector braked and got out of the car.

'Good afternoon. A bit on the warm side today.'

The elder of the men switched off his saw and gestured to his companion to do the same.

'A bit on the warm side today,' the chief inspector repeated, as he realized they would have been unable to hear a word of his first greeting.

'You can say that again,' said the man, putting down his saw.

'My name's Van Veeteren. Police. I'm a detective. Would you mind answering a few questions?'

'Eh? Er . . . yes, of course.'

He stood up straight and beckoned to the younger man, indicating that he should come closer.

'Mathias Fingher. This is my son, Wim.'

Both of them shook hands, after first wiping theirs on their trousers.

'What's it all about?'

Van Veeteren cleared his throat.

'Harrumph. The Pure Life.'

If the Finghers were surprised, they showed no sign of it.

'Okay.'

'Do you have any contact with them? You're their next-door neighbours after all – as it were.'

'Well,' said Mathias Fingher, tilting his cap over the back of his neck. 'What do you mean?'

He was evidently the one expected to conduct the conversation. His son stood a couple of paces behind, eyeing the chief inspector, and chewing gum.

'Do you ever meet any of them?'

Fingher nodded.

'Yes, of course. They buy potatoes and milk from us. Eggs and carrots, and a few greens sometimes. They come every evening to collect it.'

Aha, Van Veeteren thought. A close contact at last.

'Who actually comes?'

'It varies.'

'Meaning what?'

'Always four of them. Plus Yellinek, of course.'

'Four girls every evening?'

'And Yellinek. I suppose the girls take it in turns.'

Van Veeteren thought for a moment.

'Do you usually speak to them?'

'Well, not really. We don't usually say much. Why do you ask?'

The chief inspector put a finger to his lips, and that seemed to be a sufficient explanation. As usual. Even if respect for officers of the law might vary, people seemed to accept that this secrecy business was something you just didn't question; it was an observation he'd made many times.

Stupidity is best clad in secrecy, as Reinhart used to say.

'Do you ever talk to the girls?'

Fingher thought for a moment, then shook his head.

'No, they . . . they always stay in the background, sort of.'

'The background?'

'Yes, they always wait by the wagon until Yellinek tells me what they want. Very quiet little girls, they seem a bit . . .'

'A bit what?'

'Hmm, I don't really know. You sometimes wonder what they get up to over there.'

'Really?'

'Well, I don't want to accuse anybody of anything. People have a right to think whatever they like, and they always pay up, no problem – which is more than you could say about some folk.'

Van Veeteren wondered who the some folk might be.

'What's your own opinion of them? There are all kinds of rumours going round . . .' It was worth a try.

Fingher scratched the back of his head, and dropped his cap. Picked it up and stuffed it into his back pocket.

'God knows. I wouldn't trust any of my kids with them, that's for sure. But they don't do me any harm. As I said.'

'What about Oscar Yellinek?'

Fingher suddenly seemed embarrassed.

'I know nothing about him. Nothing at all.'

'But you know what some people say?'

It was obvious that Fingher was unsure of what to say about his unholy alliance.

'Hmm,' he said eventually. 'That he lives with his three women, I suppose.'

Aha, the chief inspector thought again. We're getting somewhere at last.

'Exactly,' he said. 'What about the girls?'

Fingher shrugged.

'No idea. But they bathe naked, and I expect they get up to all sorts of things as well . . .'

'Really?'

'According to what you hear, that is. But I know nothing . . . No, best to leave them alone and mind one's own business.'

Maybe you're right, Van Veeteren thought. But as I've come all this way . . .

'How many of them are there?' he asked.

Fingher looked as if he were counting.

'I don't really know,' he said. 'Ten, fifteen perhaps. I really don't know.'

'Do you go to Waldingen sometimes?'

Fingher shook his head.

'Hardly ever. Only if they need help with something. They had some problems with the pump, and we were there a couple of afternoons a few weeks ago. But it's usually them who come here.'

Van Veeteren took out his pack of cigarettes and offered it to them, but both father and son shook their heads. He considered taking one himself, but thought better of it and went for a toothpick instead.

'How often do their parents come to visit?'

'Never,' said Fingher. 'I've never seen an adult there – apart from that Yellinek and his three women. But they don't do us any harm, as I said. They haven't been up to something, have they?'

Van Veeteren didn't respond. Wondered if he ought to continue firing questions at them just in case, or whether it would be more sensible to save them for another occasion later on. If that should become necessary.

'I might well get back to you,' he said. 'Thank you for talking to me, Mr Fingher.'

Fingher and son nodded and took their hands out of their pockets. All four of them. Van Veeteren eased himself into the car and continued his journey along the narrow forest track. By the time he turned the first bend, he could hear the sound of the chainsaws again.

Well I'll be damned, he thought. Three of them?

Shouldn't he have realized that right away?

But the bottom line was that the range of his sexual imagination had shrunk somewhat as the years passed.

What could be more natural? he asked himself in a flash of depressing honesty.

No, enough of fantasies! Time for the lion's den.

Or was it a snake pit?

I'm still on a roll when it comes to stringing words together! he thought as he parked between the same pine trees as last time. Every cloud has a silver lining. If the Krantze thing fell through, maybe he could start writing his memoirs instead. The main thing was that he had alternative moves to fall back on . . . if it turned out that he had to choose between check or a knight gambit.

Alternative moves?

A length of bleached cotton was approaching, and he did his best to put a hasty stop to the flow of imagery.

11

There was barely room on the rickety bedside table for the necessaries. Two bottles of beer, some crispbread, a little plastic tub of marinated garlic cloves and a few generous slices of game pâté. He had found the whole lot at Kemmelmann & Sons, a little deli only fifty metres from the hotel, and when he realized that he had already been to all the decent eating places in town, he had given in to temptation. A quiet evening in his room was not a bad idea at all; it was ages since he had eaten marinated garlic, and of course there was nothing to stop him going out later on for a glass of beer or wine.

After he'd finished his homework, that is.

Satisfied with these arguments, he leaned back on the bed and slid a clove of garlic into his mouth. Followed it up with a piece of bread, a chunk of pâté and a substantial swig of beer before switching on the tape recorder and starting to listen to the fruits of his afternoon exertions.

Yellinek first.

VV: Your name, please.

OY: Oscar Yellinek, of course. Why so formal all of a sudden?

VV: Could you speak a little more clearly please, Mr Yellinek? The more turgid the contents, the more important the formalities. I thought we were in agreement on that.

OY: Words, Chief Inspector. You live in a world of empty words.

VV: Rubbish. Anyway, my requirements are simple. I want a list of names, addresses and telephone numbers of all the participants in this camp. I want to talk to your three assistants and with two of the girls. Unless I find anything that needs following up, I promise to leave you in peace after that.

[Silence for five seconds.]

VV: May I ask you to confirm that you have understood the requirements, Mr Yellinek? I trust you are not intending to continue your non-cooperation, like an itching mule?

[Where do I get it all from? Van Veeteren wondered, feeling pleased with himself. He took another chunk of pâté.]

OY: You are the instrument of power, Chief

Inspector, not of justice. You are the one holding the sword, not I. One day you will—

VV: That's enough, thank you. Save your preaching for your flock. Let me ask you a few questions first, in your capacity as the person responsible for the Waldingen camp and the spiritual leader of the Pure Life. Is it true that you indulge in sexual relationships with all three of your assistants?

[No reply.]

VV: Would you like me to repeat the question?

OY: I would like you to gather up your shame and leave the premises immediately. You have no idea what—

VV: Would such relationships be consistent with the moral values of your church and its attitude towards women?

OY: You represent a perverted and decadent society, Chief Inspector, and allow me to finish what I'm saying this time. If you want insight and guidance regarding another way of living, you can write to our church in Stamberg and your application will be treated in exactly the same way as everybody else's.

VV: I wouldn't dream of it.

OY: I'm not insisting you do.

VV: There are many people who consider you to be a charlatan, Mr Yellinek.

OY: The masses and the righteous speak different languages, Chief Inspector. I am guided by the voice of God, nothing else. If you want to insult me further, I am at your service. Otherwise I have duties to attend to.

VV: How many girls are taking part in the camp?

OY: Twelve, as I've already said.

VV: How many were there to start with?

OY: Twelve.

VV: Thank you. I think you are lying, but that's another matter. Please go and attend to whatever it is you have to do, and make sure your assistants come to see me one after the other.

OY: My conscience is clear, Chief Inspector. Yours will haunt you. Believe you me.

VV: Crap. One more thing, incidentally. In connection with the law suit against you in 1990, did you undergo any kind of mental examination?

OY: Of course not.

VV: Oh, excuse me – if you had done, it's clear, you wouldn't be sitting here now.

OY: You are exceeding your authority, Chief Inspector.

VV: I have an inner voice that guides me.

OY: Remember that I have warned you.

VV: Go away. But make sure the people I want to speak to come to see me.

OY: On the Day of Judgement you—

VV: Thank you, that's all for now.

The chief inspector switched off the tape recorder and took two more garlic cloves with pâté. Washed it all down with beer, which he first swilled round and round inside his mouth; the aftertaste of Oscar Yellinek was not something to be taken lightly. Then he fast-forwarded for a few seconds before pressing the play button again.

VV: Your name?

UF: Ulriche Fischer.

VV: Age, place of residence and occupation?

UF: Forty-one. I live in Stamberg and work in the Pure Life church.

VV: Doing what?

UF: Various things, mostly practical chores.

VV: Are you married?

UF: No.

VV: What are your tasks here at the camp?

UF: We share all the work. Cooking, washing up, laundry and cleaning. We assist Yellinek, of course.

VV: Do you partake in the teaching of the girls?

UF: Yes, at times.

VV: In what way?

UF: I've no intention of talking to you about that kind of thing.

VV: Why not?

[Five seconds of silence.]

VV: Has Yellinek forbidden it?

[Silence.]

VV: How long have you been a member of this sect?

UF: I've been in the Pure Life since 1987.

VV: Are you in a sexual relationship with Yellinek?

[Silence.]

VV: If you continue refusing to answer my questions, I'll take you away from here and subject you to an entirely different kind of cross-examination.

UF: That's up to you, Chief Inspector.

VV: Is it true that you dabble in driving out devils?

UF: Those are your words, not mine.

VV: What the hell do you mean by that?

UF: I'd be grateful if you didn't swear in my presence.

VV: Yellinek was found guilty of indecency and illegal compulsion six years ago. What do you have to say about that?

UF: It was an unjust verdict. There is a higher authority.

VV: Can you explain this principle of purity?

UF: I don't think you would be receptive to my
teaching.

VV: But your little girls are receptive?
[Silence.]

VV: Is it not the case that Yellinek's ideas are so
infantile that they are most suited to children
and the mentally retarded?

UF: You are insolent. I had expected more correct
behaviour.

VV: Now listen here. Your church is based upon
three principles. Prayer, self-denial and purity.
I ask you to explain one of these principles, and
you choose to remain silent. What the hell do
you expect me to think?

UF: You can think whatever you like. It's up to every
individual to decide how to deal with the big
questions, and what to make of their lives.

The chief inspector reached out his hand and switched off
the tape recorder.

Why do I lose control so quickly? he wondered.

Is it just the heat and the feeling of impotence, or is
there more to it? He pressed fast forward; the rest of
the conversation with Ulriche Fischer had proceeded with
neither of them trusting the other, he was well aware of

that, and nothing had emerged that could support the theory that a girl had disappeared.

It took him some time to find the right place on the tape. Before continuing he finished his simple meal and lit a cigarette. Adjusted the pillows and leaned back in order to concentrate better on the conversation with Mathilde Ubrecht. It was a bit more fruitful, he suspected. But perhaps not so much.

It depended what you were looking for, of course.

MU: My name is Mathilde Ubrecht. Thirty-six. I work for the Pure Life church.

VV: Thank you. Do you know why I want to talk to you?

MU: I think so.

VV: The police have been tipped off that a girl has disappeared from the camp. Do you understand that we have to investigate that information?

MU: Yes. But nobody has disappeared.

VV: You're sure of that?

MU: Yes.

VV: May I ask you a hypothetical question?

MU: Please do.

VV: If it was in the interests of your church, would you feel able to tell lies in a police cross-examination or in a court?

MU: I don't understand the question.

VV: All right, I'll re-word it. If Oscar Yellinek urged you to say certain things to me, would you do so even if you knew they were lies?

MU: I don't believe that Yellinek would do such a thing.

VV: What do you think of Oscar Yellinek?

MU: He's a great man.

VV: What do you mean by that?

MU: He is in contact with Eternal Life and the One True God. It is a blessing to be in his vicinity.

VV: Do your fellow sisters think the same way?

MU: Of course.

VV: I see. And your confirmation candidates?

MU: I'm sure they do. You notice it as soon as you come into close contact with him.

VV: Really? Can you give me an idea of the form the teaching takes?

MU: Yellinek talks to the girls. We pray together. We try to cast out evil thoughts and purify ourselves.

VV: How?

MU: In various ways. By means of certain exercises. By prayer. By letting ourselves go . . .

VV: What do you do when you let yourselves go? [Silence for a few seconds.]

MU: I don't want to talk about this with outsiders. It's easy to misunderstand. You have to be initiated

in order to see it in the right way, it needs
training . . .

VV: Do you make love to Oscar Yellinek?

MU: We live in intense harmony and intimacy.

VV: Even sexually?

MU: We are biological beings, Chief Inspector. We
don't impose the same limits as you do, that's
the difference between the Pure Life and the
Other World.

VV: The Other World?

MU: The world you live in.

VV: What have you to say about Yellinek being in
prison for indecency and other crimes?

MU: Jesus Christ was crucified to redeem our sins.

VV: Do you compare Oscar Yellinek with Jesus Christ?

MU: Of course.

[Another, quite long silence, apart from a noise
that sounded like a heavy stone being pushed
over the floor. It was some time before Van
Veeteren realized that it wasn't a stone, but a
groan. Coming from him.]

VV: Do your confirmands also live in intense
harmony and intimacy with Oscar Yellinek?

MU: Of course not. Not in the same way.

VV: But the girls are sometimes naked in his presence.

MU: It's not the way you think it is, Chief Inspector.

We are surrounded by ill will and slander, just
like . . .

VV: Like what?

MU: Just like the first Christians.

VV: So you compare yourselves to the first Christians?

MU: There are a lot of similarities.

[Silence. Then the scraping sound of a chair.
A match being lit and then blown out.]

VV: Thank you, Miss Ubrecht. I don't think I have
any more questions to ask you.

'For Christ's sake!' muttered the chief inspector, hopping
over the conversation with Madeleine Zander, the woman
he had spoken to the first time he visited Waldingen. I can't
face the same drivel all over again! he thought. The only
things about her that were different from the others were
that she had been a member since the very start, and that
she had been married. Madeleine Zander was the eldest of
the three – forty-six years old – and she had a grown-up
daughter from a marriage that presumably lasted just long
enough to conceive her and bring her into the world, the
chief inspector thought.

Well, not really thought: hoped, rather.

Later – in the car on the way back to Sorbinowo –
he had tried to recapitulate and home in on any signs of
disharmony between the three women – envy, jealousy or

something of that sort – but no matter how hard he tried, he couldn't recall any such indications in his interviews.

But then again, he had hardly set out to trap them. On the contrary. He had behaved in a friendly and gentlemanly manner all the time. Just as he always did. So perhaps it was best not to pass judgement.

That could apply to the whole of this damned business, he thought. If it were just a crime novel, it would probably be best for it to remain unwritten – it contained so little of substance.

Mind you, the same could be said of rather a lot of things.

However, here he was, no matter what. Two hundred kilometres from Maardam and eleven days from Crete.

There are waiting rooms and there are waiting rooms, he had just read in Klimke's meditations. But trains no longer run from most stations.

He decided to investigate that situation as far as Sorbinowo was concerned. He had only seen the station from a distance, but it hadn't seemed especially lively.

Just as an indication, that is.

He had spoken to two of the girls, and after some thought had chosen to take them together rather than separately. Perhaps that was a symptom of weariness, and perhaps it indicated that he was on the way to giving up –

but after Yellinek and his three pale slaves, what could one expect?

He located the right place on the tape, and started it running.

VV: Would you like to tell me your names – speak loudly so that you can be heard on the tape.

BM: Belle Moulder.

CH: Clarissa Heerenmacht.

VV: Do you know why I want to speak to you? [Silence. Van Veeteren remembered that the girls had exchanged glances before they both shook their heads in unison.]

VV: I'm from the police. It's about that girl who's disappeared from the camp. Can you tell me what happened?

BM: Nobody's disappeared.

CH: Everybody's been here all the time.

VV: How many of you are there?

CH: Twelve.

VV: But there were thirteen to start with, weren't there? [Short pause.]

BM: There's been twelve of us all the time. Stop trying to trick us.

VV: All right, if you say so. Can you tell me a bit about what you do here during the day?

CH: We do all sorts of things.

VV: Such as?

BM: We go swimming, play games. We have discussion classes and group work and so on.

VV: You like being here?

BM: Yes.

CH: It's a really fab camp.

BM: Lots of people think we do lots of strange things here at Waldingen, but we don't in fact.

VV: What do people think you do?

BM: I've no idea. But we have a great time anyway. We learn lots of terrific things.

VV: Really. Can you give me a few examples?

BM: Well, we learn what's important in life, how to live together with others, and things like that.

CH: How to be a good person, and have a pure soul.

VV: And how do you get a pure soul?

CH: You get rid of all wicked thoughts.

VV: How do you do that?

CH: There are lots of ways. You have to be really, really careful – there's evil everywhere.

BM: We're not supposed to talk about things like this.

CH: No . . .

VV: But I'm interested in learning.

BM: Then you should talk to Yellinek.

VV: Why?

BM: It's not good for us to talk about these things. We are learning important things, and you come from the Other World.

VV: The Other World?

BM: Yes.

VV: What's that?

BM: The Other World is everything that isn't the Pure Life.

VV: You don't say. And how long have you been members of this church?

CH: How long? Er, forever.

BM: Since we were very little, at least.

VV: So your parents are also members, are they?

BM: Of course. Our brothers and sisters as well. We're sort of chosen.

VV: I see. How old are you?

BM: Fourteen.

CH: Twelve . . . Nearly thirteen.

VV: Do you go to the Pure Life school as well?

BM: Did do. I've been going to an ordinary school for a year now.

CH: I'll be starting an ordinary school in the autumn.

BM: You think there's something odd about us, don't

you? It's always the same. What is it you're
trying to find out?

CH: We're having a fab time here at Waldingen.

VV: So I've gathered. I suppose it must be hard,
going to school in the Other World?

CH: We have to learn what to do in the Other World
as well. How to behave.

BM: But I don't think we should talk about that with
you either.

VV: Have you been told what you may and may not
talk to me about?
[Silence. A warning look from the elder girl at
the younger, if he remembered correctly.]

CH: No . . .

VV: You don't sound sure.

BM: Nobody's told us anything. But we know
anyway.

VV: I see. But there must be some girls who aren't
enjoying the camp as much as you seem to be
doing?

BM: Everybody's having a great time.

VV: Everybody?

BM: Why are you asking? Obviously somebody might
get a bit sad now and again. Is that so odd?

CH: I know everybody thinks it's great here. What
we are doing and learning is important.

VV: Can you tell me a bit about the three basic principles, prayer, purity and self-denial?

CH: Those are the basic principles, sort of. That's what everything is based on.

VV: What is meant by purity?

CH: You have to be pure when you meet your God, but I think—

BM: You don't understand all this. If you're not a member of the church, you shouldn't start asking lots of questions.

VV: Do you have to be naked in order to be pure?

CH: Yes . . . No.

BM: No, you don't have to be, and anyway it's nothing to do with you.

VV: Do you have visitors?

BM: No, it's not good to have visitors when we're busy learning.

VV: But you phone home now and then, I suppose?

CH: We don't phone, because—

BM: We write letters. That's just as good.

VV: So you're not allowed to use the telephone?

CH: I suppose we might be, but we don't.

VV: What's the name of the girl who was only here at the beginning?

CH: Eh? What do you mean by that?

BM: I think you should stop being so rude. You are

accusing us of lots of things you have no idea
about. It's cowardly of you to attack us like this.

VV: Why don't you have any boys in your church?

BM: Of course we have boys in the Pure Life, but not
at this camp. They have one of their own. I don't
think we want to talk to you any more now.
[Five seconds of silence. The sound of chairs
scraping.]

VV: All right. Let's leave it at that. Run away and
wash your souls, and tell that Yellinek to look
up Isaiah 55:8.

BM: Eh?

VV: There's a book called the Bible. I thought you
were familiar with it.

CH: Isaiah?

VV: Yes, 55:8. So, off with you now, and wash
yourselves clean!

He stopped the tape and slumped back onto the pillows.
Lay there motionless for several minutes, searching for a
way of putting into words the emotions careering around
inside him.

Or a metaphor at least.

But there was nothing. Nothing occurred to him,
and no thoughts crystallized in his brain. Only the word
'impotence', which was beginning to feel like an old

123

acquaintance by this time. A disconsolate, ancient relative determined not to die, but who refused to be cast out – perhaps because of the very relationship.

He sighed. Noted that the bottles of beer were unfortunately empty, and stood up. Went over to the window and looked out over the lake, where the last canoeists of the day were mooring at the jetties. It was a few minutes after half past nine, and shades of blue were busy transforming the evening light into mellow summer darkness.

A July night, Van Veeteren thought. 'A summer night's no time for sleep', or something along those lines – who had written that?

No matter, the thought had merit. A little evening stroll and a glass of white wine seemed to be in order. To help him shake off the thought of that old acquaintance, if nothing else.

And to help him make up his mind to leave here. There was no longer any substantial reason for him to continue this putative investigation. The debt he owed Malijsen could surely be considered paid – no matter how you calculated it – and it was hard to see any rational reason for launching more attacks on the Waldingen camp. No matter how hard one might try to find one.

Mind you, perhaps old Borkmann had a point when he used to claim that: Reason has an elder sister, never forget that. She's called Intuition.

12

She finally found the body long after the sun had set. Darkness had begun to spread through the pine trees, and for one confused moment she wondered if it wasn't just an illusion after all. A bizarre mirage, this sudden sight of a girl's white skin gleaming at her through the brushwood – perhaps it would disappear the moment it occurred to her to close her eyes.

But she didn't close her eyes. The inner voice that had led her here would not allow her to close her eyes. She would have to act, to undertake the incomprehensible task it had given her.

There was no arguing, she must do it.

Where did it come from, this voice that drove her? She didn't know, but presumably it was the only source of strength available to her in the nightmare she was experiencing. The only thing that kept her going, and made her take these measures and steps – it must be something based inside herself nevertheless; a side of her that she had never in her life needed to make use of, but it had now kicked in and made sure that whatever had to be done really was in fact done. A sort of reserve, she thought, an unknown well from which she could scoop out water, but over which – at some point in the distant future, may God please ensure that she soon got there! – she must place a heavy lid of forgetfulness. Plant the grass of time upon it: I am the grass; I cover all, as the poet said – why on earth should she think of poetry now? – so that neither she herself nor any other person could suspect what she had used its water for. Or even that it had been there.

In the distant future.

The well. Her strength. The inner voice.

It was very dark now. She must have been standing there, staring at the incomprehensible, for an incredibly long time, even if she hadn't been aware of it. She switched on her torch for a moment, but realized that light would do her no favours in these circumstances, and switched it off again. Pushed some twigs aside and pulled out the whole of the thin, naked body. Bowed down on one knee and took hold of it under its back and under its knees; was briefly surprised by the stiffness in the muscles and joints, and was reminded fleetingly of the body of a little foal when she had been present at a failed birth many years ago.

The body was not heavy, below forty kilograms for sure, and she was able to carry it with little difficulty. She hesitated for a moment, wondering about various alternatives, but eventually came to a place where she could hear that inner voice once more. Carefully – as if displaying some kind of perverted respect no matter what the circumstances – she placed the body in a half-sitting position against the trunk of an aspen tree: an enormous aspen with a whole sky of whispering leaves – and began to cover it over with what she could find in the way of branches and twigs and last year's husks.

Not to hide it, of course. Merely to shield it a little in the name of dignity and propriety.

When she had finished it was so dark that she couldn't see the result of her work, but for the sake of respect and reverence, she stood there for a while, head bowed and hands clasped.

Perhaps she said a prayer. Perhaps it was merely a jumble of words passing through her mind.

Then she suddenly felt a white-hot flash of terror. She retraced her steps rapidly and collected the spade from where she had left it. Continued on to the road, and hurried away as fast as her legs would carry her.

13

'Intuition?' said Przebuda, and smiled over the rim of his wine glass. 'Surely you're not telling me that you are troubled by doubts as far as intuition is concerned? Myself, I rely upon it without question, I simply think it's a talent that has skipped a few stages – in the chain of cause and effect, that is. Or gives the impression of having skipped them. It's a bit more advanced, but there's no essential difference. We have it, but we don't understand how we are in a position to have it. I mean, we absorb enormous amounts of information every second . . . Everything is stored away, but only a tiny portion of that gets as far as our active consciousness. The rest stays there, sending out its signals – usually in vain, simply because we are so unreceptive. Let's face it, we're only human after all.'

Van Veeteren nodded, and stretched out his legs under the table. It was Monday evening, and he was slumped back in an old leather chair in Andrej Przebuda's large living room-cum-study. He'd been sitting there for quite a while, sipping an outstanding Chateau Margeaux '81 and nibbling slices of pear with Camembert. Smoked. Dinner had been eaten in the company of Eisenstein, de Sica, Bergman and Tarkovskij, and only when they had left the table and sauntered over to the armchairs did the conversation turn to the matter that was the chief inspector's motive for his stay in Sorbinowo.

Which had now been extended by a further day.

'Presumably it's the same phenomenon as occurs in connection with new discoveries in the natural sciences,' said Przebuda. 'The researcher already knows the answer, he's seen the final solution before he actually gets that far. Or glimpsed it, at least. If that weren't the case, he would presumably be in no state to discover it. The bottom line is that we need an advance image of the conclusion. I think Rappaport writes about this, Sartre as well, of course. Pierre and the cafe and all that, you know. It's another side of the cognitive, that's all. A sort of . . . Well, what should one call it? The avant garde of knowledge, perhaps?'

'Hmm,' said Van Veeteren. 'A chain that hangs together despite the fact that several links are missing. I'd like to see the public prosecutor who falls for that kind of thing. But you are no doubt right in principle. God knows, of course I believe in intuition.'

'And what's your impression of Waldingen, then?' Przebuda asked, lighting his pipe that kept going out.

Deliberately or accidentally. 'The problem with smoking a pipe,' he added, 'is that it goes out as soon as you talk too much. I have to admit that it happens to me now and again. Well?'

The chief inspector sighed.

'I don't know,' he admitted. 'I'll be damned if I can work out what I really think. The people we are dealing with are pretty moronic, and they sort of get in the way and conceal the point at issue. Perhaps some kind of intervention would be justified no matter what – God only knows what rubbish they are drumming into those poor girls. But that falls some way short of actually murdering somebody. I can't really say I've found evidence to suggest that anybody really has disappeared . . .'

Przebuda was still preoccupied with his pipe.

'Only a trace of a suspicion.'

The chief inspector leaned back and clasped his hands behind his head; he let his gaze wander around the book-lined walls and was struck by a sudden illusion of being in the middle of an encyclopaedia. Przebuda's interests seemed to embrace everything from the financial state of the steel industry in the eighties and fishing quotas in the Arctic Ocean to cultural anthropology and Provençal love lyrics. A newspaperman of the old school, obviously; an incorruptible journalist who – given sufficient time – was quite capable of writing an article on more or less any subject at all. Although he tried to exclude it, Van Veeteren had to admit that the setting of this evening's conversation reminded him of something else as well. The classic crime novel hero – the case-hardened detective who gathers together all the facts in his head and then solves the case while sitting with his pipe in a winged armchair in his library.

Although on this occasion it was Przebuda smoking the pipe. Van Veeteren was smoking cigarettes.

So perhaps it was his host who would come up with the solution, not himself.

If a solution was needed, that is. Perhaps all the goings-on didn't amount to an equation – wasn't that the conclusion he had reached? No missing girl, and no case in fact. Nevertheless there was something special about this room; the only thing missing, of course, was a chessboard. But Przebuda had already admitted that chess was a pastime that had never managed to capture his interest.

Something that indisputably made the game even more unique than it already was, Van Veeteren thought. But pastime! Surely that was little short of blasphemy!

'Needless to say I have a few notes,' said Przebuda after a few seconds of silence. 'In case you are interested. I thought I might write half a page last summer when they were last here. The Pure Life . . . I suppose I thought I'd try to dig down into the sect itself, as it were. Not just the summer camp. Anyway, I interviewed the shepherd and took a few photographs, but I eventually decided to shelve the project.'

'Why?'

Przebuda shrugged.

'I don't really know. Some jobs you just drop, period. I think it had something to do with the impression they made. I found it a bit distasteful, to be honest. I take it you understand what I mean.'

Van Veeteren nodded.

'That Yellinek and his four fancy women.'

'Four?'

'Yes indeed. There were four women who took care of all the chores out there in the forest. Much younger than he was, and, well, I suppose that gave me cold feet, or however you might want to put it. And I don't particularly want to give dodgy people like that free publicity. Has he brought the same harem with him this year as well?'

'Three,' said Van Veeteren. 'Only three.'

Przebuda burst out laughing.

'Ah well,' he said. 'Perhaps he's beginning to run out of steam. If they observe other Muslim traditions, maybe they have the right to be satisfied as well. What's the routine? Two nights out of three?'

'Every other night, I think,' said the chief inspector.

'There are various trends. You don't happen to have the names of the women who were here last year, do you?'

Przebuda raised an eyebrow, and then his wine glass.

'Why do you ask?'

'It's just a thought that struck me,' said the chief inspector.

'All right, I'll take a look,' said Przebuda. 'But first, your very good health.'

'Cheers,' said Van Veeteren.

Przebuda stood up and went over to his desk, which was piled high with documents. It formed a triangle in a corner of the room, and must have been over two metres square. He switched on a lamp and began rummaging through a collection of red and green files at least a metre high. After a while he returned with one of them, and took out a bundle of unsorted documents.

'So, let's have a look,' he said, taking a pair of glasses from his breast pocket. 'I don't really know why I bothered, but I did actually take a few pictures of them. Yes, here we are.'

He picked out a photograph and studied it critically for a few seconds before handing it to Van Veeteren. The chief inspector looked at the picture. It was obviously taken on the terrace outside the main building. In the early evening sunshine, to judge by the light and the shadows. Oscar Yellinek was leaning against the rail, flanked by four women, two on each side. Despite the fact that they were unremarkable, he had no trouble in identifying three of them. But to the left of Mathilde Ubrecht and with one hand resting on Yellinek's shoulder was a dark-haired, unknown woman. She seemed a bit younger than the others, and unlike the rest of them had managed to raise a smile, aimed at the camera. Without a doubt she was easily the prettiest of them all.

'Hmm,' said the chief inspector. 'Do you have their names?'

'Could be,' said Przebuda. 'Does it say anything on the back?'

Van Veeteren turned the picture over and read:

'Fr. l.: Ulriche Fischer, Madeleine Zander, O.Y., Ewa Siguera, Mathilde Ubrecht'

Ewa Siguera? he thought, and took a sip of wine. Sounds like a character in a novel.

Przebuda had managed to light his pipe again, and blew a few puffs of thick smoke over the table.

'Well,' he said, 'I think I'd already decided by then that I wasn't going to run the story. What are you angling for?'

The chief inspector thought for a moment, continuing to scrutinize the photograph.

'No idea,' he said. 'I suppose you could call it some sort of avant garde knowledge.'

'I see,' said Przebuda with a smile. 'Maybe we should

take a look at the rest of the papers anyway. I have quite a bit on Yellinek, if I remember rightly. Although I don't think I made any notes about kidnapping. Still, the best things are always written between the lines. Don't you think we ought to crack open another bottle, by the way?'

'This heat certainly makes a man thirsty,' said Van Veeteren.

'Religion is a multifaceted thing,' declared Andrej Przebuda quite a while later. 'Personally, it's something I've left behind me; but I can't say that it hasn't left its traces.'

Van Veeteren waited.

'My parents, all my family were practising Jews. When the heat was turned up and we realized what was really in store for us – my father was the most clear-sighted of the whole family – they placed me and my sister with a Catholic family in a little village miles away from anywhere. They kept us hidden on their farm for four years; we were the only two to survive. Ironically enough our hiding place was less than fifty kilometres from Auschwitz. Ah well, then I married a woman from India; she died six years ago and is buried in the Reformed Cemetery here in Sorbinowo.'

The chief inspector nodded.

'Any children?' he asked.

'A handful,' said Przebuda. 'Neither more nor less. Eleven grandchildren. But I've dropped the religion, as I said.'

'And you weren't inspired to take it up again when you met the Pure Life?'

Przebuda smiled.

'No, but perhaps we ought to be grateful to them because they look after quite a few people who would otherwise be locked away in an institution. At society's expense, of course. But this business of the children is another story. Perhaps you should send in an undercover agent to find out what really goes on. Maybe a bright thirteen-year-old with a mobile phone . . . But I assume you have more urgent matters to keep you occupied.'

Van Veeteren nodded in agreement.

'Too right we have,' he said. 'For my part I'll be going on holiday in just over a week, so unless somebody comes along with a missing young lassie in the next twelve hours, I'll be on my way. I can't claim to have achieved much at all. The film club and this evening were the only useful things, to be honest. But they are not to be sneered at.'

'Glad you think so,' said Przebuda.

'May I take these papers about Yellinek as bedtime reading?' the chief inspector asked. 'I can call in and leave them in the editorial office tomorrow morning, before I leave.'

'Of course,' said Przebuda, spreading out his arms. 'So you're not thinking of letting go of the thread just yet?'

Van Veeteren stubbed out the evening's final cigarette.

'No,' he said. 'I'll hang on to it until it breaks of its own accord. That's a bad habit of mine I've had for years.'

He got up from the armchair and noticed immediately that the last glass of Burgundy had been stronger than he'd thought.

There won't be a lot of reading done tonight, he thought. It'll probably be more a question of trying to stay awake long enough to get into bed before I fall asleep.

Which was of course no more than a pious hope – especially in view of what lay in store for him during the rest of the night.

But as yet he hadn't the slightest bit of knowledge about that – be it empirical or intuitive.

14

In normal circumstances – when he wasn't standing in as chief of police in the Sorbinowo police district – he would naturally have delegated all calls in a situation like this to his answering machine. No question. He and Deborah had nestled down at opposite ends of the new Wassmeyer sofa with a box of chocolates within easy reach; the film starring Clint Eastwood hadn't yet got as far as the first ads break, and a pleasant, warm breeze was wafting in through the open French windows. Gently and tenderly he was massaging her bare feet.

From a purely physical point of view, it was more or less a perfect evening.

'Phone call,' said Deborah, sliding a chocolate between her red lips.

Kluuge sighed, and heaved himself up from the sofa. The nearest telephone was in the bedroom, and he closed the door behind him, so as not to disturb his wife's enjoyment of the film.

Typical, he thought. But if you're on duty, that's the way it is.

'Chief of Police Kluuge.'

'Hello?'

That was quite enough for him to recognize the voice. In a mere split second, Clint and his wife and the chocolates were banished from his mind.

'Yes, Kluuge here.'

'It's me again.'

'So I hear. What do you want?'

'I want to give you a tip.'

'A tip?'

'There's the dead body of a girl at Waldingen.'

'We are busy investigating . . .'

'I know. But you're not getting anywhere. If you go there and find the body, perhaps you will believe me.'

'I don't believe there is a body,' said Kluuge. 'You keep on calling just to draw attention to yourself. We have—'

'Drive out to the summer camp.'

'Eh?'

'I'll describe the way for you.'

'The way to where?'

'To the body. I'll tell you exactly where it is, so you can go there and look at it. Then you might understand that I'm telling you the truth.'

Kluuge gulped.

'Er . . .' was all he could manage.

'A hundred metres past the camp buildings there's a little path off to the right. Go down it, and just after you've passed a big boulder on your left you'll see an enormous aspen tree. She's lying just a few metres behind the rock. It's no more than fifteen metres off the path.'

'Hang on a minute,' said Kluuge. 'I must fetch a pen.'

'You don't need one,' said the woman. 'A hundred metres past the main building. A path to the right. Close to the aspen behind the big boulder. You'll find her there.'

A mass of questions suddenly piled up inside Sergeant Kluuge's brain, but before he could ask any of them, the caller had hung up.

Oh hell! he thought. Hell and damnation!

He thought for fifteen seconds, then dialled the number to Grimm's Hotel. It rang twelve times before anybody in reception answered, and the only information he received was that Mr Van Veeteren had gone out several hours ago without leaving any indication of where he was going. Nor when he would be back.

Kluuge hung up. Stared out through the open window. Darkness was slowly embracing the warmth of summer still dancing outside. Grasshoppers were chirruping away. The clock on the bedside table indicated 22.20.

What the hell should I do now? he wondered. Some-where deep down inside him he could hear a faint voice whispering that he should go back to the sofa. Simply return to Deborah and her warm tootsy-wootsies. The easy way out, of course, would be to simply forget the whole business and pretend that nobody had called. That he'd never heard a word about a dead little girl or a path or a boulder. But shame at the very suggestion that such a thought could ever have occurred to him soon took the upper hand. Grew bigger and redder.

Never, he thought. No chance. I must take full responsibility now.

He thought for a few more minutes, then called Grimm's Hotel again and left a message for the chief inspector:

Red-hot tip in the Waldingen case. Have gone there. Kluuge

Five minutes later he had already kissed his wife goodnight and was on his way out into the night.

So as not to stir up any unnecessary suspicions, he parked the car some way short of the summer camp. Switched off the lights and set off walking along the dirt road. A full moon had risen over the lake, and made it possible to overcome the darkness. He began walking slowly along the narrow road – extremely carefully, and on the very edge so that his footsteps were swallowed up by grass and soil.

By the time he passed the main buildings, it was five past eleven and all the lights were out except for two. But he didn't see a single person, nor could he hear any noises to suggest that somebody was around. Without pausing, he continued along the slight upward slope on the other side, counting his steps, and after about fifty metres he lit his torch and began looking for the path.

He found it with no difficulty. Before turning into it, he switched off the torch. Stood stock-still in the darkness for a few seconds, and listened again. But all he could hear was the faint soughing from the tops of the trees, the unceasing scratching of the crickets and an occasional love-sick frog from the edge of the lake. Resolutely, he switched the torch on again, and strode out along the path.

Fear took hold of him just as he was aiming the beam from his torch at the gigantic boulder. It suddenly occurred to him that the madwoman on the telephone maybe wasn't quite as silly as he had presumed, and that it could be time now . . . Maybe it was only a matter of seconds before he was confronted by his first corpse. He could feel his mouth going dry almost instantaneously at that very thought, and his pulse pounding so relentlessly that he could hear his own blood.

He raised his torch and shone it into the trees.

There was no doubt. No doubt at all, to be honest; he raised the beam to shine into the crown of the tree, and could see with no shadow of a doubt that it was an aspen, a gigantic aspen growing just a few metres behind the boulder. Its whispering crown was hovering high above him in the darkness like a harbinger of evil deeds and God only knew what else. He shuddered, and shook his head. Imagination, he told himself. Nothing more than imagination. Fantasy, superstition and old wives' tales. He walked around the rock and shone his torch onto the lower part of the trunk. Carefully shifted to one side with his foot several fallen leaves and twigs, and when he leaned forward to look more carefully he could see clearly – as clearly as possible – that the whitish object sticking out from the undergrowth was in fact a hand.

A perfectly normal, quite thin and bloodless little girl's hand – and he had just enough presence of mind to move swiftly several metres to one side before sicking up both Deborah's broccoli pie and the eight chocolates he had managed to consume while watching the television.

And it was clear to Sergeant Kluuge that at this very moment – this solitary, eternally long moment in the middle of the forest – he had been subjected to an experience which would cast its shadow over all other experiences for as long as he lived. Both negative and positive. Past and future.

I've just grown up, he thought in surprise. Grown up. It felt like having been cast out into a foreign, desolate land; a harsh but inevitable reality that he knew he would never be able to push to one side, or behind him, or indeed ever to get away from.

There was something else there as well: a sort of bitter satisfaction that was not to be denied, and that he couldn't really come to terms with.

But this was not the right time for such speculation. He wiped his mouth with the back of his hand, switched off the torch and hurried back to the car.

15

Reinhart always used to claim that there was really only one foolproof method of kick-starting an investigation that had come to a dead end: drink a pint of whisky and four beers, and when you've gone to bed it's guaranteed that within twenty minutes the phone will ring and you'll be saddled with another corpse.

Perhaps it wasn't quite as bad as that this warm evening in Sorbinowo, but when Van Veeteren read the two messages left by Kluuge, he decided he'd better take a long, cold shower before stepping out into the darkness.

A summer night's no time for sleep! – the memory came back to him. Perhaps certain thoughts ought to be punctured before they had a chance to float up to the surface, he thought as he stood in the shower, trying to rinse the Burgundy out of his face. They had such a damned awkward tendency to become self-fulfilling prophecies!

But nevertheless his ability to concentrate was slowly coming back.

What the hell had happened out there?

Actually, Kluuge's two messages had been as plain as a pikestaff. Especially the second one:

Dead girl in Waldingen. Reinforcements on the way. Kluuge

I wonder if the press is there already, Van Veeteren thought as he stepped out of the shower. The bright young girl in reception didn't seem to have had any difficulty in understanding the sergeant's bulletins, at least. The chief inspector wondered if he ought to call Przebuda, maybe he hadn't yet gone to bed; but he decided not to. Better to have mercy on him and let him have a decent night's sleep. In any case, his time as a front-line reporter must surely be over by now.

When he climbed into the waiting taxi, it was a few minutes short of one o'clock. According to the receptionist Kluuge's second message had arrived just before midnight, so there were grounds for assuming that both forensic and medical officers were already in Waldingen. Unless he was much mistaken, teams from Rembork would be closest at hand, but of course Kluuge would know all about that.

'What the hell do you want to go out there for in the middle of the night?' asked the podgy driver, and yawned so widely that the back of his neck was covered in creases.

'Let's go,' said Van Veeteren. 'Switch off the radio and cut the talk.'

There were three other cars at the scene in addition to Kluuge's. Sure enough two of them were from Rembork, and apart from the crime scene team they had also brought two detectives. Van Veeteren went over to the third car and peered inside: a young man with a beard and glasses was clutching a mobile phone. The chief inspector reached in through the open window and snatched the phone from his grasp.

'What the hell . . . ?'

'Van Veeteren, Detective Chief Inspector. You are getting in the way of the investigation. Who do you work for?'

'*Allgemejne.*'

'All right. If you lie low for an hour, I promise to give you correct information instead.'

The young reporter hesitated.

'How do I know you're not tricking me?'

'I never trick anybody,' said Van Veeteren. 'Ask your editor-in-chief, he knows me.'

Kluuge appeared out of the darkness.

'She's lying up there,' he explained, pointing along the road. 'One of the Rembork boys is examining her. And the crime scene team is there as well, of course. She is . . . She's been strangled and raped in any case, that's very obvious.'

'How long have they been here?' asked the chief inspector.

Kluuge checked his watch.

'Half an hour or so. I found her at round about twenty past eleven.'

Van Veeteren gestured towards the summer camp. There were lights in some of the windows in the main building, but the wings were in darkness.

'What's the state of play in there?'

'I don't really know,' said Kluuge. 'The other detective is there, but I haven't had time to check. Shall I go with you to . . . to where she is?'

Van Veeteren lit a cigarette.

'It'll be better to let them work in peace for the time being,' he said. 'I think I'd like to investigate what's going on with the church crowd first. If you stay in the car, you can show me the body later.'

Kluuge nodded and opened the car door. The chief inspector was about to leave, but paused.

'How are you feeling?' he asked.

'Not so good,' said Kluuge.

'I understand. Sit in the car and keep warm. I'll see if I can fix some coffee.'

He left the sergeant and the cars and set off for the

buildings. Stumbled a couple of times over hidden roots and very nearly fell over, but managed to get as far as the terrace in one piece. Knocked on one of the illuminated windows, and was let in by Sister Madeleine, sullen as ever, wearing a large shapeless dressing gown made of the same unbleached cotton as usual. She deigned neither to look at nor speak to him, merely escorted him, silently and bare-footed, into a little room that appeared to be used as an office. Papers, a few files and a pile of Bibles were strewn over a desk. The other sisters, each in identical dressing gowns, sat on chairs, and standing by the window was the second of the police officers from Rembork. It was obvious that he was in the middle of interrogating the three women.

And it was equally obvious that he was getting nowhere.

Van Veeteren looked round the poky room. Then he asked his colleague for a private conversation, and they both went into the corridor.

'What did you say your name was?'

'Servinus. Detective inspector.'

'Van Veeteren,' said the chief inspector. 'Let's keep our voices down so that they don't catch on to our strategies.'

He gestured towards the closed door. Servinus nodded.

'How long have you been grilling them?'

Servinus looked at his watch.

'Grilling and grilling,' he said. 'Five minutes at most.

They'd been fast asleep, so it took some time . . . But I think we have a bit of a problem.'

'Oh yes,' said Van Veeteren. 'What kind of a problem?'

'They don't say anything.'

'What do you mean?'

Servinus scratched the back of his head in irritation.

'Well, it looks as if they've decided not to cooperate.'

'What the hell . . . ?'

'Exactly. They just don't answer questions, as simple as that. Do you have any idea of what kind of a place this is, in fact? They seem to be a bit, er, how shall I put it—'

'I know what they're like,' said the chief inspector. 'We can go into that some other time. Where's Yellinek? That's the most important thing just now.'

'Who?'

'Oscar Yellinek. Where's he hiding himself away?'

Servinus shuffled uncomfortably and started to look worried.

'Who's this Yellinek? I've only just arrived.'

Van Veeteren felt something ominously cold starting to creep up his spine. It can't be true, he thought.

'You mean you haven't met Yellinek?'

Servinus shook his head.

'And they haven't mentioned him?'

'Not a word. But then, they barely open their damned mouths.'

The chief inspector clenched his fists and muttered something dripping with venom.

'Come on,' he said eventually. 'I must see this with my own eyes.'

He marched back to the room. Flung open the door, burst in and stood straddle-legged in the middle of the floor.

'Okay,' he growled. 'Where's your blue-eyed boy?'

The sisters huddled closer together on their chairs and stared at their naked feet. The chief inspector waited for five seconds, grinding his teeth loudly. Then he went to the desk and slammed his fist hard down on it.

'Where is Oscar Yellinek?' he roared. 'Answer when you're damned well spoken to! There's a girl lying dead in the woods, murdered. Raped and strangled, and you can count on your bloody sect being disbanded from this very moment! Well?'

Madeleine Zander raised her head slowly and looked him in the eye.

'Be careful what you say, Chief Inspector,' she said in a low voice. 'We are innocent, and you have no right to make these groundless accusations. We have decided not to cooperate with you.'

'We are not going to answer your questions,' added Ulriche Fischer.

'Where is he?' bellowed Van Veeteren. 'You have three seconds in which to come up with an answer!'

Madeleine Zander cleared her throat and clasped her hands on her knee. The other two sisters did the same. Lowered their gaze and seemed to be lost in thought. No doubt they're praying to their dodgy Lord, the chief inspector thought. Bollocks to that!

'You're hiding him.'

No reaction.

Van Veeteren gritted his teeth and thought for a moment. Looked at the clock. It was ten minutes to two.

'I thought you took it in turns to go to bed with him. Whose turn was it this evening?'

Madeleine Zander looked up and snorted indignantly.

'Or do you usually have a foursome?'

He glanced at Inspector Servinus, who was looking more and more baffled. He could feel the warmth from the Burgundy returning to his cheeks. Or was it merely his anger and his blood pressure?

'Are you suggesting that he's disappeared?' he asked.

None of the women answered. Van Veeteren snapped a toothpick and threw it onto the floor.

'Now listen here! One of your girls is lying in the woods out there, murdered. Your goddamned high priest is on the run. I couldn't care less what pious conclusions you draw, but I know what I think. Servinus!'

The inspector gave a start.

'Stay here and keep an eye on the Three Graces. We'll lock them up in a police van as soon as one arrives. The poor girls can carry on sleeping for now. Do you know if any female police officers are on their way here?'

'I think so,' said Servinus. 'That Kluuge guy had sent for some.'

'Good,' said the chief inspector.

He paused briefly. Tried to look out into the pitch darkness, and took three or four deep breaths in an attempt to cool down. Then he turned back to face the three women.

'It's my duty to inform you that you will be arrested on suspicion of no end of disgusting things that I'd rather not go on about now. Murder, assisting murder, protecting a criminal, to name but a few.'

'You have no right—' began Madeleine Zander.

'I thought you had vowed to remain silent,' said Van Veeteren, interrupting her. 'May I suggest that you stick to your word. And shut your trap!'

Servinus coughed discreetly. The chief inspector took another deep breath, then turned on his heel and left the room.

For Christ's sake, he thought when he had gone out into the darkness again. It feels like a film. A really awful B-movie with tenth-rate cutting and unsynchronized sound. An unadulterated turkey!

Perhaps it had something to do with the wine, but although it was past two by now, he didn't feel tired in the slightest. On the contrary. He felt full of energy. Raring to go.

Then he remembered what this was all about.

Time to take a look at the bottom of the barrel. No alternative, of course.

As usual.

The *Allgemejne* reporter seemed intent on accompanying them, but the chief inspector shoved him back into his car. Instead it was Kluuge who led the way with his torch. The chief inspector recalled having said something about coffee, but with any luck the mere mention of it and the implication that he cared would suffice. The sergeant had been a bit shocked by his experiences, that had been obvious. No wonder.

The forensic officers – two young men in green overalls – had cordoned off the crime scene with red-and-white police tape, and installed a couple of floodlights to illuminate the site. Van Veeteren stopped a few metres short, so that he didn't need to see too much. A balding man in his fifties approached and introduced himself as Suijderbeck, detective inspector from Rembork.

'Van Veeteren. How does it look?'

Suijderbeck shrugged.

'Pretty awful. Girl aged thirteen or fourteen. Raped.

Crushed larynx, I think. She was lucky in that it happened in reverse order.'

'What do the forensic guys say?'

'Dragged here, presumably,' said Suijderbeck. 'There's nothing to suggest that the violence actually took place here. But it's early days yet.'

'Sperm?'

Suijderbeck shook his head.

'Apparently not.'

'But raped nevertheless?'

'Penetrated, in any case,' said Suijderbeck with a sigh. 'With something. And maltreated here and there.'

Van Veeteren shuddered. An elderly, hunch-backed man appeared behind the inspector. He introduced himself as Dr Monsen, and seemed to ring a bell, the chief inspector thought. Rightly, as it turned out.

'Van Veeteren?' exclaimed the newcomer when he realized who it was he was talking to. 'What the hell are you doing here? Moved you on, have they?'

The chief inspector ignored the joke.

'Do you know what this is all about?' asked Monsen. 'What goes on at this place, I mean?'

'I'll tell you about that later.'

'I bet you will. Do you want to take a look?'

Van Veeteren sighed and put his hands in his pockets.

'I suppose I'll have to.'

He walked round the boulder and one of the kneeling forensic officers. Focused on what he couldn't avoid seeing.

Leaning against the trunk of a large aspen tree – grotesquely illuminated by the floodlights – was the thin body of a little girl. Van Veeteren had had plenty of time to prepare himself for the sight, but the unedited reality nevertheless hit him like a punch in the solar plexus. The same old punch he'd felt so often before. Here and there – mainly around the groin, the neck and the chest – the pale corpse was stained by large dark patches, and her thighs were striped with dried blood. Her head was twisted almost unnaturally to one side, her tongue was sticking out slightly between her lips, and her eyes were fixed in an expression of pointless terror.

Clarissa Heerenmacht. He could even remember her name.

He worked out that it must have been about a day and a half since he'd been talking to her in that large room at the summer camp.

Then he felt a moment of dizziness before an attack of heartburn returned him to reality.

There's something here that doesn't add up, he thought before turning back into the darkness once more.

FOUR

23–28 JULY

16

The forest was dense and full of brushwood.

He saw no sign of any animals or humans, but he could hear church bells ringing in the distance. Perhaps that was meant to give him the guidance he needed. But the chimes were faint and thin; they also seemed to shift slightly from one moment to the next, and the sound of his own steps in the blueberry sprigs and his heavy breathing constantly threatened to drown out the bells. He was forced to stop occasionally, cup his hand to his ear and listen for the peals; and every time he paused it was even more difficult to shake off the feeling that he'd been going round in circles, and was in fact standing on exactly the same spot as a few minutes previously.

Under the same aspen; that pale body of the little girl with the dark patches seemed familiar, to say the least. Or perhaps the whole forest was full of murdered teenagers, although that seemed undeniably somewhat exaggerated. He wiped the sweat off his brow with the sleeve of his jacket, and hurried on his way, stumbling over stones and fallen branches and tufts of grass. At last the bells were beginning to sound louder. A few minutes later he came to the edge of the forest and could see the church in the valley below, by the dark river. The last of the congregation were making their way in; he spurted down the final slope and just managed to slip inside as the heavy door started to close.

It was his own wedding; nevertheless he could feel no relief at having just made it in time. Only a certain sad feeling of resignation weighing down on his forehead and shoulders as he stood right at the back in the gloom, trying to recover his breath. His bride was already in place in front of the altar, waiting there in her wedding dress of pale, unbleached cotton; but her shock of hair was a promising chestnut-brown colour. He wasn't sure if this was good or bad, on the whole. The congregation was lost in some sort of prayer, it seemed, and the bells were still chiming loudly as – with considerable dignity – he walked down the central aisle towards his future wife. When he glanced furtively in each direction, he could see that there wasn't a single person he knew in the pews. Nothing but stern, unfamiliar faces, row after row of them; and nobody paid him the slightest bit of attention.

He finally reached the altar and placed his hand hesitantly on the bride's shoulder; she spun round with a start

– so violently that the cheap wig she was wearing slipped to one side – and he could see that it was Renate. The same old Renate as ever, damn her, and with a sly smile on her lips she hissed: 'Yesss! Now I've got you! This time you won't get away!' And when, filled with despair and justified anger, he turned to the priest – who had just washed his hands in a chalice of veined marble and was about to begin the rituals – he saw that the man had long, mouse-coloured hair and taped glasses, and realized he was in cahoots with the bride. There was no doubt about that at all. They were smiling at each other, the priest and the bride, and he had to acknowledge that the game was lost. The whole forest was full of dead girls, he was going to have to marry Renate again under the auspices of this accursed pagan prat, and no matter how desperately he searched through his suit pockets he couldn't find his police pistol. The fact was of course that he'd forgotten it in some desk drawer in his office at the Maardam police station, as usual, and as he sank down in resignation – in a ridiculously long slow-motion sequence – to kneel beside his triumphant bride, the bells became even louder.

Swelled and contorted themselves in polyphonic variations that would have driven the old master Bach into a state of delirium, and eventually became so bizarre and unbearable that he realized he would have to put a stop to it all if he were not to lose the very last dregs of his sanity.

He stretched out a hand, lifted the receiver and answered.

It was Kluuge.

The chief inspector sat up and cleared his throat so loudly that he missed whatever the sergeant began by saying.

'What did you say?'

'Good morning, Chief Inspector,' Kluuge repeated. 'I hope I didn't wake you up?'

'Of course not,' said Van Veeteren, as usual, and fumbled for his wristwatch on the bedside table.

'It's half past eleven,' Kluuge informed him. 'I thought we'd better get going, so I've summoned the others to a meeting at two o'clock, to run through what's happened so far.'

The others? Van Veeteren wondered – but then he began to recall what had happened during the night, and who had been present. A rapid subtraction suggested he could hardly have slept for more than four hours, and how Kluuge could sound so damned bright and cheery was a mystery. He preferred not to think about the possibility of it having to do with age and general condition. Not just now, at least. He cleared his throat again.

'Sounds good,' he said.

'At the police station, naturally,' said Kluuge. 'But there's something I'd like to consult you about first, Chief Inspector.'

'Go ahead,' said Van Veeteren.

There followed a few seconds of silence.

'I don't really know how to put this, but the business of who is responsible and so on . . .'

'Responsible?'

'Yes, I mean who's going to be in charge of the investigation. Obviously you are the one with the most experience and all that, but even so I thought I ought to volunteer to do it. I mean, I'm the acting chief of police, and so it comes within my remit, so to say . . .'

Excellent, the chief inspector thought. Carry on, young man!

'. . . So if you don't object?'

'Of course not,' said Van Veeteren.

'And I think it would be a pity to disturb Malijsen in the middle of his holiday.'

'I agree,' said the chief inspector.

One hundred per cent, he thought.

'Obviously I hope you will stay on and give us a hand. I mean, you have so much experience . . .'

'Naturally,' said Van Veeteren. 'No need to say another word about it. Did you say two o'clock?'

'Yes, two o'clock,' Kluuge confirmed. 'And I've arranged

a press conference for half past four. I'd be grateful if you could be present at that as well, Chief Inspector.'

'If I live that long,' said Van Veeteren. 'I assume nothing significant has happened during the morning?'

'Not a lot,' said Kluuge. 'The women are in isolation at Wolgershuus, as we said, and the youngsters are still at Waldingen. The police nurses have been relieved, and two psychologists are due at one o'clock.'

'And nobody has said anything?'

'No. They're still staying silent. We'll probably have to discuss how to interrogate them in future. Or what do you think? It's all a bit tricky . . .'

'You can say that again,' sighed Van Veeteren. 'But let's hope it's just a matter of time.'

'Could be,' said Kluuge. 'But it must be easier to break down a teenaged girl than one of those madwomen.'

'Be careful about the words you use,' the chief inspector warned. 'It can be a good idea to think before you speak to journalists, if nothing else. They like to quote people. Silence can be golden sometimes, not just for members of sects.'

'Okay,' said Kluuge. 'I'll remember that. I'll see you in a couple of hours, then.'

'Yes,' said Van Veeteren.

'Thank you,' said Kluuge once more.

Madwomen? the chief inspector thought when he'd hung up.

He didn't like it, but whether it was the circumstances or the sergeant's choice of words that should be stigmatized, he wasn't really sure.

The thunderstorm blew in from the south-west, from the direction of Waldingen, and as he ate his brunch on the terrace he was able to watch it approaching rapidly over the edge of the forest on the other side of the lake. The flashes of lightning and claps of thunder entertained him for quite some time before the first heavy drops landed on the corrugated plastic roof over his head, and the temperature dropped drastically by at least ten degrees.

The cloudburst lasted for nearly fifteen minutes, but when it was at its height it seemed to him that the surface of the lake below the hotel, previously so misleadingly calm, had been transformed into a maelstrom, nothing less than a witch's brew, and the far side of the lake disappeared behind a wall of seething, lashing water.

The wrath of the elements, the chief inspector thought. No wonder.

When it had passed over and he had just signed the bill, he could feel how the air had suddenly become more breathable. In big gulps. After a week of suffocating shortages of oxygen in the brain, it was suddenly possible not only to think a clear thought, but to remember it.

I don't think I'm made for the Mediterranean, unfortunately, he thought grimly as he left the table.

It wasn't difficult to guess what effect the heavy rain must have had on the efforts of the police dogs at Waldingen. If there were any trails out there in the forest, they certainly wouldn't be any easier to follow after rain like that.

As flies to wanton boys are we to the gods, he suddenly thought. And when they pull the strings, we dance at their beck and call. They send down buckets of rain, and we stand there with freshly washed faces.

With his briefcase tucked under his arm and two toothpicks wandering around his mouth, he set off towards Kleinmarckt in the centre of the little town. He tried to avoid the rivulets and torrents, but the gutters and grates were not designed to cope with such vast amounts of water, and by the time he reached Florian's, he was soaking wet well up his shins. But he was surprised to find that this was not an especially unpleasant state to be in – invigorating, rather; and a few minutes later he entered the Sorbinowo police station feeling alert and ready to concentrate. Ready to cope with whatever was thrown at him.

We shall solve this lot of crap as well, he thought. Sooner or later.

17

Servinus and Suijderbeck had evidently been instructed to stay on in Sorbinowo. They were sitting beside each other underneath an oil painting of Malijsen's predecessor – a certain J. Stagge – and it was immediately obvious to Van Veeteren that they had even fewer hours of sleep under their belts than he had. Possibly none at all. They had all split up outside the summer camp at about six that morning, and it was by no means impossible that the pair of them had been on duty all the time since then. Inspector Suijderbeck was half-lying in his corner with one leg stretched out in front of him at a strange angle, and it dawned on the chief inspector that he must have some kind of artificial limb. From just under the knee, it seemed. The fact that Van Veeteren hadn't noticed it before bore witness to his being somewhat under the weather.

Come to think of it, he couldn't recall ever having come across a detective officer with a wooden leg before, and he wondered in passing about the circumstances behind it.

Presumably they were not nice – but this was hardly the time or place to go into that.

Kluuge was sitting at the other end of the table with a large notepad at the ready in front of him. He seemed just as perky as he had sounded on the telephone, and Van Veeteren realized that the metamorphosis in Kluuge was still continuing. He bade everyone 'Good morning' and sat down on the only empty chair.

'Good afternoon,' said Kluuge. 'Okay, now we can start.'

'Is this the full team?' the chief inspector asked.

Kluuge shook his head.

'No. We have two colleagues out at Waldingen as well. Female inspectors from Haaldam. And then there's Matthorst at Wolgershuus, keeping an eye on the women. And I suppose that patrol is still combing through the forest; but they'll have finished by this evening, presumably.'

'Presumably,' said Van Veeteren, examining his soaking wet shoes.

'Shall we run through where we've got to so far?' suggested Suijderbeck, suppressing a yawn. 'I really must grab a few hours' sleep soon. I expect we'll have to stay here for a few more days? Don't you think?'

He glanced at his colleague on the sofa.

'Mm,' said Servinus before yawning in turn. 'In any case

I've no intention of getting into the car and driving back to Rembork just now. This is a bloody awful situation, don't you think?'

'It certainly is,' said Kluuge. 'I think we ought to get down to the facts now, don't you? So, the girl was called Clarissa Heerenmacht, and as far as we can tell she was murdered some time on Sunday evening. The day before yesterday, in other words. All traces of rigor mortis had gone by the time I found her, so the doc says it couldn't have been later than ten o'clock at night. Probably not before six either, but we can't be sure of that yet. What time was it when the chief inspector spoke to her?'

'About two,' said Van Veeteren.

'Pretty rough sexual violence on the lower abdomen,' Kluuge said. 'Strangled by extremely hard and prolonged pressure on the larynx, probably not at the location where she was discovered. No clothes have been found. No finger-prints on the body either. Well, that's about it so far. Any comments?'

'Sexual violence on the lower abdomen?' said Suijder-beck. 'In other words, it's not at all certain that we have a case of straightforward rape. I reckon we should bear that in mind.'

Van Veeteren nodded. Kluuge wrote something on his pad.

'What are you implying?' wondered Servinus, looking sceptical.

'I dunno,' said Suijderbeck. 'I just think it's worth bearing in mind.'

He took out a pack of cigarettes and looked round to see what the reaction was. Kluuge nodded, and produced an ashtray. Van Veeteren indicated that he had nothing against being offered one.

'Have you made contact with the parents?' asked the chief inspector, having taken a deep drag.

'No,' said Kluuge. 'It seems there isn't a dad, incidentally. Not any longer, that is. The mother is on a coach tour in India, so it'll probably be some time before we can get in touch with her. But there's an aunt on her way here – we had a bit of luck in finding her.'

'Luck?' said Suijderbeck. 'Why was that lucky?'

A good question, Van Veeteren thought. Kluuge hesitated.

'Well, identification if nothing else. There has to be a relative in order to make it legal.'

'Yes, well,' said Servinus, sitting up straight on the sofa. 'That detail will no doubt sort itself out. But isn't it about time we really started to get stuck in? It seems a bit like playing blind man's buff at the moment, I have to say . . .'

'Of course,' said Kluuge. 'It was a bit much last night.

Well, what can one say? Anyway, it all started a week ago when that anonymous woman made the telephone call . . .'

Van Veeteren leaned back on his chair and closed his eyes while Kluuge recapitulated what had happened before, for the benefit of his colleagues from Rembork. Tried to switch off and instead started to wonder how many times he'd been in a situation like this during all his years as a detective.

All those years.

It must have been hundreds of occasions, and then hundreds more. But even so he was aware that he could recall each and every one of them. Every single case. Always assuming he had the required time. There was something special about these opening gambits, he thought; something almost unique. At this early stage, when most of the logical structure that was always there behind every act of violence – behind most of what human beings said and did as well, of course – was hidden and inaccessible. Camouflaged and disguised.

But then it struck him that perhaps the term 'opening gambit' was wrong. Wouldn't it be more accurate to think in terms of the final confrontation? The only thing they had to go on was the final move, and what it was all about was reconstructing from the end-game positions: with the king (the murdered high school teacher, the poisoned restaurant owner, the strangled and raped teenager) surrounded and in check under the spotlight, they had to go back to the beginning and work out all the moves from the very start.

Until you finally managed to blow away all the mists and the clouds of gunpowder, and concentrate on the chessboard without distractions; work out what had actually happened. And why.

And then – the final denouement – look up and identify your opponent at the other side of the board.

The perpetrator.

Hmm, he thought. A bit overdone perhaps, but nevertheless not a bad image for how things could turn out, a description of the vocation he had made his own. He made a mental note to consider and assess the logic of it all, when the time came – when the time came to write his memoirs. He was finding it more and more difficult not to keep thinking about them. It was remarkable how often they had kept imposing themselves upon his thoughts of late. Was it mere coincidence, mere chance – or was it more than that? A pointer? Time to get out?

'But holy shit!' exclaimed Servinus, intruding upon his thoughts. 'That means there could be another one!'

Van Veeteren opened his eyes. Servinus looked as if he were petrified. Suijderbeck was staring up at the ceiling. Kluuge was leaning back in his chair, apparently having concluded his summing-up of the circumstances thus far.

'Exactly,' said the chief inspector, clearing his throat. 'There's plenty to suggest that she's in good company.'

'Oh shit!' said Suijderbeck.

'And they're still refusing to say anything, are they?' asked Van Veeteren, snapping a toothpick.

Kluuge nodded.

'Both the sisters and the youngsters. It's presumably exactly as you said: they've had it drummed into them that this is some kind of test they're being subjected to. In order to be accepted into the church, or into heaven, or wherever. They have to be strong and not cooperate with us, no matter what. Presumably they've been brainwashed good and proper, and they've been promised no end of rewards as long as they do as they've been told and say nothing.'

'Eternal life, perhaps,' suggested Servinus.

'Us and them,' said Suijderbeck.

Kluuge nodded again.

'Something like that,' said the chief inspector. 'This is the crucial battle. The Pure Life versus the Other World.'

'Eh?' said Servinus.

Van Veeteren shrugged.

'Well, they seem to live in the shadow of categories like that. The worst of their fads will fade away after a few days,

I hope . . . Because there's nothing to support them. But that's only my assessment.'

'So the chief inspector is suggesting that we should wait until they make a false move?' wondered Kluuge.

Van Veeteren scratched his head and waited for a few seconds before answering.

'I don't know,' he said. 'There might be the odd shit-stirrer among them. We can keep our eye on them and pick out the leader types. That Belle Moulder, for instance.'

Kluuge made a note. Servinus sighed deeply and rubbed his eyes.

'Is it really such a good idea to keep them cooped up there?' he asked. 'Or even possible, come to that? The whole business will surely be in the newspapers this evening and tomorrow morning, so no doubt we'll have the parents breathing down our necks before we know where we are . . . I gather there's been something on the radio already?'

'It is a problem,' Kluuge admitted. 'Although we've sorted out the practical side. So that they can stay there for a few more days at least. We've fixed food and that sort of thing.'

'But they're also a gang of wackos as well,' said Servinus. 'The parents, I mean.'

'Wackos?' Kluuge queried.

'Sheep,' Servinus explained. 'They prefer bleating to thinking.'

'For Christ's sake, one of them has to start talking soon,' said Suijderbeck, obviously annoyed. 'They know that one of their friends has been murdered. Possibly two. Surely they're bright enough to realize that . . . well . . .'

'Well?' the chief inspector prompted.

'Oh shit,' said Suijderbeck. 'I'm so tired I'm beginning to see double. So you're really saying that this Yellnek—'

'Yellinek,' said Kluuge.

'That this Yellinek's charisma is so damned strong that he can put a muzzle on his three mistresses and a dozen teenage girls while he slinks away from the crime scene, no problem at all, and scurries off out of harm's way? Beyond belief, and that's what I'll think when I wake up as well!'

'Hmm,' said Kluuge. 'I don't know. But this seems to be a pretty peculiar sect, and we might just as well be clear about that before we go any further.'

'All right,' said Suijderbeck with a sigh. 'Maybe you're right. But what the hell should we do next?'

'Hmm,' said Kluuge again and checked his watch. 'First of all we'd better cope with the press conference, and then I suppose we don't have a lot of choice. Keep on questioning them until they crack, I guess. Both the girls and the ladies at Wolgershuus. Or till somebody cracks, in any case. What does the chief inspector think?'

Van Veeteren stood up and walked over to the window. Turned his back on the others and gazed out over the unsettled sky, swaying back and forth.

'Well,' he said eventually, 'of course we should interrogate them while we're waiting. But we mustn't forget to ask ourselves what the hell has been going on out there. Or what we think has been going on, at least. I have my doubts, myself.'

'What?' said Kluuge. 'What do you mean by that, Chief Inspector?'

But he didn't receive a reply. The notorious detective inspector simply stood there, swaying back and forth on his heels, his hands clasped behind his back. Suijderbeck lit his fourth cigarette in the last half-hour, and Servinus had leaned back and fallen asleep with his mouth open wide.

Huh, Sergeant Kluuge thought. It's not easy, being in charge of a murder investigation. It needs somebody who's up to it, no doubt about that.

18

He had spent a lot of time and effort on his equipment, but evidently it wasn't appropriate even so. Not in everybody's eyes, that is.

'Are you going to take all that stuff with you?' asked the young man with a crew cut and sporting a buttercup-yellow tracksuit.

'Naturally,' said Van Veeteren. 'Is it a problem?'

'No, of course not. But cushions and an umbrella . . . ?'

'Parasol,' insisted the chief inspector. 'Protection from the sun. As you may have noticed, it looks like being another hot day. The cushions are for my back and my head – I happen to know how uncomfortable it is, sitting in a canoe, and I intend being away all day. Well, are you going to rent one to me, or aren't you?'

'Of course,' said the youth, a becoming shade of red appearing to contrast with the buttercup yellow. 'I beg your pardon. So, which one would you like? It's thirty guilders per day, plus a hundred-guilder deposit.'

Van Veeteren took out his wallet and paid.

'That one,' he said, pointing at one of the red Canadian canoes lined up neatly beside the boathouse. 'The wider it is, the better.'

The young man carried the canoe to the water without needing any assistance, then held on to it while the chief inspector loaded on board the cushions, his briefcase and the parasol. And then himself. For a nerve-racking second, before he flopped down onto the bottom of the boat, he thought it would capsize; but once he had settled down and adjusted the cushions behind his back, he smiled and nodded to the young man, who gave him a good push, sending the canoe gliding over the mirror-like water.

Not bad, he thought as he began paddling cautiously alongside the bank lined with alders. Not bad at all.

Heading east, that's how he had planned it. Upstream out, downstream back. Mind you, in this early morning stillness the canoe was gliding along so effortlessly that he doubted if there was any current at all. Ah well, no doubt it would make itself felt when he came to some narrower stretches.

He paddled for a hundred strokes before checking his watch. A quarter to nine. Carpe diem! he thought. Dipped his hand into the cool water and rinsed his face. Took off his shirt and shoes, and set off again. Calmly and rhythmically. The temperature was still only about twenty degrees, at a guess; but there was no doubt – as he had explained to the buttercup-yellow youth – that it was going to be a hot day. Another one. But it would be hard to think of a more acceptable way of spending it, surely?

Poor Kluuge, he thought, in a moment of generosity and sympathy.

But if you are only a consultant, you may as well act like one.

In his briefcase he had – apart from newspapers and tooth-picks – two bottles of mineral water, a bag of newly baked buns (from the bakery next door to Grimm's) and a few tomatoes. That was all. No beer, no cigarettes.

It was intended to be that sort of day. One of those days when you get things done, and even so feel younger when you go to bed in the evening than you did when you got up in the morning. As somebody or other – presumably not Reinhart – had once put it.

It was also meant to be a day when, in peace and quiet – one might even say in splendid isolation – he would have an opportunity to put what had happened back there in Waldingen under the microscope.

Mainly that sort of day.

Weigh up the pros and cons, whatever they may be, and listen to the voice of his intuition – it hadn't been very audible thus far, but then, if he counted Monday – when they had discovered Clarissa Heerenmacht's dead body – as day number one, this was only the morning of day three. There again, if he started with his arrival in Sorbinowo, he would have to admit that nearly a week had passed by already.

So the chances of his coming up with something or other during his day on the dark waters should be rather more than mere pious hope. Might he be able to find a foothold, and clear his mind of irrelevant junk and prejudices?

Those were the thoughts passing through the chief inspector's head as he paddled along the river. Left, right, left, right. He had to keep adjusting his course – he was finding it a bit hard to stick to the rhythm he'd learned many moons ago, but what the hell? This wasn't a display.

It was only when he'd progressed quite a long way up the river, and was beginning to feel the strength of the current, that he felt able to divert the whole of his attention to the thoughts building up in his mind. To the case.

Clarissa Heerenmacht. Waldingen.

The Pure Life. The anonymous woman.

The murderer?

He slowed down; contented himself with just an occasional stroke of the paddle to prevent himself from drifting backwards between the wooded banks. This was countryside, not an urban area. Nothing but coniferous forest teeming with brushwood, and a scent of alder and aspen. The trees leaned over the water: roots and branches reached out across the narrow river, bridges were few and far between. After no more than an hour, he found himself in the midst of what could almost be termed a wilderness – and he understood even more clearly the attraction the Sorbinowo region must have for all categories of outdoor types.

But enough of forest air and bucolic romanticism! The case. Concentration.

He started with the previous day. Forced his thoughts back to the press conference, which he had to admit Kluuge had conducted admirably. The connection between the murder and the Pure Life had been toned down to a minimum – Clarissa Heerenmacht was one of the girls who had been staying at the camp, she had left the site in unknown circumstances, and then been found dead in the forest. That was all.

No tracks. No clues. Not a word about anonymous telephone calls.

And no indications or theories to follow up. So far. But all available officers had been put on the case, and they were doing whatever could be done. No doubt the gentlemen of the press would understand that the police had to be careful about what they made public in these early stages? Excuse me, and the ladies of the press as well, of course.

And so on. It had lasted for over twenty-five minutes, and the chief inspector had only needed to speak on two occasions. Another good mark for Kluuge, no doubt about it, especially as both Servinus and Suijderbeck had been too tired even to open their mouths. Except when they needed to yawn.

Before setting out he had glanced through the two newspapers he had with him in his briefcase. Naturally space was given to the murder – the link between summer and murder and a young girl had an obvious appeal for headline writers, but even so there was considerable restraint. They were holding back, simple as that. No doubt the evening tabloids would make a meal of it, but Van Veeteren didn't think he could have made a better job of the press conference than Kluuge had managed.

And most important of all, presumably: not a word about the disappearance of Yellinek, the women who refused to speak and the silent confirmands – for the simple reason that Kluuge hadn't mentioned any of that. Obviously it was only a matter of time before these details became known; but the important thing was to make use of as many hours – preferably days – as possible before that happened.

And best of all: to break through the silence before the newspapers realized that it existed.

When he came to think about it, he noted that he wasn't at all sure why those thoughts were so important – this business of shielding that damned prophet and his silent congregation from the eyes of the world.

Why?

No reasonably plausible answer occurred to him. Only an intuitively demanding call of duty, which of course wasn't remotely like what he really thought should happen to that damned circus, but nevertheless he recognized its existence.

A sort of tipping point probably, he thought. Not unlike the dilemma the police found themselves in whenever it came to protecting Nazi thugs from counter-demonstrators. It was obviously not a good advertisement for the police if the skinheads were manhandled and perhaps even killed while the police hid round a corner, cleaning their nails.

Or?

Anyway, he didn't like thinking about the Pure Life. The moment he began to reflect on that self-denial and purity lark, and the innocent young girls, he was filled with disgust, and only wanted to forget about it all. Didn't want to know.

So why not let the press pack loose on them? Why not put the sanctimonious prats in the pillory?

All right, he thought. It must be my motherly instinct being triumphant once again.

Or was it simply a certainty that if the general public and the media started poking around in this religious backwater, things would become intolerable? From both a moral point of view, and that of investigating the case. Perhaps that was a more likely explanation after all.

After these humanistic musings – and feeling empowered by the almost clinical systematic he had employed so far – he decided to concentrate his attention on the main problem.

Who had murdered Clarissa Heerenmacht? And why?

The image of her dead body suddenly loomed in his mind's eye. The spotlight in the dark forest. Her pale skin. The marbling and the blood. He recalled that she hadn't even made it to her thirteenth birthday, and he could sense the feeling of impotence coming on once more.

Oh shit! he thought, rinsing his face with clear, cold water. I shouldn't have bothered to look at her. I should have refused. My quota of suffering – other people's suffering – is already filled.

Perhaps it's time to lie low for a while, he decided, in order to dispel the gloom. I don't need to enter the heart of darkness.

After a few problems he managed to tether his Canadian canoe by wedging it underneath a projecting root. It swayed a little in the current, but seemed to be comparatively secure even so. He opened his umbrella to shield him from the worst of the sun. Drank half a bottle of mineral water and ate a bun. Adjusted the cushions and settled down. Then waited for a minute or so until a fairly precise and developable premise occurred to him, but the only thing in his mind was the same old question:

What the hell is all this about?

Not especially precise, he was the first to admit that.

Let's take it in chronological order, anyway:

First: An unknown woman calls and reports a missing person. When she thinks the police reaction has not been good enough, she calls again.

Question: Who is she?

Another question: Why does she call?

He lay still for quite a while without moving so much as a finger, allowing these questions to wander back and forth in his mind. Especially the second one – what the devil was her motive for telephoning the police? But in the end he gave up. No trace of an answer occurred to him, and no unexpected reflections cropped up.

Secondly: Four days later the same woman calls again. Gives detailed instructions as to where to find a murdered girl. Sergeant Kluuge follows the directions and discovers poor Clarissa Heerenmacht, not quite thirteen years old, taking part in the Waldingen camp . . . Raped, strangled, dead. (But still alive as recently as the previous day – on the Sunday afternoon – when he himself had questioned her about goings-on in the sect, the Pure Life.)

Conclusion one: If the unknown woman had been telling the truth on the first two occasions, she couldn't have been referring to Clarissa Heerenmacht.

Conclusion two: It seemed not totally improbable that there could be another dead girl in the forest around Waldingen.

Oh hell! the chief inspector thought and took a tomato. He must keep all this at arm's length. Next?

Let's see . . . Thirdly: Oscar Yellinek – prophet and spiritual shepherd of the infernal Pure Life sect – goes up in smoke in connection with the death of Clarissa Heerenmacht, having first instructed the whole of his flock – ewes as well as lambs – to remain silent. Conclusion?

Conclusion? Van Veeteren thought. Yes, what the hell can one conclude?

He closed his eyes and tried once again to open his mind to any thoughts that might occur; but the only thing to arrive was a question mark.

But eventually two – ridiculously simplified – alternatives.

Number one: Oscar Yellinek had raped and murdered Clarissa Heerenmacht (and perhaps also another or others of his young confirmands), and then done a runner in order to escape justice and the day of reckoning.

Number two: Yellinek had nothing to do with the girl's death, but had chosen to go to earth rather than expose himself to all the cross-examinations and harassment he knew would be the inevitable consequence of the situation.

Commentary on number two: Yellinek was a cowardly bastard. That corresponded with earlier observations.

Necessary corollary of number two: Yellinek must have known about the murder of Clarissa Heerenmacht before the police did!

The chief inspector closed his eyes. Wrong, he thought. It might just be that he knew she had disappeared.

But no doubt the whole line of argument was a ridiculous oversimplification, as already said. About as thin and tenable as a soap bubble, you could say. He sighed. Decided to change track. Systematics are all very well, but it might be time for a spot of less logical thinking.

But before the chief inspector could turn his attention to that, he realized that he would soon be confronted by a very different kind of problem.

How? he thought. How – in this the best of all worlds – can a bloke manage to pee from a canoe? A curse on that damned mineral water!

*

For the rest of the day – especially on the journey back – Chief Inspector Van Veeteren spent most of the time thinking about that inner landscape.

What could it be that was going on behind the neutral and expressionless faces of Madeleine Zander, Ulrich Fischer and Mathilde Ubrecht? And what was simmering away inside the grim-faced teenaged girls?

Not to mention how long they'd be able to keep it up.

Yesterday evening he'd visited both the camp and the psychiatric clinic where the women were locked up in isolation. He hadn't bothered to attack the wall of silence himself, merely sat and watched as Kluuge and the detectives from Rembork tried to break through. It wasn't exactly an unmissable event, but the sergeant was obviously right in suggesting that one of the girls would crack first.

But it was difficult to ignore the unethical aspect of the situation. Or at least, he had difficulty in doing so. The whole business stank of dodgy and dirty goings-on. As far as the young girls were concerned, that is. Of course it was the role of the police to get stuck into whatever turned up – but to subject youngsters to ruthless interrogations with the aim of making them betray a sacred promise – and in other words betray their faith – well, that was pushing things a bit.

Never mind that Yellinek is mad. Never mind the Pure

Life's obscure teachings. Never mind the murder. It was an inner landscape that somebody was intending to crush, and dammit all, safety nets were going to be needed.

When all these misguided individuals woke up. For surely they would eventually wake up?

Perhaps what is written between the lines really is best.

Things were a bit different with regard to the locked-up women. He would have nothing against giving them a bit of a grilling. It wasn't impossible that he might have a chance to do so that evening – Servinus and Suijderbeck had agreed to spend the day interrogating them, and the fewer rests the women had, the better, presumably.

An even more attractive thought, of course, was the possibility of coming face to face again with Yellinek himself. But on Van Veeteren's own terms this time. On home ground, as it were. Sitting at a rickety table in the filthiest and smelliest cell he could find. Looking him in the eye and giving him a really hard time.

But there was nothing he could do about that. Yellinek wasn't around. All they had was fourteen witnesses who refused to say a word. No openings. No threads.

But no matter what, he would have liked to spend some time wandering around that inner landscape. It could have taught him a great deal.

People are unfathomable, he thought.

That's why we can understand them, he added after a few seconds' paddling.

When the chief inspector berthed skilfully and elegantly at the jetty close to Grimm's Hotel, he had been away for over seven hours, and as far as the basic questions were concerned – Who? and Why? – he was more or less back where he started.

But he had made up his mind to follow a particular line. Or to hold a particular series of meetings, rather – there were people he would like to exchange words with and ask a few specific questions.

Always assuming it was possible to get hold of people at this time of year. That was something that couldn't be taken for granted.

The youth with the crew cut had changed into a green tracksuit, unless it was a different person altogether. The chief inspector stepped ashore without getting his feet wet, and declared himself satisfied with both the canoe and the trip as a whole. He then walked straight to the cafe and ordered a dark beer.

I don't want to feel thirty years younger than I did this morning, he thought, and so bought a pack of West as well.

Miss Wandermeijk – young Mr Grimm's fiancée, if he'd understood the situation rightly – brought him his beer, and also a message from Kluuge. It had arrived only ten minutes ago, and suggested that a little breakthrough had taken place.

It wasn't possible to be more specific than that. Kluuge had evidently learned to be a bit more reticent in his correspondence, which of course – like several other things – had to be seen as a step in the right direction. The chief inspector tucked the fax into his back pocket, but chose to enjoy both his beer and a cigarette before calling the police station.

'Kluuge.'

'It's me,' the chief inspector explained. 'Well?'

'One of the girls has started talking,' said Kluuge.

'Excellent,' said Van Veeteren. 'What does she have to say?'

'I don't know,' said Kluuge. 'She's on her way here now, with Inspector Lauremaa.'

'Brilliant,' said the chief inspector. 'I'll be there in a moment. Don't lose her.'

19

When Van Veeteren entered the chief of police's office, the car from Waldingen still hadn't arrived. Kluuge was sitting at his desk, his bronzed arms contrasting with his light blue tennis shirt, but the chief inspector noticed that he looked both older and more tired.

'A hard day?' he asked as he flopped down on the sofa.

Kluuge nodded.

'It's sheer chaos out there,' he said. 'We'll have to do something about those psychologists. They act like defence lawyers and bodyguards as soon as we get near any of the girls. Makes you wonder whose side they're on.'

'I recognize the phenomenon,' said Van Veeteren. 'What about the parents? Have they started rolling up?'

'No, they haven't in fact.' Kluuge stood up and started wiping his brow with a wet wipe. 'Not yet. Four have been in touch, but we told them that the situation is under control and that we would like to keep the girls here for a few more days at least. Besides, they don't want to go home.'

'Really?'

'It seems to be a part of their holy oath, or whatever the hell it is they've sworn, that they should stay on. I don't know, but I suppose we might find out now that one of them has started talking.'

'Hmm,' muttered the chief inspector, examining a toothpick. 'What's she called?'

Kluuge threw the wipe into the waste bin and consulted a sheet of paper.

'Marieke Bergson. I wasn't there; it was Lauremaa who called. About an hour ago.'

He looked at the clock.

'I don't understand what's holding them up.'

'You don't know what she's said, then?'

Kluuge shook his head.

'No idea. Shall we have a cup of coffee?'

'I think so,' said the chief inspector. 'It might be an idea if you could conjure up some Coca-Cola and that sort of stuff as well. Whatever else the Other World has to offer . . .'

Kluuge nodded and left the room in order to delegate the food question to Miss Miller. Van Veeteren inserted the toothpick and waited.

★

The girl's name was Marieke Bergson. She looked pale, and her eyes were red with weeping.

When she came into the office with Inspector Elaine Lauremaa from the Haaldam police – and also a grim-looking but well-dressed child psychologist with her name, Hertha Baumgartner, taped to her chest – the chief inspector had a fleeting impression of a shoplifter who had just been caught red-handed.

Perhaps that was more or less what Marieke Bergson felt like. She sat down sheepishly on the edge of the chair she was allocated, clasped her hands in her lap and stared hard at her red gym shoes.

Lauremaa sat down next to Van Veeteren. The psychologist stood behind the girl with her hands on the back of the chair, looking at all those present in turn with a sceptical expression on her face, clenching her teeth so that her mouth became no more than a narrow stripe.

Kluuge cleared his throat twice, and introduced all present. That took ten seconds. Then there was silence for another five.

Somebody ought to say something, Van Veeteren thought – but instead there was a knock on the door and Miss Miller appeared with a tray of coffee, soft drinks, crisps and various other refreshments.

'I'd like you to think carefully about what you say,' said the psychologist when Miss Miller had withdrawn.

'That sounds like a good idea,' said Van Veeteren.

'Marieke has made a difficult decision, she is under a lot of pressure and I don't really think she ought to be exposed to cross-examination. I think that ought to be said.'

Lauremaa sighed. She was a rather sturdily built woman in her fifties, and the chief inspector immediately felt a degree of sympathy for her. Probably a woman with three children of her own and plenty of common sense, he thought. But perhaps not much of a diplomat.

Kluuge had no children as yet, but even so managed to serve up coffee and gave the impression of having reacquired some of his earlier irresolution.

It's up to me, Van Veeteren thought. Just as well, I suppose.

'Perhaps it might be easier if there weren't so many of us,' he suggested.

'I'm not shifting from Marieke's side,' said the psychologist.

Lauremaa and Kluuge exchanged looks. Then Kluuge nodded in agreement and stood up.

'I think we'd better record this,' said the chief inspector.

Kluuge and Lauremaa left the room. A minute or so later Kluuge reappeared with a tape recorder.

So, here we go again, the chief inspector thought.

★

'What's your name?' he asked.

'Marieke,' said the girl, without looking up.

'Marieke Bergson?'

'Yes.'

'Is your mouth feeling a bit dry?'

'Yes.'

'Drink a drop more Coca-Cola – that usually helps.'

The psychologist gave him a withering look, but Marieke Bergson did as he'd suggested and sat up a bit straighter.

'How old are you?'

'Thirteen.'

'Where do you live?'

'In Stamberg.'

'And you're in year six?'

'I'm just going up into year seven.'

'But you're enjoying your summer holiday at the moment?'

'Yes.'

'At the camp here in Waldingen?'

'Yes.'

'If I've got it right, there's something you want to tell us.'

No response.

'Is that right?'

'Yes. Maybe.'

'Would you like me to ask you questions, or would you prefer to tell me about it yourself?'

'Questions . . . I think.'

'Okay. Have another bun if you'd like one.'

The chief inspector took another sip of coffee. He had the impression that the colour of the girl's face had deepened by several degrees, but the psychologist still looked like a plaster cast.

No doubt she has domestic problems, he decided, then resumed his questions.

'Do you know what's happened to one of your friends?'

Marieke Bergson nodded.

'Clarissa Heerenmacht,' said the chief inspector. 'She's dead.'

'Yes.' Her voice quivered somewhat.

'Somebody must have killed her. I expect you understand that we have to try to catch whoever it was that did it?'

'Yes. I understand that.'

'Will you try to help us?'

Another nod, and another sip of Coca-Cola.

'Can you tell me why your friends don't want to help us?'

'They told us not to.'

'Who did?'

'The sisters.'

'They told you that you shouldn't answer questions put to you by the police?'

'Yes. We weren't to say anything.'

'Did they explain why?'

'Yes. It was a test. God would test if we were strong enough . . . To be able to continue.'

'Continue with what?'

'Er . . . I don't know.'

'Continue to stay at the camp?'

'I think so.'

Marieke Bergson couldn't suppress a sob. Judging by her red eyes, she had been crying a lot. He hoped that she had wept sufficiently to keep her head above water. Most probably neither he nor the psychologist were sufficiently skilled to cope with a teenage breakdown. He recalled fleetingly a few failures in such circumstances from his own past.

'So they said you'd be sent home if you helped us to find the murderer?'

'Yes . . . Well, no, that wasn't what they meant. But everything just seemed to go wrong . . . I mean, they can't have known what had happened last Monday . . .'

'But they didn't change anything after they'd got to know?'

'No.'

'And you don't want to go back out there to the camp?'

'No.'

Her answer was so faint that he could hardly hear it. A whisper so that not even God could catch on to what she said, he thought.

'How did you get to hear that Clarissa was dead?'

She hesitated.

'It was . . . er . . . we knew on Sunday evening that she wasn't there any more. She wasn't there at assembly, nor at the evening meal. But they didn't say anything then.'

'Nothing?'

'Not until Monday morning. Then Sister Madeleine told us that she'd gone home.'

'Hang on a minute. Can you remember the last time you saw Clarissa?'

Marieke Bergson thought that one over. Looked him in the eye for the first time, without averting her gaze, as she bit her lip and seemed to be thinking about it.

'It was last Sunday,' she said. 'In the afternoon. We had a free period, four o'clock I think it was, and I know that she and some of the others went down to the road. Yes, that would be about half past four, I think.'

'You had a free period?' Van Veeteren asked. 'So you should really have been doing something else?'

'Yes, we were supposed to be having role play.'

'Role play?'

'Yes. About the Ten Commandments.'

Van Veeteren nodded. A timetable change, he thought. Why? That was less than two hours after he'd got into his car and driven away from there.

'And you're quite sure that you didn't see her again after that.'

She thought that over again.

'Yes. I didn't see her after that.'

'Do you know who was with her?'

'Yes, I think so.'

'We'll come back to that,' said Van Veeteren. 'So you knew that Clarissa was no longer at the camp on Sunday evening – or at least, not on Monday morning. When did you discover that she hadn't in fact gone home, but was dead?'

'That was, er . . . when you came and woke us up and told us. And we saw her. Although we . . .'

'You what?'

'We didn't believe you. That was the fact of the matter.'

'But you saw her, didn't you?'

'Yes.'

'I don't understand. Do you think you could explain it a bit better?'

'We'd expected you to come from the Other World and say terrible things. That was the test, I suppose you could say.'

'But even so you understood that Clarissa really was dead?'

Marieke Bergson gave a sob.

'Yes, when I saw her I understood that, of course.'

The chief inspector nodded. He was the one who had insisted they should see the dead body, and although he'd had his doubts about it afterwards, he now conceded that it had been the right thing to do.

The situation had required firm action.

But for Christ's sake! It was incomprehensible that none of the young girls had broken down when confronted with what had happened. Five o'clock in the morning, summoned out of their warm beds in order to be faced with the sight of a murdered friend. Only the face, admittedly, but still?

On the other hand he'd gone no further than making the girls file past the ambulance and look in through the doors. And he hadn't started cross-questioning them immediately. He'd allowed them an hour for breakfast first. Deep down he was well aware that the whole set-up was a sort of revenge on the tight-lipped sisters – but maybe he could have saved a day if he'd put the boot in a bit harder?

Put the boot in a bit harder? he thought. What on earth am I going on about?

'Was there anything else?' asked the psychologist, and

he realized that he must have been lost in thought for quite some time.

'Yes, of course,' he said. 'There's a lot more.'

'Is there a toilet?' asked Marieke Bergson. 'I need to . . .'

'Just outside, over there,' said Van Veeteren, and switched off the tape recorder.

When she came back, she took the initiative straight away.

'There's the Katarina thing as well,' she said.

'Katarina?'

'Yes, she was also at the camp to start with, but then one morning they said she'd gone home. She'd done something silly. We've been friends since last spring . . .'

'What was her second name?'

'Schwartz. Katarina Schwartz. She had the bed next to me.'

'Katarina Schwartz,' repeated the chief inspector, noting it down. 'Is she also from Stamberg?'

'Yes.'

'How old?'

'Thirteen, nearly fourteen. She moved to Stamberg last spring. She used to live in Willby before.'

'I don't suppose you remember her address and telephone number?'

'Yes, I do.'

'Can you write it down for me?'

He slid a notepad and pencil over the table. Marieke Bergson wrote down the details, her tongue in the corner of her mouth. When she'd finished she slid the pad back again. The chief inspector examined her round, school-girlish handwriting for a few seconds before continuing.

'So, she'd done something silly, you said. Can you tell me any more about that?'

Marieke Bergson hesitated and bit her lip.

'She swore at Yellinek. She had the devil in her body . . . I thought it was a bit odd, although I knew her; the others thought so as well. We were supposed to pretend she'd never been there.'

'Why?'

'I don't know, but I suppose it was right. She'd been silly, she had the devil inside her, and it was best to forget her. I could hardly remember that she'd ever been at the camp until yesterday, when . . .'

Her voice died away. The chief inspector waited, but she said nothing more.

'Can you remember when exactly Katarina Schwartz disappeared?'

Marieke seemed to be working it out.

'Two weeks ago, I think. Maybe a bit less. You lose track – time doesn't pass in the usual way when you're at Waldingen.'

Van Veeteren suddenly had the feeling that he'd like to continue cross-questioning this teenaged girl for several hours, but he realized he would have to resist the temptation to put her under too much pressure. He needed to prioritize, to take the most important matters first; then he could probably try to penetrate the shadowy side of the Pure Life later on, when there was time and opportunity.

'Yellinek,' he said instead. 'Do you know where Oscar Yellinek is?'

The girl shook her head.

'You don't know?'

'No.'

'When did he disappear?'

'The day before yesterday.'

'Are you sure?'

'Yes. He wasn't there on Monday morning. He'd been called away.'

'Called away?'

'Yes.'

'What do you mean by that?'

'The Lord had called him, and he needed to be away from the camp for a few days.'

She took a few more sips of Coca-Cola, and the chief inspector closed his eyes for a couple of seconds.

'When on Monday?'

'In the morning. He wasn't there for morning prayers.

Sister Ulriche took them instead. Then she told us that God had appeared to him during the night and given him a task. It was important that we should be firm in our faith, and remain pure and worthy in his absence.'

'Pure and worthy?'

'Yes.'

'I see . . .' Van Veeteren searched for the right words. 'And what exactly does that mean?'

'I don't know,' said Marieke Bergson.

'Nor do I,' said the chief inspector. 'What do you do in order to show that you are pure and worthy?'

The psychologist raised a warning finger, and Marieke suddenly looked to be on the verge of tears. She wrung her hands and stared down at her shoes again. Van Veeteren hastily changed track.

'When did you last see Yellinek?'

'Sunday . . . Yes, Sunday evening.'

'What were you doing then?'

'It was evening prayers. Before we went to bed.'

'And he didn't say anything then, about having to go away?'

Marieke looked up, then averted her gaze again.

'No, it was late at night when he met God, as I've said already. But Clarissa wasn't around. We wondered a bit, but he didn't say anything about her. He just said that the final struggle was here, and that we should be strong and pure.'

'The final struggle?'

'Yes.'

'What did he mean by that?'

'I . . . I don't know.'

'So, it was on Monday morning you found out about Clarissa Heerenmacht and also about Yellinek's task?'

'Yes – although we knew about Clarissa already. That she was no longer around.'

'Don't you think it seemed a bit odd? That the two things happened at the same time, I mean?'

'No.'

'But I expect you talked about it?'

'No, we had to . . .'

'Had to what?'

She suddenly lost control. Marieke Bergson slid off the chair and collapsed in a heap on the floor. Covered her face with her hands and drew her knees up to her chin in a sort of twisted foetus position. And slowly a low-pitched, plaintive sobbing emerged from her body, a whimpering – unarticulated despair that he realized must come from chasms deep down in her thirteen-year-old soul. Just for a moment he had the impression that she was play-acting, but he dismissed the thought.

Poor kid, he thought. What have they done to you?

The psychologist hastened to go to her assistance. Started caressing her arms, back and hair in long, gentle strokes. When the girl had recovered somewhat, but was still curled up and lost in her own personal hell, the woman looked up at Van Veeteren.

'Well then,' she said. 'Are you satisfied now?'

'No,' said Van Veeteren. 'How the hell could I be satisfied?'

That evening he had dinner with Suijderbeck.

Servinus had returned to Rembork to spend the night with his wife and four children, but Suijderbeck had no such ties and preferred to retain his room at the City Arms hotel, where he'd already stayed for one night.

And it was in the dining room of the City Arms hotel that they sat down to eat. Right at the back in a smoke-filled corner of the packed, sepia-brown restaurant with table-cloths that had once been white and crystal chandeliers that had always been glass. Suijderbeck seemed to be even glummer than usual, and Van Veeteren began to feel a spiritual affinity.

'How were things at the loony bin?' he asked, when they'd finished ordering their meal.

'Hilarious,' said Suijderbeck, lighting a cigarette. 'If it were up to me, I'd leave the harridans there for the rest of their lives. There's no doubt that they've got the qualifications.'

'Hmm,' said Van Veeteren. 'They're still not saying anything, I take it?'

'Pure autism,' said Suijderbeck. 'The worst of it is that they are so damned superior as well – they are martyrs, and nobody else is worth a toss. They all radiate contempt.'

'The Lord's chosen few?'

'Something like that. They already know everything, don't need to condescend. Even though they have no contact with one another, I'll be damned if they don't have some kind of telepathic communication. How are things with the girls?'

'One has started talking.'

'So I'd heard. Did you get anything useful out of her?'

Van Veeteren shrugged.

'More or less what we'd expected, you could say. The girl seems to have disappeared some time on Sunday afternoon. And Yellinek the same night, presumably. Then they muzzled the youngsters. The big question, of course, is what the hell happened, and we don't know much more about that than we did before. But there seems to be another girl who's gone missing, just as we thought.'

'The Lord giveth, and the Lord taketh away,' said Suijderbeck. 'What do you think yourself?'

The waiter came with two beers.

'I don't know,' said the chief inspector. 'I'll be damned if I know. Cheers.'

'Cheers,' said Suijderbeck.

When they had drunk, they sat in silence for a while. Then Suijderbeck sighed deeply and said:

'There's only one thing we can do, I suppose.'

'What's that?' wondered Van Veeteren.

'We'll have to find out if he was screwing the girls as well.'

The chief inspector wiped the cutlery with the table cloth.

'Yes,' he said. 'I suppose we'd better do that.'

'What happened to your leg?' he asked when they had begun tucking into their main course.

Suijderbeck looked up.

'Do you really want to know?'

'Why do you ask that?'

Suijderbeck took a swig of beer.

'Because people usually take it so badly.'

'Really?' said the chief inspector, and thought for a few seconds. 'Yes, I want to know.'

'If you insist,' said Suijderbeck. 'But we'll leave it until we've finished eating.'

'Well, I was a member of the drugs squad for a few years,' Suijderbeck explained.

'In Rembork?'

'No, Aarlach. Anyway, I was hot on the scent of some really big names. One night I was in a parked car, keeping an eye on them, when it turned out that they were hot on the scent of me as well.'

'Oh dear,' said Van Veeteren.

'Bloody silly, sitting in a car on your own, don't you think?'

Van Veeteren said nothing. Accepted a cigarette and allowed Suijderbeck to light it.

'They took me to a place on the edge of town. They were going to teach me a lesson, they said. To keep my nose out of their business in future. That's all they did say, in fact. Reticent types. Anyway, they tied me up and then started the circular saw.'

He paused briefly.

'It all went so damned quickly. No more than half a second, but that was the longest half-second of my life. And it keeps coming back.'

He fell silent. Van Veeteren stared at the hand holding his cigarette. Felt something in his mind turn round and give up. He drew on his cigarette, then stubbed it out.

'Shall we pay?' he said.

'I suppose so,' said Suijderbeck.

*

Suijderbeck wanted to take a little walk before going to bed, and after they'd gone a couple of hundred metres the chief inspector asked:

'How long ago was that?'

'Five years.'

'Why did you stay in the police?'

Suijderbeck couldn't help laughing.

'A fifty-year-old with a wooden leg,' he said. 'Have you ever heard of something called the job market?'

20

At about one o'clock on Thursday, when acting Chief of Police Kluuge got into his hot car out at Waldingen – in order to drive back to Sorbinowo and be contactable at the police station during the afternoon (and possibly snatch a half-hour lunch with Deborah) – at least he was able to reassure himself that things had started moving.

Just a little bit. Following the example set by Marieke Bergson, a handful of girls had started to crack and speak about the last few days at the camp. Together with his colleagues from Haaldam – Lauremaa and Tolltse – Kluuge had spent a few hours that morning listening to their tear-soaked confessions. However, nothing specific nor of vital significance for the investigation had materialized. Not as far as they could tell, anyway. The girls had been ordered – more or less explicitly – to say nothing, and so they had said nothing.

It seemed to be as simple as that.

There was still a group of girls sticking to the party line

and saying nothing, and there were grounds for suspecting that it was this group that had put the others – the ones whose faith was beginning to wobble – under pressure. Moreover, a trio of girls had emerged, probably led by Belle Moulder (that was Lauremaa's contention at any rate), who had been the last to see Clarissa Heerenmacht alive.

Excluding the murderer, that is. Round about five or half past five on the Sunday evening these girls, including Clarissa, had been down by 'the rock' – a smooth, warm and sunny flat piece of rock a few hundred metres to the west of the summer camp – swimming in the lake. It was still unclear how the four of them had become separated, but the bottom line was that they hadn't returned to the camp together.

Clarissa Heerenmacht hadn't returned at all.

Instead, Clarissa Heerenmacht had met her murderer. Unclear how. Unclear when and where.

The families were another problem. Kluuge switched on the air conditioning and turned into the main road. Yesterday's evening papers – not to mention the television and radio – had devoted a lot of space to the case (Kluuge sincerely hoped that Malijsen really was as isolated as he had said he would be: if the real chief of police were to appear on the stage without warning, his arrival would hardly have a positive effect on the work they were doing – everybody involved agreed about that, even if nobody was prepared to say so), and most of the parents had been in touch. Shortly before Kluuge left Waldingen that roasting-hot afternoon, four of the girls had been collected by worried mums and dads – obviously after spending quite a while with Lauremaa and the psychologists. Two of the girls turned out to be sisters, a detail that hadn't been clear before.

Anyway, there were six left. Three who still hadn't said a word, two who seemed to be about to do so, and one who had made a clean breast of it and was waiting to be picked up.

Plus Marieke Bergson, of course. She was still at the police station, under the wing of Miss Miller and a Roman Catholic Sister of Mercy (the latter had turned up out of the blue the previous evening and offered her services – for professional and ethical reasons, not to mention pressure from her trade union, the psychologist had fled the scene long ago). Her name was Vera Saarpe, and she had let the girl stay at her place overnight.

It was only this morning, early on, that they had managed to contact Marieke's parents, and apparently they would be arriving during the course of the afternoon to take care of their daughter. Kluuge had spoken on the tele-phone to the mother, and established that the apple hadn't fallen very far away from the tree in this case either.

He sighed deeply. It was far from easy to keep tabs on everything, he thought.

Far from easy.

Then he sighed even more deeply – when he began to think about Katarina Schwartz, the girl who seemed to have gone missing from the camp some ten to twelve days ago. Marieke Bergson's claim regarding her sudden disappearance had been backed up by all the others who had spoken up so far, and it seemed reasonable to assume that it was this Katarina who had been referred to in the first two telephone calls from the anonymous woman.

To crown it all, they hadn't succeeded in making contact with her parents. They were evidently on holiday, touring France by car. But if in fact Katarina had simply run away from the camp, it was quite possible that she was sitting in the same car as her mother and father. Or in a rented cottage, or in a deckchair. In Brest or Marseilles or wherever the hell they happened to be. Why not Lourdes, come to that?

Servinus had been in touch with the French police, who had promised to send out SOS messages to track down the couple and their car; but Servinus had dealt with his French colleagues before, and wasn't especially optimistic.

In any case, there were indications to suggest that the girl might have had good reason to run away; but just how strong they were was something Kluuge hadn't yet established. Nor had anybody else, come to that. The probability was that this scenario was no more than wishful thinking – neighbours, friends and relations of the Schwartz family had seemed to be quite certain that Katarina had not been in the car that set off on the journey south-west the previous week.

But the timing did fit in, as Kluuge had noted when he thought the matter over. If the daughter had suddenly turned up unexpectedly the evening before they set off – well, it wasn't out of the question that she might have travelled with them the next morning without anybody else knowing.

In which case they had only one murder to solve.

Which was bad enough, of course.

It also occurred to him – as he sat in the car sweating and driving far too fast on the zigzagging road – that all these interrogations, all these telephone calls and all the various measures they were taking seemed to be irrelevant. They were simply taking up an enormous amount of time and energy and resources, without actually leading anywhere.

Apart from in circles. What little they found out was what they had already worked out for themselves.

When – and how – he would find the time and energy to sit down and think about the actual murder and how to solve it, well, he found that very hard to see just at the moment.

Is this the way it always was? he wondered at the back of his mind. In all the cases I've been involved in?

Merwin Kluuge sighed yet again, and checked his watch.

A quarter to two.

That meant a window of twenty minutes for Deborah. Half an hour at most.

I must buy her some flowers on Friday, he thought. No time for that today, that's for sure.

At about the same time as Merwin Kluuge gently – but perhaps not quite as gently as was his wont – stroked his wife's stomach and his as yet unborn son, Van Veeteren left Elizabeth Heerenmacht to allow her to say farewell to her murdered niece down in the cold-storage room at Sorbinowo hospital, to which the battered body had just been moved after two and a half days at the forensic clinic in Rembork.

Elizabeth Heerenmacht was not a member of the Pure Life church – although after spending half an hour in her company the chief inspector found it hard to understand why not. She seemed to have all the qualifications, to put it mildly: that was the harsh conclusion he had drawn, unfortunately.

But perhaps that was a bit unfair, given the nature of this grim and roasting-hot day. It was difficult not to be prejudiced when the sweat was flowing freely, then froze to ice down in the mortuary before starting to pour off him again when he emerged once more into the sun.

Earlier in the morning he had devoted quite a lot of time to another woman – the mysterious Ewa Siguera. At least, he wanted to convince himself that she was mysterious, that there was just as much mystery about her in reality as there was about her name and her smile in the photograph Przebuda had taken of her the previous summer.

Rubbish, he then thought in a moment of pungent self-criticism. That kind of thinking would be more appropriate in a novel.

But what the hell was one supposed to do? he thought. The less contact you had with the opposite sex, the more fond you grew of it – or of certain examples of it, anyway. Nothing new about that.

He had been advised by the registration authorities that Ewa Siguera did not live in Stamberg. He had also asked Lauremaa and Tolltse to confront the confirmation candidates with her photograph, but as far as he could tell nobody had come up with any helpful information.

The plot thickens, he thought with a feeling of bitter self-satisfaction. Then he removed a chewed-up toothpick from his mouth and shook his head. Oh shit! he exclaimed, I'm a travesty of a police detective! Of myself. Am I looking for a murderer, or for a woman? In the warmed-up cold sweat on my face? One with chestnut-brown hair . . . ?

After an hour's fruitless search, he called Reinhart and passed the task on to him. Asked him to track down Ewa Siguera and report back the moment he found her. There had been other possible paths to follow, of course, but as he suspected that the inspector was simply twiddling his thumbs while waiting for his holiday to begin – or devoting himself to his beautiful and newly married wife – he might as well be made to do something to earn his wages.

Reinhart had little in the way of objections. He promised loyally to get in touch as soon as he discovered anything. Within the next twenty-four hours at most.

So his assumptions about Reinhart's thumbs and his wife had been an accurate guess, the chief inspector thought.

'And how are things with the bloodhound himself?' Reinhart had asked. 'Sunbathing, swimming and fishing all day long, eh?'

'You've forgotten the wine and the women,' Van Veeteren informed him.

*

He began with the Finghers, as he could see that they were at home.

He only managed to say hello to Mrs Fingher, a sinewy farmer's wife in her fifties – she was on her way to look after a grandchild, she announced, as she hurried past him in the direction of an old, hand-painted Trotta parked on the road outside the house – but both Mr Fingher and his son Wim seemed to have plenty of time for a chat.

'It's mainly Sunday evening I'm interested in, this time round,' explained the chief inspector after they had settled down on garden chairs under a shady chestnut tree.

'Sunday evening?' said Fingher. 'Wim, go and fetch a couple of beers. Would you like a Pilsner, Chief Inspector?'

'I wouldn't say no,' said Van Veeteren, and the son went back into the house.

'Why?' asked Fingher. 'What do you want to know about Sunday evening?'

'Can you tell me what time the party from the summer camp arrived, and if anything unusual happened?'

Fingher tried to remember, and his son arrived with the beers.

'No, everything was the same as usual, as I recall it. What do you think?'

He looked at Wim, who merely shrugged.

'What time?' asked Van Veeteren.

'Seven, maybe half past. Around then. As usual.'

Wim Fingher nodded in agreement, and all three took a swig of beer. It was unusually sweet, and Van Veeteren wondered if it might be home-brewed. There were no labels on the bottles, so it wasn't out of the question.

'Good,' he said. 'Was Yellinek with them?'

'Eh? Yes, of course.'

'And four girls?'

'Yes, four.'

'Do you recognize the one who was found murdered?'

Fingher nodded solemnly.

'By Christ, yes. She'd been here several times, just like the other three. This is a right bloody mess, if only I'd had any idea I'd have . . .'

'You'd have what?' wondered Van Veeteren.

'Huh, I'll be buggered if I know. Castrated that damned black-coated bastard, for instance. I'm damned if I know how anybody can send their kids to a place like that. We only have Wim here, but if I had a daughter I swear I'd lock her up if there was anybody like him around . . .'

His anger suddenly seemed to put a lid on his words, and he fell silent. Van Veeteren took another swig and allowed a few seconds to pass before continuing.

'Did you notice anything special about him last Sunday?'

'That bastard,' said Fingher. 'No, I don't think so. What do you say, Wim?'

Mathias emptied his glass in one swig.

'No,' said Wim. 'I only saw him in passing, but he seemed the same as ever.'

'Nothing unusual about the girls either?'

Wim shook his head. His father belched.

'No,' he said. 'They just stood there holding on to the cart, as usual.'

'Hmm,' said Van Veeteren. 'Will you promise to contact us if you should think of anything? Anything at all that might seem tasty.'

Tasty? he thought. I'm losing my way with words.

'Of course,' said Fingher, scratching his head. 'Obviously we'll do anything we can to help. But I have to say I'm fucked if I know what you're after.'

Van Veeteren ignored the criticism.

'Last Monday, then?' he asked instead. 'I assume Yellinek wasn't here then, in any case.'

'Correct,' said Fingher. 'Only one of the women came on Monday.'

'No girls?'

'Not a single one.'

'Did she explain why?'

'Explain? Did she hell. Just stood there looking like a fart in a bottle, trying to be posh – as if she was God's mother's cousin or something.'

Van Veeteren cleared his throat.

'You're not religious yourself, I take it, Mr Fingher.'

'No fucking chance,' said the farmer and belched again.

'Same here,' said his son.

The chief inspector emptied his glass.

'Ah well, thank you,' he said. 'I won't disturb you any longer. But do get in touch if you think of anything . . . As I said.'

'Of course,' said Fingher, and began shepherding the chief inspector back to the road.

'Sunday evening,' he said, fixing the twelve-year-old with his eyes.

The girl, whose name was Joanna Halle, was gazing down at the table and rubbing her wrists nervously.

'Sound a bit more friendly, perhaps,' whispered the young psychologist into his ear.

'Would you like to tell me a bit about what you were doing last Sunday evening?' Van Veeteren tried again. 'When you were down by the rock, swimming.'

'We were swimming,' Joanna Halle explained.

'I see. Who, exactly?'

'There was me and Krystyna and Belle. And Clarissa.'

'And you were swimming?'

'Yes,' said the girl.

An intelligent conversation, this, Van Veeteren thought. Gliding along as if on rails.

'Were you friends, the four of you?'

'Yes . . . No, not exactly . . .'

'What do you mean?'

Don't they teach pupils how to speak in school nowadays? he wondered.

'We were just . . . sort of.'

'Really? What time was it when you were there, roughly speaking?'

'I don't know, but we were back at six o'clock in any case, that's when we have dinner.'

'Did anything special happen when you were down there by the rock?'

'No – what do you mean, something special?'

'I don't know. What did you talk about?'

'Nothing special.'

'You didn't fall out?'

'Fall out?'

'Yes. Do you understand what that means?'

'Yes, but we don't fall out at the Pure Life, only Other people do that.'

'Are you telling me the truth?'

'Clear.'

Clear? the chief inspector thought. I'd better arrest

more children so that I can learn how to communicate with them.

But Marieke Bergson and the others hadn't caused any problems of that kind, so he decided for the moment that it was Joanna Halle who was a bit hard to get through to. Not himself.

'Were all four of you together all the time?' he wondered.

'Can't remember.'

'Do you remember how you left there?'

Joanna Halle seemed actually to be thinking for the first time.

'I was with Krys,' she said.

'Krystyna Sarek?'

'Yes.'

'So Clarissa and Belle Moulder were together?'

'I think so.'

'But you don't know?'

'Yes, they were still there when we left. Or at least, Belle was.'

'But you didn't see Clarissa when you left the rock?'

'Yes, she must have been there.'

'Come on, you must make your mind up. Was Belle on her own or were they both there when you and Krystyna left?'

'They were both there.'

'Sure?'

'Clear.'

The chief inspector sighed and glanced at the psychologist, but she looked as inscrutable as a potato in glasses. *Das Ding an sich*, he thought grimly. The thing in itself.

'But you didn't see Clarissa later on at all?'

'No . . . No, I didn't.'

'Do you remember if you saw Yellinek at all when you got back here?'

'Yellinek?'

'Yes. Will it be easier if I ask every question twice?'

The psychologist glared at him.

'No, that's not necessary,' said Joanna Halle. 'No, I didn't see Yellinek until we went to the farm.'

'So you're saying you were one of those who went to collect the milk last Sunday evening?'

'Of course. It was my turn.'

She looked at him in a way he realized was meant to express mild contempt.

'Who else was there?'

She thought for a moment.

'Krys and the sisters.'

'The sisters?'

'Yes, Lene and Tilde.'

Van Veeteren nodded.

'Let's go back to the rock where you went swimming. Did you notice anybody else while you were there?'

'No, we were the only ones there.'

'No other grown-ups either?'

'No.'

'And nobody else you recognized?'

'No, I said there was only us there.'

'How long were you there?'

'I dunno . . . Not all that long.'

'Did you notice if Clarissa was worried at all?'

'No . . . No, she was the same as usual.'

'And there was nothing else about her that made you think?'

'No.'

'She didn't say she wanted to be on her own, or anything like that?'

'No.'

'And there wasn't anybody who was nasty to her in some way or other?'

'We are never nasty to one another, I've already told you that.'

No, you little goose, the chief inspector thought as irritation threatened to get the better of him. But the fact is that Clarissa Heerenmacht met her murderer some time after you'd returned back home – and it could possibly have been you.

'Are you thinking of leaving this church now?' he asked.

Joanna Halle's face turned a deep red, and he couldn't decide if she was angry or embarrassed. Neither could she, it seemed, and so she burst out crying instead.

'Thank you, that's all,' he said, and hastened out into the sunshine, with the psychologist's eyes sticking daggers into his back.

It was three-quarters of an hour later, when he pulled into a petrol station just outside Sorbinowo, that he realized the fourth estate had by now caught up with the police.

SEX PRIEST ON THE RUN!

it said in bold print on the billboards.

NEW CLUE IN THE GIRL MURDER!

He wondered for a moment if somebody had leaked the information to the press, but then he realized that the information must have come from the girls who had already left Waldingen – and perhaps also the Pure Life – behind them.

Ah well, he thought. Time to put on a false moustache and hide away in the woods, I reckon.

There's a time for everything.

21

On Friday, when they met to assess progress on the Clarissa Heerenmacht case, the temperature in acting Chief of Police Kluuge's office was 33 degrees Celsius. And it was still only morning; it was also the first time the whole investigation team had assembled in the same place.

'We are presumably the only idiots in town who are sitting indoors,' said Suijderbeck.

'Presumably,' said Servinus.

In addition to the pair of officers from Rembork, those present comprised the two female inspectors from Haaldam – Elaine Lauremaa and Anja Tolltse – plus team leader Kluuge and the consultant, Chief Inspector Van Veeteren from Maardam police. Six individuals in all. The team leader was wearing shorts, but that was not obvious when he was sitting at his desk.

'The media have been making a bit of a meal of it,' said Suijderbeck, producing a copy of *Neuwe Blatt*, which devoted its front page and two more full pages to developments in the Sorbinowo forests.

And to the Pure Life. Speculation was rife in all the media regarding the absent spiritual leader and goings-on in the sect. The old lawsuit had been dug up, deserters had expressed their opinions with no beating about the bush, and one of the television channels had come close to flouting its own conventions regarding decency and decorum in a report on one of the girls who had left the camp and returned home – a starkly realistic, high-pressure interview with timid, stuttering parents and a red-eyed tearful thirteen-year-old trying to make their way from their car into their own terraced house on the outskirts of Stamberg.

'Well, so what, for Christ's sake?' said Servinus. 'Of course they're going to write about it! What more could they ask for? Summer. Murder. Young girl. Mad priest! If they can't sell extra copies on the back of a witch's brew like that, I reckon they might as well throw in the towel, and start devoting their attention to *Country Life* instead.'

'When was the Wanted message for Yellinek first sent out?' the chief inspector asked.

'Yesterday afternoon,' said Kluuge. 'We thought we might as well, since his disappearance had become public knowledge.'

'Quite right,' said Suijderbeck. 'As a matter of fact, I threatened the Three Sisters with Armageddon yesterday, if they failed to produce him by noon today. But they don't read any newspapers, so my conscience is clear.'

'What's all this about a condom clue?' Tolltse wondered. 'What's going on?'

'Harrumph,' said Kluuge. 'Perhaps we ought to take matters in turn. The situation out at the summer camp – I take it that's all over and done with now?'

Anja Tolltse checked her watch.

'One girl and one psychologist left. And two constables on guard. The girl will be collected in half an hour, assuming they are punctual. And I suppose we'll be in a position to sum up our efforts out there once that's done and dusted.'

'Lots of journalists?' Servinus asked.

Tolltse nodded.

'There were a few cars around when I left. They generally sneak around and take photos. They don't approach the girl – although of course there's nothing to stop them tagging on when the parents come to collect her. If they want another smutty scoop – I mean, a few of the others have been targeted.'

'Brilliant,' said Suijderbeck. 'An honourable corps of professionals, that lot. I'll be damned if I don't stop reading newspapers one of these days.'

'All right,' said Kluuge. 'Anyway, that search party is

combing the woods today as well, looking for the other girl, of course. Let's hope they don't find anything.'

'And that they don't tell the hacks what they're looking for,' said Lauremaa. 'Unless we want it made public that there's another one missing, that is.'

'I don't understand why we don't make a public appeal for information about her,' said Tolltse. 'Wouldn't it be just as well?'

Nobody spoke. Suijderbeck shrugged and Kluuge tried in vain to make eye contact with Van Veeteren, who was sitting with his eyes closed and a toothpick sticking out of the side of his mouth.

'Well,' said the chief inspector eventually. 'I don't think it matters much. In any case, she's not going to be murdered while we sit around not mentioning that she's disappeared.'

'If she's dead, she's dead,' said Suijderbeck.

'Without a shadow of a doubt,' said the chief inspector. 'No, we ought to make contact with her parents first. Shall we go on?'

'The weird sisters?' asked Kluuge, looking unusually un-comprehending.

'Excuse me,' said Van Veeteren. 'It was just a reference. *Macbeth*. What's the state of play at Wolgershuus?'

'There's not a lot one can say,' said Suijderbeck. 'All quiet on the western front, if we're going to be literary. They're in a world of their own. There might be a tiny bit of hope for Mathilde Ubrecht, but that's just speculation. Still, if we were to think of picking out one of them for a bit of . . . er . . . special treatment, she's the one I would recommend.'

'Well, that's a start,' said Van Veeteren. 'Hmm, I think I might take a trip out there this afternoon.'

'I read somewhere that you can inject alcohol into people who are a bit unwilling to cooperate,' said Servinus. 'Push up the blood content by the odd percentage point, and it's usually hard to shut them up.'

'I think we'd better stick to more sober methods to start with,' said the chief inspector. 'That seems to be a bit more ethical.'

'Ethical?' muttered Servinus. 'I didn't realize we were playing cricket.'

The chief inspector smiled inwardly, but it didn't show on the outside.

'How long can we keep them locked up on the present basis?' wondered Lauremaa. 'Don't we have to charge them soon?'

'Monday,' said Servinus. 'If nothing new happens. But none of them has asked for a lawyer, and none of them has said a word about being released, so I don't know . . .'

'It's no doubt best to play it by the book,' said Suijder-beck. 'If we don't they could use that against us later on.'

'Exactly,' said the chief inspector. 'We should be able to break them over the weekend. Is one of the ladies interested in having a go?'

He pointed his toothpick first at Tolltse, then Lauremaa.

'I have the feeling there's a bit of a gender barrier, you see.'

'Oh dear,' said Lauremaa.

'I wouldn't mind having an hour or two at home first,' said Tolltse. 'We've been here for four days now.'

'What does our team leader say?' asked Van Veeteren, using his toothpick as a pointer again.

'Well . . .' said Kluuge. 'I don't really know.'

'Sunday,' decided the chief inspector. 'I'll have a go before then, as I said, but if I don't get anywhere you can have the whole of the Sabbath to see what you two can do.'

'Thank you,' said Lauremaa. 'That'll be fun.'

'Next,' said the chief inspector. 'What else is there to discuss?'

For the first time for ages there was a trace of impa-tience in his voice. He noticed it himself, and wondered if it had to do with the heat, or the environment. Both, probably. In any case, he wished he had Münster and Reinhart at hand for an exchange of opinions.

I've been spoilt over the years, he acknowledged. Worn

out and disillusioned and God only knows what else, but definitely spoilt. I'd better bear that in mind, I suppose.

'It seems there are no known rapists on the run around here at the moment,' said Servinus, consulting a sheet of paper. 'One has just been released from Ulmenthal, but it's known for certain that he's been a long way from here. So we're presumably dealing with somebody new. Whether his name's Yellinek or something else . . .'

The chief inspector nodded.

'Next,' he said again.

'We don't have very much,' said Kluuge. 'A few more technical details, of course, after the report from forensics.'

He rummaged through a file on the desk in front of him.

'That fragment of rubber might be worth taking note of. A condom or something.'

'That's what I've been wondering about,' said Tolltse. 'Do rapists normally use condoms? I've never heard of that, anyway.'

There was silence for a while. Suijderbeck scratched his wooden leg.

'There are all sorts,' said Van Veeteren. 'Believe you me, all sorts . . .'

'Besides, it might not have been a condom,' Servinus pointed out. 'They stress that it's a very small fragment of rubber, and it could easily have been something else.'

'What, for instance?' asked Kluuge. But he received no answer.

And just for a moment it was crystal clear that the whole of the investigation team were trying to conjure up the same image in their mind's eye.

The same infernal, elusive image.

After the press conference – which this time lasted for over an hour, and the chief inspector and Lauremaa had to field many of the questions in order to help out Kluuge, who was close to exhaustion – Van Veeteren had lunch with Suijderbeck at Florian's. It was exactly a week since he'd been there the previous time, and in view of his estimation of where they were at, there was every reason to indulge themselves with a taste of the good life.

Perhaps even the very best.

'It's a bloody circus,' said Suijderbeck. 'I think I'll have eel.'

'Hmm,' said Van Veeteren, 'I associate eels with drowned corpses, forgive me. What do you mean by circus?'

'These mass media clowns, of course. But I suppose you're used to all that crap?'

Van Veeteren shrugged.

'It's not easy to get used to it,' he said. 'But there is a bit of a discrepancy even so.'

'Discrepancy?' said Suijderbeck, sniffing at his glass of beer.

'Between what's written and what's actually done. A lot more happens in the newspapers than in the investigation.'

Suijderbeck tasted the beer and nodded.

'Quite right,' he said. 'What happens and what seems to happen. Have we come up against a brick wall, do you think?'

'What do you think?' the chief inspector asked. 'The girls have gone away. The women are saying nothing. Yellinek's disappeared.'

Suijderbeck pondered for a moment.

'Katarina Schwartz,' he said.

'No trace,' said the chief inspector. 'Neither of her nor of her parents.'

Suijderbeck sat silently for a while, contemplating his beer.

'Okay,' he said eventually. 'We've reached a dead end. What do we do?'

'Hard to say,' said the chief inspector. 'But go ahead and order your eel. I'll start with some crab.'

But once the food had arrived on the table, he knew it was all in vain. There was a time for everything, true, but even to think about being hungry at this time seemed to be almost indecent. He glanced sadly over the table, where Suijderbeck was tucking eagerly into his fatty, greasy fish.

Despite all the marbled corpses of young girls. Despite all the infinitesimal fragments of rubber. Despite all the circular saws.

Perverse, he thought. One of these days I simply won't be able to stand it in this world any more.

It's only a question of time.

22

He waited for the first cool evening breeze before setting off. The sun was on its way down behind the rows of trees to the west, and he was lucky enough to be able to stay in the shade and relatively mild temperatures all the way.

Wolgershuus was located a few kilometres outside the little town, pleasantly secluded in the woods and some distance from the main road. It comprised extensive walled grounds with half a dozen separate buildings from the early twentieth century, all in the same soft, pale yellow limestone. Van Veeteren had read up on its genealogy: at the beginning a sanatorium and convalescent home for the well-heeled; later – during the war years – an educational institution for female health workers and other volunteers; and then – from the fifties onwards – a treatment centre and residential home for people with various mental and psychosomatic illnesses.

But all the time with an increasing emphasis on detaining

potentially dangerous mentally ill patients, if he had read correctly between the lines.

Even from a long way away – just after he had left the main road and started to follow the narrow, meandering tarmacked path through the forest – he could hear a voice. A plaintive wail coming from inside the grounds further up the hill. A solitary, anonymous voice forcing its way out through an open window, presumably, and hovering over the trees and the summer evening like an expression of, not to say a reminder of, the natural place of suffering in the world.

The melancholy cry of a migratory bird, he thought. A migratory bird that had stayed behind. A languageless animal's vain attempt to make contact with a cold and indifferent environment. It ceased at exactly the same moment as he came to a stop outside the locked gates. But nevertheless it seemed to linger like an unfilled silence under the trees, and he paused for a few moments until it died away.

The Wolgershuus Clinic
Secure Psychiatric Nursing Home

it said on a blue-and-white enamel plaque, screwed directly onto the solid brick wall.

Dangerous lunatics! Van Veeteren thought. That's what

it would have said in another age – and that's probably what ordinary people still say.

Although nowadays, of course, there is medicine to make them less dangerous.

He walked over to the window at the entrance and explained why he was there. The young porter, busy solving a crossword puzzle, pressed a button and he was allowed in through a barred gate. Then he had to consult another porter behind another window, and was given instructions about how to get to where he wanted to go, and a little white plastic card as authorization.

It was the same pass as he'd been given the previous time, when he had merely sat there and listened to Servinus and Suijderbeck trying in vain to squeeze a reply out of the Weird Sisters.

This time it was his turn, and he had no intention of returning empty-handed.

He walked straight ahead along the well-raked gravel path. There was another hour or so to go before dusk, and here and there he could see small groups of people. Carers and warders in white coats; dark green interns – wearing big, loose jackets and shapeless trousers that reminded him of the crappy get-up he'd occasionally been forced to wear during his National Service long ago, at the beginning of time.

And here and there among all the greenery an

occasional recluse. A man sitting on a bench smoking, with an empty dog lead in his hand. Another lying stretched out on the lawn, apparently asleep. Under a tree a bit further away, a woman: she was leaning against the tree trunk with her forehead while carrying out slow, hesitant swimming movements with her arms.

Over everything – over the grounds, over the buildings, over the surrounding forest – stillness. A vague, almost oppressive stillness that seemed to embody not only the illusion of another land, but also another existence.

A dimension that was dangerously attractive, he was aware of that. An allure that in certain circumstances – with certain rudimentary defence mechanisms neutralized – he would find difficult to resist.

Deep down in his consciousness was a blurred image of his own father, and of a conversation between his father and his only brother. His father's words, and the inexplicable way in which he distanced himself from his own brother. Resolute steps hurrying away over the gravel, and a heavy gate slamming shut.

His own four- or five-year-old legs first hesitating, and then having to run for dear life in order not to be shut up behind the walls. And having to stay there with Uncle Bern.

Incomprehensible then. Incomprehensible now – but even so, he had inherited a portion of that attitude to life.

His own private birthmark. One of them.

He turned off to the right before coming to the main building, followed the well-trodden path down into the hollow and came to the same low, oblong building under the elms as last time. Showed his pass to a bearded young man behind another window, and was allowed in.

Sergeant Matthorst was sitting in the coffee room, smoking and watching the television. He seemed to be somewhat embarrassed at having been caught in such trivial circumstances, and was keen to escort the chief inspector to a room in one of the corridors where Mathilde Ubrecht had been held for the last three and a half days. He unlocked the door, and Van Veeteren entered.

She was curled up on her bed, reading the Bible. The same pale, unbleached cotton individual as before. The same lank, colourless hair. The same introspectiveness. The chief inspector hesitated for a moment before turning the desk chair round and sitting down opposite her, less than a metre away.

He paused. Took a toothpick from his breast pocket and weighed it in the palm of his hand. Decided it was too light and put it back again. Looked out through the barred window. Most of the view was obscured by a dense and unpruned lilac hedge. He returned to observing the woman on the bed.

Waited. Listened to the silence and the very faint noise from some air-conditioning system. After about five minutes, she closed the Bible. Looked up, and met his gaze.

'I suggest we go for a little walk in the grounds,' said Van Veeteren. 'It's a lovely evening.'

She didn't respond. Continued looking at him while leafing through the Bible and breathing through her half-open mouth. He wondered if she might suffer from asthma or some kind of allergy – it looked like it. After a while she nodded vaguely, and stood up. Matthorst, who had evidently been waiting outside the door, accompanied them along the corridor; as they passed the television room, the chief inspector gave him a nod as an indication that he could go back to watching his programme.

Or to more high-minded pursuits, always assuming he had any.

The sun had set by the time they went outside, and the groups of green and white people had gone indoors for the night. Van Veeteren let Mathilde Ubrecht choose the route, and they set off slowly in the direction of the pond at the other end of the grounds. North-west, unless he was mistaken. The evening breeze, the gentle whispering he had heard in the forest as he made his way up to Wolgershuus, had now died away altogether; the only noise remaining was their steps on the gravel, and Mathilde Ubrecht's slightly strained breathing. There was a faint aura of tension over her movements, and he was careful to keep a half-metre behind her so as not to influence her route and possible decisions.

Nor did he say a word until they came to the artificial pond with water lilies and softly murmuring water trickling out of a mythological bronze statue. They sat down on one of the brown-coloured benches and Van Veeteren lit a cigarette.

'I have three questions,' he said. 'Your silence is protecting a murderer. I take it for granted that you will give me honest answers.'

Mathilde Ubrecht didn't react. Didn't even indicate in any way that she had heard what he'd said. He inhaled deeply on his cigarette and braced himself.

'Question number one,' he said. 'Do you know who murdered Clarissa Heerenmacht?'

Silence. He contemplated the dark forest over the top of the high wall. She's not going to answer, he thought.

'No,' she said.

Van Veeteren nodded. Allowed a minute to pass. Stubbed out his cigarette.

'Number two,' he said. 'Do you know what happened to Katarina Schwartz?'

Another wait. Then she took a deep breath; he could hear the irregular wheezing in her bronchial tubes.

'No.'

'Thank you,' said the chief inspector. 'Oscar Yellinek. Do you know where he is?'

She paused longer this time, but when the answer eventually came it sounded just as definite as the previous ones.

'No.'

He sat for a while, mulling things over.

'Is there anything else you want to tell me?'

Instead of answering she stood up and made a gesture indicating that she wanted to go back indoors. He nodded, and they started to walk back through the increasingly blue silence.

Matthorst was waiting for them at the entrance, and Van Veeteren realized he must have been watching them through the window.

He didn't go inside with her, merely handed her over to a carer. But nevertheless he had a moment's eye contact with her before she vanished through the door, and it was that farewell look that accompanied him all the way back.

Through the hospital grounds. Through the dark forest. Along the sparsely lit road back to the little town.

He had received three negative replies to his three questions. But also a look that said . . . Well, what did it say?

Intuitively – before he had begun to analyse and weigh everything up – he had no doubt about the answer:

I've told you the truth. Believe me.

But then it went off the rails. Did he dare to trust her? Did he really dare to believe that this mad priestess – or whatever epithet one chose to hang around her neck – really didn't have any information worth telling him?

Be it about the murder, or the girl who had disappeared, or the shepherd who had done the same thing?

He knew that everything depended on his judgement of these matters. And of course it wasn't out of the question that she had given him a mixed bag of answers – served him up two truths and one lie, or vice versa, and as he strolled slowly back to the little town, he had the impression that his journey was not unlike the usual tightrope walk – along the blurred and tarnished borderline between true and false.

How far could he trust her? How far could he trust her three negative replies? How much was his intuition worth on this occasion?

And when shortly afterwards he sat down in the dining room at Grimm's Hotel, he still didn't know. But nevertheless, he had made a few decisions.

For after all, somebody needed to make interpretations and solve doubts. *Mene tekel*.

Mene mene tekel.

23

Suijderbeck ignored the warning notice, instead flung the gate open wide so that the whole fence shuddered. Sure enough, half a second later two fifty-kilogram German shepherds came racing round the corner of the house.

Suijderbeck stopped.

'Sit!' he roared when the beasts were only two metres away and the adrenaline swirled like a cloud of steam around their jowls.

It had the same effect as usual. The dogs were transformed instantly into two phlegmatic black sheep whose only ambition seemed to be to sink down into the earth at the feet of their newly acquired master.

'Shit-scared cowards,' muttered Suijderbeck and continued along the gravel path.

A woman in cut-off jeans and a checked man's shirt came out onto the patio, fists clenched by her sides. Suijderbeck paused and looked her up and down. Realized that a single barked command wouldn't work in her case.

Although it would have been fun to try. No doubt about that.

'Mrs Kuijpers?' he asked instead.

'And who the devil are you?'

'Suijderbeck. Police,' said Suijderbeck, walking up the steps with his hand outstretched politely to greet her.

'ID,' said the woman, instead of shaking hands.

Suijderbeck fished it out of his inside pocket. When he held it up ten centimetres in front of the woman's face, he could smell the strong drink on her breath. He decided to remove his silk gloves.

'I have a few questions to ask you,' he said. 'Would you like to come with me in the car, or can we sort it out here?'

'What the hell?' said the woman. 'Coming here and—'

'It's about the murder at the summer camp,' snapped Suijderbeck, interrupting her and gesturing with his hand towards the forest and the road he'd just come driving along. 'I assume you've heard what's happened.'

'Of course.' She immediately seemed rather more tractable, he noticed. 'Er, please sit down.'

She sat down on one of the plastic chairs on the patio, and Suijderbeck sat down opposite her.

'But we haven't done anything,' she said without being prompted. 'I mean, Henry came out last spring, and since then we've lived like angels out here.'

'You don't say,' said Suijderbeck.

'Who the hell is it?' a gruff-sounding man's voice enquired from inside the house.

'The police!' shouted the woman in a tone pitched somewhere between hope and despair.

The man appeared in the doorway. A copy of his wife, in fact, Suijderbeck noted. Big, powerful, the worse for wear. Approaching fifty, it seemed.

Mind you, only the woman sported bleached hair and a nose ring.

'Kuijpers,' said the man, extending a hairy hand. 'I'm as innocent as a newly wed virgin.'

The wheezing splutter was presumably laughter. Suijderbeck lit a cigarette. What a pair of idiots, he thought. If I just hold my tongue, they'll have confessed to illicit distilling and receiving stolen goods within a quarter of an hour.

'Anyway,' said Kuijpers. 'I gather it's about that poor girl.'

'Yes,' said Suijderbeck. 'Do you know anything about it?'

They both shook their heads. The woman hiccuped and put her hand over her mouth.

'What a bloody mess,' said Kuijpers. 'No, we've had no contact with them. As for that creeping Jesus on the run . . . No, I'm at a loss for words.'

'There was another police officer here a few days ago,' said the woman.

'I know,' said Suijderbeck. 'I just want to check a few things.'

'Well?' said the man, scratching at his crotch.

Suijderbeck took out his notebook and thumbed through a few pages.

'We know nothing about it,' said the woman nervously.

'Don't harp on about it,' said the man.

'Hmm,' said Suijderbeck. 'So you haven't spoken to any of them? Not to the girls nor to the leaders? Not at all during the summer? The camp is less than two kilometres away from here.'

The man shook his head again.

'A little group of them came here once or twice,' said the woman. 'Picking blueberries or something, but the dogs kept most of them away, you could say.'

She nodded her head at where the German shepherds were prowling around restlessly.

'Most of them,' she said again, to be on the safe side.

'All we've done is drive past the summer camp on our way to town,' said the man. 'As for talking to 'em? No thank you . . . I can't say I'm surprised at what's happened, hell no. Randy old buggers like that fucking priest – there's no saying what they can get up to.'

Suijderbeck began to draw a fat priest in his notebook.

'What were you doing last Sunday night?' he asked. 'I'm referring to Sunday last week, the night the girl was murdered.'

'What?' said the man. 'All night? I was at home of course. As usual.'

'You didn't have any visitors?'

Kuijpers shook his head, and looked enquiringly at his wife.

'No,' said the woman. 'We were on our own here.'

'Do you remember hearing anybody drive past during the night?'

'No,' said the man. 'That other cop asked that as well, but we didn't hear a thing. Mind you, we were asleep.'

'I don't suppose many cars come past your house?' Suijderbeck asked, looking for somewhere to stub out his cigarette. He eventually hit upon a shrivelled pot plant standing next to his wooden leg.

'Two or three a week,' said the man, flashing his teeth. Presumably it was a smile.

'But you don't remember anything from that night?'

'Not a bloody thing,' said the man.

'Do you have any children?'

'Eh?' said the man.

'We have a daughter,' said the woman. 'Her name's Ewa, and she moved out, er, how long ago is it now?'

'Four years ago,' said the man. 'She's twenty-four now. She was twenty when she buggered off.'

'With a foreigner,' added his wife.

'I'm not her real father,' said Kuijpers.

Suijderbeck noted it all down.

'I see,' he said, and thought for a while. 'And there's nothing else you could tell us that you think might be of use to us?'

Kuijpers frowned and his wife pulled anxiously at her nose ring.

'No . . . No, I can't think of anything at all.'

'What do you do for a living?'

'I'm off sick,' said the man, holding his back.

'Ceramics,' said the woman. 'He has a little pottery. And he paints a bit as well.'

Suijderbeck nodded and put away his notebook. Squinted up at the sky.

'It's hot,' he said. 'It must be an advantage to live so close to the lake. I suppose you have a boat, do you?'

'Of course,' said the man. 'We do a bit of fishing as well, but that used to be better than it is now. What with all the effluents and the rest of the bloody shit . . .'

'Yes,' said Suijderbeck, 'there's a lot of shit around nowadays. No, I mustn't impose upon you any longer.'

He stood up.

'Anyway, many thanks,' he said. 'What were you inside for, by the way?'

'Bank robbery,' said the man, scratching at his stubble. 'But I've served my time. It's the straight and narrow for me now.'

'I should hope so,' said Suijderbeck. 'Otherwise I'll have to pay you another visit.'

'Ha ha,' said the man, but his smile didn't stick fast this time either.

'Thank you for your visit,' said the woman.

'Bye for now,' said Suijderbeck.

The moment he left the patio, the dogs disappeared under a corrugated iron roof at the gable end of the house. Lickspittle, Suijderbeck thought. Like owners, like dogs.

He could scarcely claim that this had been an hour well spent.

But that could be said about lots of other things in connection with this bloody case, there was no denying that. Lots of other things.

'Where are you calling from?' asked Kluuge.

'Stamberg,' said the man. 'As I've already said.'

'Okay,' said Kluuge, wiping the sweat from his brow. 'What do you want?'

'I told the girl on the switchboard.'

'Could be, but now you're talking to me. Let's hear it one more time.'

'All right,' said the man. 'My name's Tomasz Banx, and I think I can help you.'

'With what?'

He made a note of the name.

'With the murder, of course. The Waldingen murder. I assume you are the man in charge, so I don't need to explain about that all over again?'

'Yes, I'm in charge,' Kluuge admitted.

'Good. Anyway . . .' Kluuge could almost hear him straightening his back and bracing himself. 'I think I know what happened – the fact is that I . . .'

Silence.

'Well?' said Kluuge.

'Do you believe in Providence, Chief Inspector?'

'I'm not a chief inspector yet, but never mind that. What do you mean by providence?'

'You mean you don't know what Providence is? It's what guides and governs our lives, of course. What brings about justice, and something we can rely on without hesitation, irrespective of what—'

'I understand,' said Kluuge. 'Will you come to the point now, Mr . . .' He checked his notebook. 'Mr Banx. We are very busy and time is short.'

'Yes, harrumph, I'm sure it is. Anyway, I can explain how this murder came about, and what its purpose was.'

'Purpose?'

'Yes, purpose. The Lord moves in a mysterious way as far as we normal, simple people are concerned, but there is always a purpose – a plan and a meaning. In everything, Chief Inspector, and I really do mean everything.'

'That's enough,' said Kluuge. 'Would you mind coming to the point instead of rambling on about all sorts of other things, or I shall hang up on you.'

'I've had a vision,' the man explained. 'And in that vision I saw how everything took place and how it all hangs together.'

'Hang on,' said Kluuge, 'hang on a minute! What's your religion, Mr Banx, can you tell me that?'

'I believe in the only one true God.'

'Are you a member of the Pure Life?'

'From the start,' said Tomasz Banx excitedly. 'From the very beginning.'

Kluuge groaned and kicked off his shoes under his desk. These damned blockheads! he thought.

'Do you know who murdered Clarissa Heerenmacht?' he asked.

Mr Banx cleared his throat solemnly.

'Nobody murdered Clarissa Heerenmacht,' he stated in a serious tone. 'Nobody at all. She was taken home by the

Lord. It was a promise and a punishment combined into one – and an amazing grace.'

'Many thanks, Mr Banx,' said Kluuge, and realized that what he had just said sounded like an idiotic rhyme from a children's book or some such thing. 'I've made a note of everything you've said.'

He slammed down the receiver and summoned Miss Miller. She appeared in the doorway half a minute later, just as cool and unruffled as ever.

'Yes?'

'Miss Miller, haven't I told you not to put any old half-witted idiot through to me? This was the third one today, and I have business to be getting on with that—'

'I understand,' said Miss Miller before he had made his point. 'Anything else?'

'No, that's all,' said Kluuge with a sigh. 'Oh, hang on – do we have any soda water left in the fridge?'

'I'll go and check,' she said, and returned half a minute later.

'No, the fridge is empty,' she reported casually, and left the room.

Like our heads, Kluuge thought, and started to take off his socks as well.

24

'But what do you think has really happened?' asked Przebuda, lighting his pipe. 'If we could perhaps go over to reality for a change.'

Van Veeteren took a sip of wine and contemplated the remains of the meal that had occupied them for the past hour. It was Saturday evening, darkness had begun to fall, and Andrej Przebuda had just been upstairs to fetch a few candles whose flickering light now illuminated the table. Just for a moment the chief inspector had the feeling that his perception seemed to be crackling: all at once he was in the middle of a film. As his eyes roamed slowly over the contents of the room, their dark outlines and barely lit surfaces, he understood what it must be like to be the camera-man for a Kieslowski or a Tarkovskij. Or even to be the eye of the camera itself. Needless to say, the setting was not coincidental or haphazard. Przebuda was not the type to overlook details. They had been talking again about film – its means of expression and its prerequisites when it came to creating, and making invisible things visible. Or perceptible, at least. This special raster capable of transforming a simple two-dimensional screen into something that could make the multifaceted and irrational world into something perfectly clear and comprehensible. In the right hands, of course. There were so many bunglers as well – so incredibly many.

'Reality?' responded the chief inspector after blinking away the illusions. 'Oh, that . . . I suppose I think far too much. There are too many oddities in this business, and it's not easy to keep them at bay. Or too many oddities in that sect, to be more precise. All those damned idiotic practices and sick ideas tend to twist the whole perspective. Away from what is basic. I seem to remember we talked about this last time.'

'And what exactly is basic?' Przebuda asked, blowing out a thick cloud of smoke that momentarily turned the table and the remains of the meal into what looked like a miniature battlefield.

'The basic fact,' resumed the chief inspector when the smoke had dispersed, 'is that a girl was murdered out at Waldingen last Sunday evening. If we can concentrate on that, and forget about all the other goings-on associated with the Pure Life – well, maybe we might get somewhere.'

'I understand,' said Przebuda. 'Anyway, reconstruct last

Sunday afternoon for me and see where we get to. I'm all ears.'

'Hmm,' said Van Veeteren. 'I find it a bit difficult to accept that you serve me up this magnificent dinner, and then have to sit and get involved in my work as well.'

'Nonsense,' said his host. 'Do you think I'm happy at the thought of a desperado prancing around in our forests? Besides, may I remind you that I run a little newspaper – so let's not go on about whose work we're getting involved in.'

The chief inspector conceded and took another cigarette. It was becoming a habit again. Hadn't tasted pleasant for several days now, but once he got away from here, he would make a point of laying down strict and more precise limits. For several things.

'All right,' he said, sitting up straight. 'If you insist. Harrumph! Sunday afternoon, we'll start with Sunday afternoon. I spent a couple of hours out there. Talked to Yellinek, all three women and two of the girls. I won't pretend that I pulled any punches, not much at least, and when I left at three o'clock I had the impression that I'd stirred things up a bit – set a few things in motion, but the question is: what exactly?'

He paused, but Przebuda continued to lean back in his chair on the other side of the table, observing him over the rim of his half-full glass. He looked studiously serious.

Possibly with a touch of lenient indulgence. The chief inspector took a deep breath, and continued.

'In any case, it had put the cat among the pigeons as far as the rest of the afternoon was concerned. The planned activities – some kind of group work based on the Commandments, it seems – were cancelled, and the girls were given a few hours off instead. They could do whatever they wanted, more or less, a most unusual circumstance as far as we can make out. The norm was to keep them occupied with sanctimonious prattling from morning till night. Hour after hour, non-stop. With no opportunity to pause and reflect, which was presumably the point. I've no idea what Yellinek and his fancy women got up to for the rest of that afternoon, but presumably the four of them were hiding away somewhere, holding hands. Discussing the situation, or something of the sort. Anyway, the evening meal was served at six o'clock as usual, apart from the fact that Yellinek wasn't present. Soup with vegetables and noodles, bread and butter and cheese. A bit spartan, you might think, but nothing unusual.'

'Yellinek?' wondered Przebuda.

'Wasn't there for the meal, nor did he take part in the preprandial prayers. Nevertheless, he accompanied a quartet of girls to fetch fresh milk from Fingher's between seven and a quarter to eight, or thereabouts. Then he turned up again shortly after nine, or so we've been led to believe. He took evening prayers as usual, but before that the girls had been informed by the women that the Pure Life had been attacked by the Devil, and that major and crucial things were under way.'

'What the hell?' said Przebuda, putting down his pipe. 'They say things like that?'

Van Veeteren nodded.

'Most certainly,' he said. 'But if we go back a bit and concentrate on the girls instead: they spent their hours of freedom in the late afternoon in various ways. Some went swimming in the lake, others lay down to read – indoors or outdoors – and needless to say, only the wishy-washy stuff available out there: lives of the saints, parish magazines and other such trash. Some of them went for walks in the woods, and four of them went to the place they call the bathing rock. I'd been talking to two of those girls a few hours previously: Belle Moulder and Clarissa Heeren-macht. All four of them went swimming, but shortly before half past five or thereabouts the other two made their own way back to the camp – it's only about five hundred metres, no more. The two left were Belle and Clarissa, aged four-teen and twelve respectively.'

He paused briefly, but his host didn't move a muscle.

'Half an hour later the elder girl was in the dining room, saying grace. The younger one, Clarissa . . . well, she was probably still alive, but was presumably together with her murderer. In any case, she hadn't many hours to live.'

'Ugh,' said Przebuda, taking off his glasses. 'No, I don't want to exchange jobs with you. Sorry, I hope you'll forgive me. But what did that Belle have to say? Wasn't that her name?'

The chief inspector nodded.

'Belle Moulder. And that's our problem. At first she didn't say much at all. Of all of them, she's the one who held out longest. She's evidently some kind of leader for the whole group – and not particularly good at it, if I've interpreted the indications correctly. And when she eventually did come out with something, I think she was lying. She claimed that she wanted to go back to the camp from the rock with Clarissa, but that Clarissa wanted to be alone for a while in order to think something over. So she left her there.'

'I see,' said Przebuda. 'And what do you think really happened? Always assuming that you have an opinion on that score.'

'I think she gave her a good telling-off,' said Van Veeteren.

'A telling-off?' said Przebuda, starting to scratch out his pipe with a matchstick. 'Why?'

'Because she'd been a bit too outspoken when I talked to them.'

'Aha,' said Przebuda. 'And had she been?'

The chief inspector sighed.

'The hell she had. But then, that's the way they are.'

Przebuda pondered for a while.

'Hmm,' he said eventually. 'I can't see how this could be of vital significance. The older girl left the younger one, either on friendly terms or after a quarrel. What difference does it make?'

'I don't know,' said Van Veeteren. 'Maybe none at all. But there's another little detail. The indications are that Belle Moulder also had a tête-à-tête with Yellinek later that evening – some time after evening prayers, but before bedtime. About half past nine. Several of the girls say they saw them together. It's all a bit vague, to be sure, and she denies it.'

'And what would the implication be if she did in fact talk to Yellinek?'

'Hard to say. The most likely thing is, of course, that he wanted information about Clarissa Heerenmacht. He must have realized that she was missing by this time, in any case. If he was the one who killed her, he obviously knows more about that than anybody else.'

Przebuda nodded and began filling his pipe.

'I understand,' he said. 'I think I get the picture. Would you like another glass?'

'Is it really necessary?' wondered the chief inspector. 'Well, just a few drops, then.'

Andrej Przebuda stood up and walked over to the corner cupboard.

'And then what?' asked Przebuda. 'Down at the rock, I mean.'

'A good question,' said the chief inspector. 'Well, then – presumably within fifteen minutes of Belle Moulder leaving her – the murderer comes into the picture. Either he's down there on the rock already, or he turns up somewhere as she's on her way back to the camp. I don't think the girl decided to give dinner a miss, even if that's not impossible, of course.'

'You say "he",' Przebuda commented.

'Let's assume it's a man,' said the chief inspector. 'He rapes her, and strangles her to death. And then we come up against the next complication.'

'Really?'

'The location,' the chief inspector explained. 'I'd like to think there's some kind of logic even in the most perverted patterns of behaviour – we've discussed this before. The murderer kills her somewhere or other, and all we can say with certainty is that it didn't happen where we found the body. There are no signs of a struggle or violence around that place, which indicates that she must have been taken there afterwards. Either immediately after the murder, or later. By the killer, or somebody else.'

'By the killer or somebody else . . . ?' Przebuda repeated, raising an eyebrow.

'The reason for moving the body is also a bit intriguing,' Van Veeteren went on. 'You would usually move a body in order to hide it, but in this case it looks like the intention was just the opposite – to help us to find it.'

Andrej Przebuda nodded.

'That woman on the telephone . . . ?'

'Yes,' said the chief inspector. 'I'd be grateful if you'd refrain from writing about her. Perhaps we're barking up the wrong tree, but the investigation team has decided to keep her existence secret for the time being. Well, what conclusions do you draw?'

Neither of them spoke for quite a while. Van Veeteren eyed the pack of cigarettes on the table in front of him, but didn't take one. Instead he clasped his hands behind his head and leaned back. Wondered if he'd remembered all the essentials, or if he'd left out any details.

And if it was possible to come to any sensible conclusions.

'Two,' Przebuda decided in the end. 'Two conclusions. She seems to know what she's talking about, and she wants to help the police. That woman, I mean.'

Van Veeteren said nothing.

'Two questions as well,' said Przebuda. 'Why? And who the hell is she?'

'My friend the editor is bubbling over with intelligent questions,' the chief inspector declared. 'But there's another one.'

'I know,' said Przebuda. 'How? How the hell can she know so much?'

'Exactly,' said Van Veeteren. 'I've been grappling with these imponderables for several days now. Who is she? How come she knows? Why does she want to help us?'

'But the fact no doubt is . . .' Przebuda began, and then held back.

'What?'

'Surely the implication is that it'll be sufficient to get an answer to one of those questions. Solve one and the others solve themselves. Don't you think?'

The chief inspector sighed.

'Presumably,' he said. 'But how about making a suggestion? Surely an experienced old newspaperman like you should be able to manage one out of three?'

Przebuda burst out laughing. Then he cleared his throat and turned serious.

'No,' he said. 'But surely it's not possible for the chief inspector's intuition to have been fast asleep all week? Do you think it's one of them? Those women at the summer camp, that is?'

Van Veeteren contemplated the flickering candles for ten seconds.

'I don't know,' he said eventually. 'But I think I can exclude one of them, in any case.'

'Better than nothing,' said Przebuda.

They set off at a leisurely pace on a stroll past the cemetery on the western edge of the town, along a meandering path for pedestrians and cyclists to the residential area of Kaasenduijk – where acting Chief of Police Kluuge lived with his Deborah – and then a semicircular route back into Sorbinowo from the north. One hour in all, two and a half kilometres through the fragrant summer's evening. To start with Przebuda maintained a non-stop commentary on items of interest they passed by – buildings, local landmarks, flora and fauna (mainly mosquitoes and cattle of the black-and-white variety) – but he eventually grew tired of that and they returned to the agenda they seemed to have agreed was inevitable.

'This Yellinek character – I take it he does a runner in the middle of the night, is that right?'

'Same as before,' muttered the chief inspector. 'We don't know. None of the girls saw him after a quarter to ten on the Sunday evening, so we assume he must have cleared off before dawn in any case. There's one girl – but only one, *nota bene* – who thinks she heard a car starting at some point during the night.'

'A car?'

'Yes, they had a car out there, an old Vauxhall, registered in the name of Madeleine Zander. Yellinek doesn't even have a driving licence.'

'But it was still there next morning?'

'Yes. Parked in the same place as usual. She – or one of the others – might have driven him somewhere during the night, but we have no proof or confirmation.'

'How else would he have been able to get away?'

Van Veeteren shrugged.

'The devil only knows. So it's certainly most likely that he disappeared with the help of that car, but where does that get us?'

'What about neighbours out there?' Przebuda wondered.

'The Finghers in one direction,' said Van Veeteren. 'They had a bit of contact with the campers. And there's a couple by the name of Kuijpers a bit deeper into the forest. There was somebody at home in both places that night, but nobody heard a car. But that doesn't mean a thing, of course. The probability is that Yellinek's hidden away in the home of one of his church members somewhere, but there are getting on for a thousand of them, so we need considerable resources if we're going to make a serious search. Obviously the police in Stamberg are pouncing on as many of them as they can find, but they don't seem to be making any headway. And of course it's holiday time. And on top of that is the refusal to cooperate.'

'Oh dear,' said Przebuda, wafting away a cloud of gnats. 'Things aren't exactly stacked in your favour.'

They continued in silence for a few minutes.

'Why?' said the editor eventually, having followed his own train of thought to the next halt. 'Why did he run away if he's innocent? Doesn't that suggest he's the culprit?'

'That's very possible,' said the chief inspector. 'Although he had good reason to go under cover in any case. He's been in trouble with the police before, and if girls suddenly start disappearing from his camp he's bright enough to realize that he's on the spot. It's obviously disgraceful of him to run away like that, but by no means beyond comprehension. We must never lose sight of the fact that we're dealing with an arsehole. A king-size arsehole.'

'So you're saying there's a logical explanation, are you?'

'Without a doubt,' said the chief inspector. 'I've been thinking about it, and I reckon it would have been odder if he'd stayed around. Especially in view of this other girl that's missing – remember this is just between me and you: you're the only editor in the whole country who knows about that – and even more so when you take into account what a shit that Yellinek is.'

'I see,' said Przebuda. 'Although I don't really get what the implications are. There's nothing to link Yellinek and his hangers-on directly with these terrible happenings, is there?'

'No,' said Van Veeteren with a sigh. 'No very strong link at least. As far as I can see it's possible we're dealing with some anonymous lunatic wandering about in the forest.'

'With no link to the Pure Life?'

'No link at all.'

'Well I'll be damned!' said Przebuda.

'But on the other hand, it's just as likely that they are the ones responsible.'

'Of course,' said Przebuda. 'One or other of them.'

He paused to light his pipe, then he and the chief inspector immersed themselves in private thoughts as they strolled, at a very gentle pace, side by side along what was in fact the home straight of Sergeant Kluuge's jogging track. But not even the editor was aware of that geographical fact.

'Ah well,' said Przebuda as they approached the built-up area again. 'Whichever way you look at it, it's a very nasty business. I hope you can sort it out. But I must admit that I've got nothing much to contribute, I'm afraid . . . Anyway, I think we're coming to a parting of the ways. That's

Grimm's down there, as you can see – but if ever you need a Dr Watson again, my tiny brain is at your disposal.'

'Thank you,' said Van Veeteren. 'Two tiny brains are better than one, I suppose.'

They said goodbye, but before Andrej Przebuda had climbed even five of the steps up to Kleinmarckt, he paused.

'Do you think you're going to solve this case?' he asked. 'Do you usually solve your cases?'

'Most of them,' said Van Veeteren.

'But you have some unsolved cases, do you?'

'One,' admitted the chief inspector. 'But let's not go into that. Every new day brings enough problems, as I've said before.'

'You can say that again,' said Przebuda, and Van Veeteren thought he could hear his friend smiling in the darkness. 'Goodnight, Chief Inspector. May the angels sing you to sleep.'

No, Van Veeteren thought grimly when Przebuda had disappeared. Let's not start thinking about the G file as well. We've got enough on our hands without that.

By the time he strode through the milk-white glass doors of Grimm's Hotel, his dejection had caught up with him.

We ought to have talked about other things, he thought. We ought to have focused on something else.

Katarina Schwartz, for instance. Or Ewa Siguera. Or potential violent criminals in the area. I'm damned sure he'd have been able to come up with something useful if we'd done that!

But perhaps his self-criticism was unfair. In any case, the disappearance of the Schwartz girl was still something they'd managed to keep away from the journalists – after nearly a week under the spotlights. That was probably due more to good luck than good management; and besides, one might ask if there was any point in keeping it secret. Perhaps, perhaps not.

And they hadn't heard a word from the French police.

Becalmed, the chief inspector thought (although he had only been in a sailing boat twice in the whole of his life – both times together with Renate). For the whole of that Saturday in Sorbinowo there had hardly been a breath of wind, and the case had not moved forward even a fraction of an inch.

Becalmed.

He recalled the potentially meaningful silence up at Wolgershuus the previous day, and realized that there was more to coming to an end and dying than people generally imagined.

Madeleine Zander and Ulriche Fischer! he then thought

with a feeling of disgust as he stood at the reception desk, waiting for his key. Were things really so bad that he would have to tackle them as well?

When the night porter eventually appeared, it transpired that there was another woman's name to frustrate him.

Albeit in a slightly different way.

Reinhart had left a message for him. It was short and sweet:

There's no damned Ewa Siguera anywhere in this country. Shall I continue with the rest of the world?

Van Veeteren's reply was more or less just as stringent:

Europe will be enough. Many thanks in advance.

Ah well, he thought when he had eventually gone to bed, I suppose I might just as well carry on as planned, no matter what.

25

The second of the victims of the sect murderer – as several newspapers would call the person concerned – was discovered at about six on Sunday morning by a sixteen-year-old boy scout and a fifteen-year-old girl guide who were part of a biggish group on a hike in the forests north-west of Sorbinowo. At the pair's urgent request, no attempt was made to find out what they were doing some three kilometres away from their tents at that time in the morning, but Chief of Police Kluuge – who was once again the first on the scene – naturally had his suspicions.

The body of the young girl was under a pile of brushwood and dry twigs about twenty metres from the narrow road from Waldingen to Limbuis and Sorbinowo, and the distance to the nearest of the summer camp buildings was no more than a hundred and sixty metres or so. The distance between where the two bodies had been discovered was measured later and found to be about three times that, and perhaps one could reasonably have expected that the police team that had spent two days searching the area after the first murder would have found the body; and perhaps also – Kluuge thought à propos of nothing in particular – the unusually pale colour of the girl guide's face might have had to do with the fact that she found it hard to forget what she had been doing next to, and even hidden behind, the pile of twigs in question.

In any case, that was the conclusion he drew as the three of them sat on a stack of logs watching the sun rise over the trees to usher in a new day, waiting for the medical team and the crime scene officers to arrive – and he was also aware that these irrelevant speculations only came into his head as a way of keeping his thoughts under control.

When he compared the Katarina Schwartz who had spent almost two weeks in the form of a dead body, reduced to a mass of chemical processes, with the photograph of a smiling young girl with blonde plaits he had in his wallet, there was no doubt that his thoughts needed all the distractions they could possibly get.

I've grown old, he thought. Even though it's no more than a week since I grew up.

The first report from more or less all the experts at the scene was ready by shortly after one p.m. and confirmed that the dead child was Katarina Emilie Schwartz, thirteen years old, resident in Stamberg. She had been raped (no trace of sperm) and strangled, suffered pretty much the same type of injuries as the other victim, Clarissa Heeren-macht, and had probably met her killer somewhere between twelve and sixteen days earlier. No clothes – nor indeed any trace of clothes – had been found at or in the vicinity of the place where the body was discovered, and it was considered to be highly likely that the girl had been killed at some other location. The press communiqué issued later in the afternoon contained all known details of the tragic discovery – apart from the fact that the police had known about the girl's disappearance for quite a while.

At the same time the police issued two Wanted notices.

One was a repeat of the appeal for information about Oscar Yellinek.

The other was new and aimed at tracing the girl's parents.

By coincidence, a little later that same afternoon a fax arrived from the French police: Mr and Mrs Schwartz had been traced to a so-called *gîte* on a farm in Brittany. Before the sun had set over Sorbinowo that long Sunday, the unfortunate couple had set off on the journey home in order to be confronted as soon as possible by the earthly remains of their daughter.

And when old Mrs Grimm – the hotel's owner who was at bottom indifferent to anything not connected with royalty or Bohemian porcelain – checked through the hotel ledger even later that evening, she found that not only was every room taken, but that the number of guests who had given their occupation as 'journalist' or something similar was strikingly large.

As for Mr Van Veeteren (watchmaker and horologist), who had been staying in room number 22 for the last ten days, by midnight he still hadn't returned from the excursion he had set out on that morning.

But as he seemed to have left most of his belongings in his room, she was not particularly worried that he might have run off with no intention of returning to pay his bill.

After all, he had given the impression of being an honest man, on the whole.

FIVE

28–31 JULY

26

For the first fifteen kilometres or so he felt almost like a successful fugitive.

Only very slightly guilty. A bit like when he was at school, he recalled, on one of those early summer days when he skipped French or Physics and instead cycled with a like-minded friend down to the canal to watch some girls swimming. Or rode out to Oudenzee to lie back on the beach and do some surreptitious smoking.

Playing truant, in other words. There was no doubt he had left Kluuge and the others in the lurch. And hence there was no doubt either that Krantze's was quite a satisfactory alternative, all things considered.

Nevertheless, it was rather remarkable that he was able to keep the whole business at a distance. That's how it felt, at least, as he sat behind the wheel in the sparse morning traffic. Servinus had informed him about the new discovery by telephone at about eight o'clock. The body of the second little girl. After overcoming his initial feelings of disgust and repugnance, he had spoken in turn to Kluuge, Lauremaa and Suijderbeck several times during the course of the morning, but he had not cancelled his plans.

He hadn't driven out to Waldingen to see the circumstances for himself, and didn't feel guilty about that – or only very slightly so, as already stated. But he had been aware of a feeling of weariness swelling inside him, and it was essential to keep that at bay – that bank of clouds spreading across the landscape of his soul and casting over it a shadow of death, the dark skies of tiredness and loathing . . . and once again he was struck by this attack of poetic eloquence. He had known that this was going to happen, of course. He'd been waiting for this selfsame discovery all these days, and now confirmation had arrived.

So perhaps this eagerness to keep things at a distance was no more than a defence against impotence, when all was said and done. Prepared in advance and defendable, in a way. After all, he wasn't a young beginner any more. He'd been through this kind of thing before.

Rather too often.

'I have a few possible leads,' he had explained. 'Probably nothing of importance, but I think it's best if I follow them up. You can manage on your own. I mean, this is what we've been expecting, isn't it?'

Kluuge hadn't dared to protest. He'd indicated that further reinforcements were being sent, and hoped that the chief inspector would soon be back.

'We shall see,' said Van Veeteren. 'If I find I'm not getting anywhere, I might even be back by this evening.'

That was a blatant lie, of course. He was intending to spend at least two nights in Stamberg, and it was only for the sake of appearances that he hadn't checked out of Grimm's altogether.

Still, rather a bill for four nights instead of two – something bound to raise an eyebrow in the accounts department – than having to cope with the sight of another abused little girl.

Or having to explain why he couldn't face up to that prospect. That was simply the way it was. His decision was not negotiable.

And now, as he analysed and contemplated these thoughts and decisions in more detail – as the kilometres rolled past and Boccherini oozed out of the speakers – he was a bit surprised: but it was surprise tinged with resigned weariness. Even these thoughts were affected. Nothing to get excited about, and there was nothing he could do about it.

I've had enough, he thought. I don't want to stand gaping at yet another dead thirteen-year-old. I've reached a full stop, at last. Everything is clear now, I've caught up with myself.

The decision is made.

He stopped about halfway – after eighty kilometres or more – at a service area not far from Aarlach. Clouds had been building up all morning, quite a strong north-westerly wind was blowing over the open fields, and his guess was that it would be raining before nightfall. Nevertheless, he sat down at one of the outside tables with a cup of coffee, a bottle of mineral water and the early editions of the evening newspapers. Both *Den Poost* and *Neuwe Gazett*.

There was nothing there about the second murder in Waldingen, not yet; but needless to say, it wouldn't be long before he was confronted by the headlines. It wasn't all that hard to work out the likely wording. Nor was it difficult to imagine the tension to which the investigation team was subjected.

Nor the hunger of the hordes of reporters who were at this very moment flocking to the Sorbinowo forests in order to sink their teeth into the fresh corpse of another little girl.

Well, no – not all that fresh. It would be a couple of weeks old by now.

That hardly made the situation any better.

He shuddered in disgust, and drained the bottle of mineral water.

Then he lit a cigarette and tried instead to concentrate on what lay in store for him in Stamberg. Enough of all those thoughts about running away.

His discussions with Inspector Puttemans took about an hour, and all the time he sat watching the progress of rain-drops trickling slowly down the uneven surface of the windowpanes. He wasn't sure why, but there was some-thing about those thin, irregular trickles that appealed to him, and that he was unwilling to lose contact with. He didn't want to miss the moment when one of all those raindrops suddenly felt that enough was enough, and decided to trickle upwards instead. Yes, something of the sort was no doubt what fascinated him. Something to do with rebellion and spiritual affinity.

Or possibly with the first stages of Alzheimer's, he was suddenly horrified to think.

When the discussion was over they shook hands. Putte-mans went home to his family and the roast duck that awaited him, as it did every Sunday. Van Veeteren had declined in friendly but firm fashion the offer to partake of the meal – instead he stayed at the police station for a while and telephoned several of the people whose names his colleague had presented him with. He arranged to meet them the following day, and when he hung up after the last of the calls, he saw that it was still raining.

And that the drops were still trickling downwards.

He remained at the station for another twenty minutes, reading through the notes he'd made on the conversation with Puttemans. He smoked another cigarette, whereupon it stopped raining. He left the police station and wandered aimlessly around the centre of town for a few minutes. Changed his mind and left a couple of bars without actually entering them, on the grounds that they looked as uninspiring as his motive for entering them in the first place. But shortly after five o'clock he found a hotel that corresponded more or less to the calibre he'd been looking for.

Glossman's, it was called. Off the beaten track. Small. At least fifty years old.

A modest-looking dining room with white tablecloths, and television in every room.

The latter was something he'd just have to put up with. He checked in and explained that he intended to stay for two nights. Possibly one or even two more. He picked up a couple of beers in reception, then indulged in a lengthy and refreshing bath in their company while thinking thoughts more or less martial in nature.

*

In view of its age and significance, the town of Stamberg contained a number of churches dating from various centuries and built in different styles (including the so-called Moorish basilica at the heart of the old town, with its altar by Despré or one of his disciples). But when Van Veeteren eventually found his way to the sanctuary of the Pure Life, he realized that a different kind of spirituality held sway here.

Completely different. Obviously late-sixties architecture – in so far as there was any such thing as architecture at that time. Dirt-grey concrete with occasional infusions of cheap red brick. Disproportionate windows apparently distributed at random. A sports hall or a secondary school closed down for the summer were the first thoughts to enter the chief inspector's mind. The impression of neglect and melancholy was striking: the overgrown flower beds and the dandelions in the gaps between the paving stones were a clear indication of activity that had been suspended. Not to say abandoned. It was summer, and the arable land of the soul was lying fallow.

Godforsaken! he decided, and kicked an empty beer can into the overgrown lilac hedge. And it was off the beaten track as well. In something that resembled an industrial park – with characterless, oblong factory buildings and deserted streets with no pavements. Not exactly your church in the heart of the village. Having completed a tour of the outside of the building, he was aware that there were also external forces conspiring to keep the faithful at bay.

'Murdering bastards' was sprayed in shaky, fifty-centimetre-high letters over the entrance doors at the gable end. A bit further along, the graffiti urged readers to 'Kill the swine'; combined with a large number of 'Fuck' messages and other obscenities, the overall impression was depressing. He also had the feeling that most of the graffiti was recent: that these young, anonymous al fresco artists had most probably been creating their masterpieces in the last few days.

Or nights, to be more accurate.

The Other World, he thought, and turned on his heel to put the whole wretched business behind him.

But, it suddenly occurred to him: if it really was the case that the persecution of the first Christians was a part of the dogma in the catechism of the Pure Life, then here was grist to their mill.

But given the current circumstances, that could hardly provide much consolation.

After a lengthy dinner in the almost deserted dining room, he returned to his room just in time for the ten o'clock news. He switched on the television, and lay back on his bed.

It was a twenty-minute broadcast, and he noted with a heavy heart that almost half of it was devoted to happenings in the Sorbinowo forests.

Pictures from the places where the bodies had been found – both of them. Pictures of the summer camp buildings, and of both the dead girls – albeit while smiling and still alive. Information about their age, where they lived, their interests. Instructive maps complete with crosses and arrows. Long-winded summaries of the investigation to date, followed by interviews.

First of all Kluuge, who looked sweaty and embarrassed, and hardly gave the impression of trustworthiness, it unfortunately had to be said. Then Suijderbeck, who came out with four swear words in a mere thirty seconds and seemed to be having difficulty in refraining from suggesting that the sleek-haired reporter might consider going to hell.

And to round it all off, a picture of the press conference as a whole – something which allowed the first ray of hope to illuminate the surface for some considerable time.

Or at least, that is how Van Veeteren saw it. The two places on the far right of the five-man police panel were occupied by no less than Inspector Reinhart and Constable Jung – no, Inspector Jung as he now was – and even if neither of them seemed able to raise a smile (Reinhart looked as if he were sitting on a heap of broken glass), the chief inspector couldn't help but notice that his cheek muscles kept twitching – his own cheek, that is, his right one.

Obviously, any such thoughts faded away as soon as his friends and workmates withdrew; but the very fact that they had unexpectedly turned up to support him definitely gave him a faint feeling of confidence and cautious optimism. For the first time for a very long time.

I wonder if they've booked rooms at Grimm's, Van Veeteren thought. Perhaps I ought to give them a ring.

But on second thoughts, he desisted. Instead, he devoted the next two hours to reading all the documents associated with the Pure Life and its members, given to him by Puttemans; and when he had finished, his conclusion was that it had most probably been a waste of time.

Like so much else.

27

Nevertheless, he phoned them the next morning.

'We have nothing to do with the investigation,' Reinhart explained. 'We've come here to track down an ancient detective chief inspector who's disappeared.'

'I'm on his trail,' said Van Veeteren. 'No need to worry.'

'Glad to hear it,' said Reinhart. 'What the hell are you doing?'

'I'm just following up a few leads.'

'That's a quotation.'

'Could be. In any case, I'll be back tomorrow, or the day after. How are things?'

'Bloody awful,' said Reinhart. 'You must know that. Who's done it? That Messiah-prat?'

'Quite possibly,' said Van Veeteren. 'I don't know.'

'Where's he hiding, then?'

'I've no idea. Maybe here. There are at least five hundred households in Stamberg that would be prepared to put him up. Most of them have been investigated, but you never know.'

'No, you never do,' said Reinhart, lapsing into one of his hacking morning coughs before continuing. 'I find it a bit hard to imagine you wandering around, knocking on doors; but that's not my problem. Anyway, if he's not the one, who is it?'

'In that case it's somebody else,' said Van Veeteren.

'I'll make a note of that,' said Reinhart. 'And what does the chief inspector think I should use my little grey cells for on a day like today?'

Van Veeteren thought for a moment.

'Finding the murderer,' he decided. 'Yes, that would improve your situation quite a bit.'

'I'll make a note of that as well,' said Reinhart. 'If you phone this evening, I'll give you a report. By the way, to be serious for a moment . . .'

'Yes?'

Three seconds passed.

'I don't like this business at all.'

'Nor do I,' said Van Veeteren.

Another pause, presumably while Reinhart fumbled after his pipe and tobacco.

'Child murderers like these are the worst set of bastards I can think of.'

'All the more reason to make sure we catch them,' said the chief inspector.

'Exactly,' said Reinhart. 'I'll do whatever I can. By the way, what are our colleagues like?'

'They've passed the test,' said Van Veeteren. 'Suijderbeck is probably the best.'

'The one with the wooden leg?'

'Yes.'

'Okay, so long for now,' said Reinhart and replaced the receiver.

The woman eyed him first for quite a while through the peephole in the door, and made him hold up his ID in front of the tiny hole before starting to unlock. This complicated procedure took another half-minute, and he began to wonder if she was quite right in the head.

But perhaps they're all like this, he thought, when she'd finally finished and he was able to step inside the cramped vestibule. All the mutton-heads in this naively sanctimonious flock.

But then again, given what certain newspapers had written and the contents of some graffiti, maybe there were good grounds for barricading oneself in these days. If you wanted to avoid coming in excessively close touch with the Other World. Who was he to judge?

Her handshake was cold and damp. She led him into the living room and invited him to sit down on a flowery sofa in front of an oval table laid with tea and cakes.

'Help yourself,' she said, in a shaky voice.

'Thank you,' said Van Veeteren.

She poured out some pale-looking tea from a pot, and he observed her furtively. A slim and somewhat anaemic woman. Forty plus, he guessed. The same sort of anaemia as displayed by the Three Graces in Sorbinowo, he noted, and wondered what it could be due to.

A state of spirituality that was on the way to suffocating all bodily functions and needs? The triumph of the will?

Or was it just his usual prejudices and traditional thoughts about gender roles? Hard to say. Nevertheless Renate turned up briefly in his mind's eye. Glared reproachfully at him and disappeared.

'Can you tell me something about your church?' he wondered. 'What you do, how you are different from other communions, that kind of thing.'

She put her cup down on the saucer with a clinking noise.

'Well . . .' she began and cleared her throat several times. 'We believe in the living God.'

'I see,' said the chief inspector with an encouraging nod.

'In the living God.'

Van Veeteren took a cake.

'Jesus is in our midst.'

'Yes, I've heard that said.'

'Anybody who has seen the light of faith . . .'

'. . . ?'

'It's a blessing to be a part of it.'

'So I gather,' said the chief inspector. 'And how long is it since you joined the Pure Life?'

'Two years,' she said without hesitation. 'Two years, two months and eleven days. It was during the spring campaign that Christ revealed Himself to me.'

Van Veeteren took a sip of tea, which tasted like warm water with a hint of mint. He swallowed it with some difficulty. Looked up and eyed the picture on the wall behind the woman's back instead. Quite a large oil painting featuring a group of people dressed in white in front of light-coloured birch trunks and a pale, slightly shimmering sky. Porridge, he thought. Against the light. Anyway, carry on, for God's sake!

'You can't possibly imagine what it's like,' explained the woman, now with a fresh dose of unctuousness in her voice. 'You really can't! If you really understood what it was like to live in the light, you would break away from your old way of life this very day.'

'Hallelujah,' said Van Veeteren.

'Eh?'

'Excuse me. Can you tell me about Oscar Yellinek instead? I take it you know what's happened in Waldingen.'

The woman clasped her hands in her lap, but said nothing. Her lively optimism had vanished into thin air. He realized that he'd offended her. Already.

'Have you ever been there?'

She shook her head.

'What have you to say about Yellinek?'

'Oscar Yellinek is our leader.'

'I know that.'

'He's our link with the living God.'

'How?'

'How? Well, he has contact because of his purity and his nobility.'

'I understand,' said Van Veeteren. 'Do you know where he is just now?'

'No.'

'But you know that he's run away from the camp at Waldingen?'

'Yes . . . No, not run away.'

'What would you call it, then?'

'He's simply following the voice of God.'

'The voice of God?'

'Yes.'

'Have you read what's being written in the newspapers? A lot of people think it's Yellinek behind the murders.'

'That's impossible. That's all lies and slander. Some people are full of jealousy and malice, that's why they say things like that. Christ was also persecuted . . .'

The roses of indignation were coming into bloom all over her neck and cheeks. The chief inspector waited for a few seconds, trying to catch her eye.

'Are you sure about this?'

'Oscar Yellinek is a holy man.'

'And that gives him the right to protect a murderer, does it?'

'I don't understand what you mean.'

'Don't you? It's the easiest thing in the world to understand. Do you agree that these girls are dead?'

'Yes, I assume—'

'That they have been brutally raped and murdered?'

'Yes, but—'

'Do you think it would be right to allow their murderer to go free?'

'No, of course not—'

'So how can you defend the only people who could give us information about it all by choosing not to say anything? Go on, I'd like to have an answer to that question.'

She said nothing.

'Do you know where Oscar Yellinek is?'

'Me?'

'Yes.'

'Of course not.'

'Do you think it's right to say nothing?'

'I don't want to talk about this. I think—'

'The murderer is still free because the Pure Life refuses to cooperate with the police,' the chief inspector persisted. 'You are all hand in hand with criminals, killers, and . . . and with the devil himself. There are some people who believe that you are Satanists, did you know that?'

She didn't respond this time either. Van Veeteren said nothing. Leaned back in his chair and observed her silent confusion for half a minute. Realized he had overstepped the mark, but it was far from easy to adapt to every single situation. He changed track.

'Are you acquainted with the three women who were present at the camp? Ulriche Fischer, Madeleine Zander and Mathilde Ubrecht?'

She shrugged half-heartedly.

'A bit.'

'What do you mean by that?'

'We all belong to the same family.'

'In the Pure Life?'

'Yes.'

'But those three are not among your closest friends?'

'I mix more with some of the others.'

'Have you any friends who are not members of your church?'

She hesitated for a moment.

'Not real friends, no.'

'So you abandoned all your circle of acquaintances when you discovered Jesus two years ago, is that it?'

'No, you don't understand . . .'

Publicans and sinners, Van Veeteren thought.

'Why is your church abandoned, can you tell me something about that? I went to see it yesterday. Don't you have any meetings at all during the summer?'

'We have . . . We have a period.'

'A period?'

'Yes.'

'What kind of a period?'

'Solitariness and heart-searching.'

'Prayers, self-denial and purity, that sort of thing?'

'Yes, although those are the cornerstones. They apply all the time.'

'So there are no services when the shepherd isn't there?'

'No. Why . . . ?'

'Why what?'

'Why are you so angry with me?'

Because I get nothing but heartburn all the time, the chief inspector thought.

'I'm not angry. Can't you try to explain why those women have chosen not to cooperate with the police?' he tried once more. 'If Yellinek is innocent.'

She shrugged again.

'I don't know.'

'Is it because Yellinek has told them not to?'

No reply.

'Do you know if all three have a sexual relationship with him?'

She didn't react as he'd expected.

She didn't react at all. Simply sat there in the light blue armchair, with her teacup on her lap and her mouth like a razor blade.

'Or does every woman in the congregation have a relationship with him?'

Perhaps as a sort of initiation rite, it occurred to him. But for God's sake, there must be several hundred of them! And there were other men in the congregation, albeit not many of them. The woman's eyes shifted several times between her teacup and the knot of his tie. Then she said:

'I think I must ask you to leave me in peace now. I don't think you are a good person.'

Van Veeteren cleared his throat.

'Thank you,' he said. 'I can assure you that nothing would please me more than to leave you now. But the fact is that I have a job to do. My task is to find a murderer, and if you prefer we could drive to the police station and continue our conversation there.'

She gave a start, and put down her teacup. Clasped her

hands more tightly and closed her eyes. He ignored the gesture.

'Just a few more questions,' he said. 'Do you have any children?'

She shook her head.

'Have you been married?'

'No.'

'Do you think there's anything you know that could be of use to us in this investigation? Anything at all.'

She shook her head once again. He stood up. Have you ever been in bed with a man? he wondered.

Not until he was in the hall did he fire off his final question.

'Ewa Siguera, by the way. Who's she?'

'Siguera?'

'Yes.'

'I've no idea. Can't you leave me in peace now? I need to be alone.'

He saw that she was starting to twitch. Little tics around her eyes and mouth, and he wondered if she suffered from some somatic illness or other, on top of everything else.

'All right,' he said. 'I won't disturb you any longer. Thank you for a very instructive conversation.'

He tried to open the door, but it was only when his hostess helped him with two of the locks that he was able to step out into the fresh air again. He listened to the bolts being shot, one after the other, and took two deep breaths.

For Christ's sake, he thought. Is there a single member of the church who would pass a mental examination?

Or even a test to prove they were ready to start school?

Then he remembered that the woman who had just locked herself in was supposed to be a primary school teacher, according to the telephone directory. His mind went blank for a moment.

A teacher?

But perhaps one could entertain a pious hope that her teaching activities were restricted to the church's own private academy. That would limit the damage somewhat.

Nevertheless, what about the children? He descended the stairs with long, almost desperately long strides. Irrespective of whether they live in the Light or in the Other World, what kind of birthmarks would be inflicted on anybody who had to endure a schooling of that kind? Ineradicable for ever and a day.

Give me strength! Van Veeteren thought as he hurried down the street. Oh shit!

He could feel not the slightest trace of that liberal religious tolerance he had flirted with a few days previously.

Red wine, he decided instead. It was only eleven in the morning, but not a minute too soon for a glass and a cigarette. For Christ's sake.

28

The bar was called Plato's Cave, and as he sat there among the shadows he devoted his thoughts mainly to the topic that had cropped up during his latest conversation with Andrej Przebuda.

The premise that assaulting children – subjecting them to some kind of abuse, and in one way or another robbing them of their childhood – was in fact the only crime, the only deed, that could never be forgiven.

With the possible exception of accusing somebody – wrongly – of having done so.

What a balance, he thought. What an incredibly delicate balance! In one pan of the scales all the children that had been the victims of incest without the culprit being punished.

And in the other all those who had been punished, despite the fact that they were innocent.

For there certainly had been witch-hunts. Lots of them.

It was not a new problem, but the lopsided paradox

that kept nagging inside him, and also haunted this case, seemed to him more and more repulsive with nearly every hour that passed.

With every hour and every pointless interrogation.

It would be nice to be a mere shadow, he thought as he looked around at the walls.

Or sitting under a plane tree in Spili.

During the afternoon he talked to two more people who had seen the light. A man and a woman, in that order. Both were aged about thirty-five, both were single, and they had been members of the church for five and six years respectively. The man – a certain Alexander Fitze – gave the impression of having remained in childhood, slow-cooking, until he was well turned twenty, Van Veeteren thought. He picked his words extremely carefully, as if the letters were made of bone china, but even so managed to give the impression of being strained and nervous. He reminded the chief inspector of an old language teacher he'd had as a young teenager: he had behaved in roughly the same way for a few months before he broke down and hanged himself in the attic.

The woman's name was Marlene Kochel and she was more phlegmatic, built like a seal and with a lisping, laid-back tone of voice. But as far as their evidence was concerned, what the chief inspector was obliged to listen to that increasingly hot afternoon was strikingly similar.

The same almost clinical lack of solid information when it came to the actual teachings and beliefs behind the Pure Life.

The same putative phrases about light, purity and the sublime life.

The same devoted outpourings with regard to Oscar Yellinek, his divine gifts and his unadulterated nobility.

The same pious drivel. Time after time Van Veeteren found himself thinking about something else while the tirades followed one after the other before biting their own tail. Or sitting and observing – studying – his interviewees from an entirely different point of view from that usual in such circumstances. Or what ought to be usual.

A distrait and exhausted listener who, instead of listening to and trying to form an opinion about what was being said (and assessing its credibility), devoted himself mainly to wondering what kind of a strange creature was sitting in the chair opposite, babbling (or lisping) away. Churning out these pointless harangues without the slightest basis in either the real world or any kind of logical structure. Words, words, words. In a language he didn't understand.

Almost a different species. Something fundamentally incomprehensible.

But then again – a thought that was never far away from

his mind – he could be the caged animal. The object of study. Lonely and abandoned, staring out through the bars at a whole world of . . . yes, that was the point: incomprehensibility. *Folie à deux*, he thought. There is no such thing as objective reality.

'What are your views on the theodicy problem?' he asked at one point.

'What did you say his name was?' asked Mr Fitze with a nervous smile.

In matters of a more tangible nature – nudity, exorcism, confirmation classes and suchlike – the conversations did manage to throw light on a few places, but by no means all. Of course there were gatherings in the nude. One of Yellinek's central ideas was evidently meeting your God in the same unencumbered and unconstrained state as when you came into the world. And as for driving out sins, or even devils, it was naturally a big advantage if the sinner was wearing as few clothes as possible. It made the process more effective – surely even a secularized detective chief inspector could see that?

Declared Marlene Kochel with a sly smile.

Another fact that was embraced without hesitation as a matter of course was that angels and God the Father Himself were in the habit of striding naked through heavenly pastures – so why not start getting used to it on this side of the border, especially if you happened to be one of the chosen few? Children and adults alike.

Yes, why not?

But carnality? No. Eroticism and licentious behaviour and uncontrolled screwing (the chief inspector's term, which he kept to himself)? Certainly not. This was denied firmly and with such promptitude and lisping frenzy that he realized he wasn't going to get any further along this track – but on the other hand it made him suspect that things were not as above board as was being maintained.

Neither Alexander Fitze nor Marlene Kochel had any comment to make on the prophet and his stable of fancy women at the camp. It seemed to be a matter way beyond the comprehension of a detective chief inspector; a spiritual state of such significance that one could only feel giddy at the very thought. Feel giddy and shut your trap.

To put it in plain English.

And so, on the whole, Van Veeteren did not feel much wiser when he finally emerged into the bustling street after the last of the conversations. But then, not much more stupid either; and what needed to be done first was to place the whole afternoon in parenthesis and add it to the case notes. One of several.

Especially as he had received no help regarding Ewa Siguera on this occasion either.

Ah well, the chief inspector thought with the insight

that experience brings. I've grown a bit older again with a degree of dignity intact.

Then he realized that it was almost six o'clock and he hadn't much more than an hour to spare, if he was going to be able to listen to what his body was telling him about an evening meal.

The meeting with Uri Zander was arranged for half past seven, and as he understood it, the address was somewhere in the suburbs.

So, food! And no shilly-shallying over the menu.

It took him less than five minutes to find a seat and order a substantial portion of meat in one of the restaurants opposite the railway station.

That's enough of ethereal exploration and ecstatic experience to be going on with, he thought, selecting a toothpick while he was waiting to be served. My spiritual needs have been satisfied for the next two years.

Despite all the good intentions, his second evening in Stamberg turned out rather differently.

Nothing wrong with the beef steak, but it joined forces with the dark red wine and his own feelings of inertia with the result that instead of venturing out into the unfamiliar suburbs, he called Mr Zander from the telephone in the entrance and postponed the meeting until the following day. Then he stayed put for another hour with a cheese board and a couple of scandal-mongering evening papers before returning to his hotel as dusk fell.

Two beers, the ten o'clock news on the television (this evening with the events at Sorbinowo crammed into a mere minute and a half) plus four chapters of Klimke's *Observations* took him past midnight, and he fell asleep with a vague but very familiar guilty conscience, without having brushed his teeth.

A sign of decadence, no doubt about that, and during the whole day he had barely devoted a thought to Ulrike Fremdli or Krantze's antiquarian bookshop. However, as soon as he entered the land of dreams, it was these two major matters that demanded his attention. But perhaps, as a tiny pulse of emotion that still hadn't dozed off suggested, that was precisely what everything boiled down to.

Dreams.

29

Reinhart emptied his glass of lemon-flavoured mineral water, and gestured to the waiter for another.

After having been exposed to ten hours of more or less continuous information (with breaks for a couple of hours' sleep and individual lavatory visits), he and Jung had withdrawn to a quiet and comparatively cool corner of the Grimm's Hotel dining room. It was eleven in the morning, but as yet the lunch guests had not started arriving. A few television reporters were gathered around a window table, drinking a few morning Pilsners, but it was clear that they weren't on the ball yet.

'Well,' said Reinhart, 'what do you think?'

'Not a very nice story,' said Jung.

'It certainly isn't,' said Reinhart. 'Not even judged by our standards.'

'No,' said Jung. 'What do *you* think?'

Reinhart shrugged.

'I don't know. But if VV has gone to Stamberg, it's not

impossible that the answer is there somewhere. He usually manages to stumble into something crucial when he's out and about.'

Jung nodded.

'Or maybe he's just got sunstroke,' suggested Reinhart as he was served with another bottle of lemon-flavoured mineral water.

'Or washed his hands of it all.'

Reinhart took out his pipe and tobacco.

'Hmm,' he muttered. 'It wouldn't be like him to walk away from something like this; but there are rumours in circulation.'

'Yes indeed,' said Jung, yawning. 'Well, what do you reckon we ought to be doing? I don't think that Kluuge went out of his way to issue instructions. He seemed to be hoping that we'd be able to solve it all for him . . . Us or VV, that is. Or that other lot, although I doubt if they're up to it, to be honest.'

'Pious hopes,' said Reinhart. 'In any case, I think we ought to get going. Like the acting chief of police, I have a pregnant wife and I'm damned if I want to be away for a minute longer than is necessary.'

'I didn't know about that,' said Jung. 'May I congratulate you?'

'Of course you may,' said Reinhart. 'Anyway, where do you want to start?'

Jung pondered.

'Finding Yellinek would be a good idea.'

'You're a genius. Where are you thinking of looking?'

'Good question,' said Jung. 'Mind you, a Wanted message has been issued, so perhaps that problem might be solved without my help. I have the impression his fizzog turns up on every single television programme just now. Maybe all we need to do is wait for him to turn up.'

'Or for something else to turn up,' said Reinhart, contemplating his pipe. 'But by Christ, I have to say that this shitty mess turns my stomach over . . . Still, if you're not going ferreting around after false prophets, what else do you have on your wish list?'

Jung drank a pint of mineral water before answering.

'That loony bin,' he said eventually. 'Wolgershuus, or whatever it's called. If nothing else, it could be interesting to take a look at those women.'

'And listen to the silence?' Reinhart suggested.

'Why not?' said Jung. 'Silence has a lot to say for itself.'

As if to emphasize the wisdom of that remark, Reinhart said nothing for half a minute while gazing out at the sunshine and scraping around inside the bowl of his pipe with a lace table napkin.

'Hot again today,' he commented thoughtfully. 'All right, you can lean on the priestesses. Give them a taste of your usual unassuming style, and let's see what happens.

I don't think our colleagues have got anywhere using their approach.'

'Okay,' said Jung. 'It's important to make the best of your talents. And what are you intending to do?'

'Well,' said Reinhart, 'I suppose all that's left for me is the young ladies of a more tender age.'

'Good hunting,' said Jung, standing up.

'Many thanks,' said Reinhart. 'See you later this afternoon.'

Belle Moulder looked sullen and scared. And as insignificant as they come, Reinhart thought, especially as he'd spent over two hours on the phone and in the car in order to get to her.

After the dramatic break-up of the camp at Waldingen, the girl had evidently spent a couple of days at home in Stamberg before being despatched to an aunt in Aarbegen with similar religious convictions. She was expected to spend the rest of the summer holiday there saying her prayers, bathing in the river and undertaking long, invigorating bicycle rides supervised by two corpulent cousins – in order to lick her wounds and recover from the traumatic days in the Sorbinowo forests, one assumed.

But that was no criticism of the Pure Life. God forbid.

Edwina Moulder welcomed him in shorts and on a

yellow garden hammock, and it soon became obvious that she had no intention of leaving her niece alone with the police officer.

Not for a second, Reinhart decided on the basis of the determined expression on her face. He spent a couple of moments considering the circumstances and his subsequent strategy, then he fell into line and sat down on the garden chair designated for him, under the parasol.

'I'm sorry to trouble you,' he began, 'but we have to find the madman who's committed these murders.'

'We understand that,' said Edwina Moulder.

'Good,' said Reinhart, glancing at the girl. 'I had intended to take Belle with me to the police station – but naturally it would be better if we could sort things out here instead.'

'Belle really has told you everything she knows, and besides—'

Reinhart raised a warning finger.

'Steady on now. Your niece was one of those who obstructed the police more than anybody else at the beginning of our investigation, so everything depends on whether or not she is prepared to cooperate.'

'What . . . ?'

'As long as you don't interrupt, you are welcome to sit in on our conversation,' Reinhart explained. 'But I must insist that you don't say anything. Is that clear?'

'What? You come here and—'

'Is that clear?' Reinhart said again.

'Hmm,' said Edwina Moulder.

Reinhart took a sip of the watery coffee. Adjusted his chair so that he didn't need to look at the very suntanned aunt, and could concentrate on the girl instead.

'Belle Moulder?'

'Yes.'

'You've spoken to the police several times already about these most unpleasant goings-on . . .'

The girl nodded at him, without looking him in the eye.

'And to start with, you behaved very badly – is that right?'

Belle Moulder examined her thumbnails

'But let's not worry about that now. I take it for granted that you are telling the truth, and helping me as much as you can. If I notice that you are making things up or refusing to answer, I'll have to drive you into town and interrogate you at the police station. Is that clear?'

'Yes, but . . .'

'Excellent. What I'm most interested in is what happened that Sunday evening when Clarissa Heeren-macht went missing. I take it you remember that pretty clearly?'

'Fairly.'

The girl shrugged, and tried to look nonchalant. Reinhart

couldn't help thinking about Winnifred and the child they were expecting.

Surely it wasn't going to be one like this?

He cleared his throat and tried to banish the thought.

'Why did you leave Clarissa alone down there at the bathing rock?'

'She wanted to be on her own.'

'Why?'

'I don't know.'

'Had you quarrelled?'

'No.'

'Are you sure?'

'Yes.'

'Was Clarissa upset when you left her alone?'

'No.'

'Happy?'

'She was the same as always.'

'What was she like when she was the same as always?'

'Er, like she always was.'

Reinhart took another sip of coffee. It hadn't become any better.

'And then you spoke to Yellinek.'

'What?'

'You had a conversation with Yellinek later that evening. When was that?'

'Er, it . . . it was after evening prayers.'

'What time would that be?'

'Half past nine . . . A quarter to ten, maybe. I don't know. I've been asked about that before. We don't . . . didn't . . . keep all that close a check on time at Waldingen. We didn't need to, we were always called up when necessary . . . But it was round about then.'

'Between half past nine and a quarter to ten?'

'Yes.'

'What did you talk about?'

'Clarissa.'

'Why?'

'Because she'd gone missing, of course.'

'You knew that she'd gone missing?'

'Of course. She wasn't there for dinner. Not there for PT, nor for prayers.'

'What did Yellinek want to know?'

Belle Moulder hesitated for a second.

'If I knew anything. I mean, nobody had seen her since we were down by the rock – I suppose I was the last person to see her.'

'Can you remember exactly what Yellinek said?'

'He asked if I knew where she was.'

'And what did you say?'

'That I didn't know, of course.'

'And then? You were talking for ten minutes after all, weren't you?'

'No, not as long as that. He sat thinking as well.'

'But he must have asked you other questions?'

'Yes, what I'd been doing that afternoon and so on, but nothing special.'

'Nothing special?'

'Belle has told you all that already,' interrupted Edwina Moulder.

'How do you know?' asked Reinhart.

'Eh?'

'I asked you how you could know that,' said Reinhart, angrily. 'Have you read the minutes of the police interview? If you can't hold your tongue I must ask you to go away and cut your hedge, or whatever. Is that clear?'

Edwina Moulder opened her mouth, then closed it again. Then she looked down and seemed to have decided it was best not to say anything.

'Anyway,' said Reinhart. 'What else?'

'What do you mean, what else?'

The same snooty nonchalance, he noted. Despite the fact that she still looked scared. Perhaps that's the way kids were at that age?

'What else did Yellinek have to say? Don't play the innocent, young lady.'

'Eh?' said Belle Moulder. 'He didn't say much at all.'

'He asked you not to say anything, didn't he?'

'Yes, of course. Although it was mainly the sisters who said that later.'

'Really?'

'Yes, and then we said a prayer.'

'You and Yellinek?'

'Yes.'

'What kind of a prayer?'

'Eh?'

'What sort of a prayer? What did it say?'

'It . . . No, I don't understand what you mean.'

'Repeat the prayer for me now!'

'No, I can't.'

'Why not?'

'Well, like, he was the one who did the praying. I just repeated it silently.'

He did the praying, I just repeated it silently, thought Reinhart, and sighed.

'So you don't remember the words?'

'No . . . No, I don't.'

'And this took ten minutes?'

'He sat thinking as well, as I said.'

Reinhart lit his pipe and waited for a while.

'Okay,' he said, and glanced at Edwina Moulder. 'Did he touch you?'

'What?' said Edwina Moulder.

Reinhart blew a cloud of smoke in her face.

'The final warning,' he said before turning his attention back to the girl. 'Well, did he touch you?'

'He just gave me a hug.'

'Just gave you a hug?'

'Yes.'

'How?'

She seemed a bit confused.

'From behind?'

'Yes.'

Reinhart bit hard on the stem of his pipe.

'While you were praying?'

'Yes.'

'Only then?'

'Yes.'

Edwina Moulder's suntan seemed to have ebbed out into the yellow garden hammock, and her jaws were twitching and squeaking softly.

'And then?'

'Then? Er, then he left.'

'Going where?'

Another shrug.

'I don't know. Headed for the lake, I think.'

'The bathing rock?'

'Could be.'

'But you don't know? He didn't say what he was going to do?'

'No, but . . .'

'Well?'

'I think he was going to go to the rock. He might have said that, but . . . No, I don't remember.'

Reinhart paused, but nobody said anything, neither the girl nor her aunt.

'So,' he tried again, 'you think Oscar Yellinek went down to the bathing rock some time round about ten o'clock or shortly before that, on Sunday evening?'

'Yes. Maybe, in any case.'

'Did you see him again after that?'

She paused to think.

'No . . . No, I didn't.'

'Do you know if anybody else saw him after that?'

'I don't know. But I don't think any of the girls did.'

He waited for a few moments, but she just sat there looking at her knees, especially the right one, on which he could detect the dirty remains of a plaster. He put his pipe away.

'So, you were the last one to see Clarissa Heerenmacht alive, and possibly also the last one to see Oscar Yellinek before he went missing. Have you told the police that business about him maybe going down to the bathing rock?'

She thought it over.

'No, I don't think so.'

'Why?'

'Nobody's asked me that.'

'Nobody's asked you that?'

'No.'

Typical, Reinhart thought.

Then he left the aunt and her niece to their fates, and returned to his car.

30

Uri Zander was dressed like somebody from the 1960s, and hanging over the corduroy sofa in the living room was a signed poster featuring a pop group called Arthur and the Motherfuckers. It was by no means impossible that Mr Zander was in fact identical with one of the four grim-faced youths in bomber jackets and sunglasses, but Van Veeteren didn't bother to pursue the matter.

In any case, time had left its mark on Uri Zander. His hair was now long and straggling at the sides and at the back of his neck – the top of his head was empty – and a crescent-shaped pot belly coupled with a distinctly humped back made him reminiscent of a carelessly drawn question mark.

He didn't seem particularly happy either.

'Would you like anything to eat or drink?' he asked as the chief inspector lowered himself warily into a red contraption made of soft plastic.

Van Veeteren shook his head.

'Just as well, I've got nothing in.'

He took off his round-rimmed spectacles and started polishing them on his shirt, a tight-fitting flowery garment. The chief inspector thought he recalled the pattern from one of those summers at the beginning of time – probably sixty-seven or sixty-eight – when he had been so new to the game that he occasionally found himself rented out as a uniformed representative of the forces of law and order. Whenever the regular police were short-staffed, that is – which they were all the time.

All those pot-perfumed music festivals and free-love manifestations that, in retrospect at least, seemed to have been so thick on the ground. There were pleasanter memories than those, even in his life.

'Well, as I explained,' he began, 'it's not you we're interested in, but your ex-wife. Madeleine Zander.'

'Ugh!' said Mr Zander.

'I assume you're familiar with the situation,' the chief inspector went on. 'We are busy with the murders of the young girls at Sorbinowo, and that sect she's mixed up with is involved somehow or other. There were three women present at the camp, and Madeleine is one of them . . . As you may have heard, they all refused to cooperate with the police from the very beginning. I don't know what you think of all this . . .'

'Bloody idiots,' said Uri Zander.

Ah, Van Veeteren thought. Good. He hadn't really been worried, but there was always a risk that Uri Zander might line up on his ex-wife's side. It was more than clear that this was not the case.

'That accursed church,' his host exploded. 'And that priest . . . In my view the whole lot of 'em should be locked up; they're a disgrace to the town. A disgrace to humanity, dammit.'

'So you know them all well?' the chief inspector asked.

'How can you avoid knowing about them these days?' wondered Uri Zander, putting his glasses back on. He was evidently dissatisfied with the result as he took them off again right away and started polishing anew.

'How long were you married to Madeleine?'

'Eight years,' said Zander. 'From seventy-four to eighty-two. She was only twenty when we met. Got a bun in the oven the very first time we had a shag. We were on a tour, I thought she was your usual groupie of course, but in fact she was almost a virgin and then, well, things just went on from there.'

'So you got married before the child was born?'

'Of course. Oh, I liked her a lot in those days. And it was time to stop playing around. I was getting involved in too much of this and that, if you follow me?'

Van Veeteren nodded, as always in such circumstances.

'Anyway, we settled down, I suppose you could say. I got

myself a proper job and Madeleine looked after Janis, our daughter. Maybe things could have turned out okay – in any case, we were together for eight years: most marriages come to grief a lot sooner than that, don't they?'

'Perhaps,' said Van Veeteren, who had stuck it out for more than three times as long as that. 'No more children?'

Zander shook his head.

'Nope. But when you think about it, it's obvious it was doomed from the start.'

'What do you mean?'

'Huh, I don't really know. She was young and inexperienced. I'm seven years older, and then, well, it seemed as if she felt obliged to give everything a try, once she'd got over the first flush of being a mother. And she got over that pretty damned quick, by Christ she did.'

'Tell me about it,' said Van Veeteren.

Zander finally replaced his spectacles and started groping around for cigarettes instead. He eventually found a pack under a pile of newspapers and magazines on the table. After a discreet check on how many were left, he offered one to the chief inspector and then lit up for both of them.

'Well,' he said, 'she wasn't exactly happy sitting around at home with the kid. With Janis, that is. She wasn't happy about anything, if truth be told. She had loads of ideas about every bloody thing, but nothing was good enough to keep her happy in the long run.'

'What kind of ideas?' Van Veeteren wondered.

'Everything you can think of,' snorted Zander, forcing a cloud of smoke out through his hairy nostrils. 'Every damned thing you can think of! She became a feminist, a Buddhist, a spiritualist – and in the end she became a lesbian as well.'

'Really?' said the chief inspector.

'Yes, really – although that soon passed. Everything passed. Some things lasted just for a few months, others for a bit longer, and every time she started out on something new it was as if nothing of the old stuff counted any longer. As if . . . As if she needed to start out on a new life twice a year, more or less. Not exactly a secure background for a little kid, don't you think? It was all that jumping around from one thing to another that finished me off in the end.'

'I understand,' said Van Veeteren, and he really did. 'But she seems to have stuck with the Pure Life – is that true?'

Uri Zander inhaled and nodded.

'Yes, it seems so. You might ask yourself why. I think she was there at the very beginning, that must be over ten years ago now. It would have been better if she'd stuck to another of her fads, but I couldn't give a toss about that now. Janis has flown the nest, and she has no intention of finding herself a new mum.'

'Who looked after her?' the chief inspector asked. 'After you'd separated, that is.'

'Me, of course,' said Uri Zander, with perhaps a trace of humble pride in his voice. 'For fuck's sake, she couldn't be left with that scatterbrained nincompoop! They used to get together over the weekend the first few years, but then Madeleine cleared off to the USA for six months – some fancy emancipated sect or other; I think they were at the heart of a scandal later on, but that was after she'd moved on – and since then they haven't been in touch at all. Janis wasn't interested, nor was the scatterbrained nincompoop, as I understand it.'

Van Veeteren devoted a few moments' thought to this family idyll.

'Do you know a lot about the Pure Life?' he asked eventually. 'What they get up to, that sort of thing?'

Zander puffed away at his cigarette and gazed out of the window, looking miserable.

'No,' he said. 'Only what I've read in the newspapers. And what people have been saying after these murders, of course. Obviously, I think they're a collection of right bastards, and it's a bloody scandal that they can hoodwink so many poor swine who are so stupid that they can't distinguish between a hole in the ground and their own arsehole. Youngsters and old dodderers and all the rest of 'em, just so that they can get screwed by the priest and shag one another.'

'So you think that's what it's all about, do you?'

'Yes,' Zander said. 'That's what I think. And I'm not the only one.'

Van Veeteren thought for a moment.

'What do you think about the murders?' he asked.

Zander stubbed out his cigarette and his face took on a thoughtful expression.

'I don't know,' he said. 'This Yellinek character might well be a bloody psychopath, I don't doubt that for a second: so I reckon he's the one who's done it. And now, needless to say, he's hiding away here in Stamberg, in a house owned by some lunatic woman who's a member of his congregation – there are plenty of those around. Most likely, of course, he's busy screwing her all ends up. For Christ's sake! The Pure Life? Fuck me!'

'Hmm,' said the chief inspector, glancing at the poster. 'But why are Madeleine and the rest of them refusing to say a word, do you think?'

'Because he's told them to stay schtum, of course. He's the big shagger god after all, and they obey every word he utters. I take it you know about the court case against him a few years ago?'

'Of course,' said Van Veeteren.

'Anyway, all I can say is that I hope to God you find the

bastard and put an end to him and his fucking hangers-on,' Uri Zander declared. 'It's disgusting that they're allowed to carry on as they do – and they have a school as well. Just imagine, pouring all that shit into youngsters' minds!'

Van Veeteren began to realize that he'd got as far as he was going to get, and there wasn't much point in sitting around and listening to Zander's outbursts. His host was currently fumbling around in the cigarette pack: the cupboard was evidently almost bare, and so he slid it back under the pile of newspapers.

'Your ex-wife?' Van Veeteren began. 'Madeleine. You haven't married somebody else since then, have you?'

Zander shook his head.

'Is there any message you'd like me to pass on to her? We've got them locked up in Sorbinowo, and I expect to see her tomorrow or the day after.'

Zander looked at him in astonishment.

'A message for Madeleine? I'll be fucked if I have anything to say to her.'

'Maybe your daughter might want to say something to her?'

'They have no contact with each other. I've explained that already.'

'Yes, that's right, you have,' said the chief inspector.

All right, he thought, and braced himself for the effort required to extract himself from the beanbag, or whatever it was he was sitting in. Enough for today. All things considered, he'd been presented with a pretty substantial picture of Madeleine Zander – especially if he compared it with the strangely elusive impression he'd had from the unbleached linen confrontations in Waldingen.

But whether it was going to be of any use to him was another question, of course.

They were already in the hall when his final question occurred to him. 'Ewa Siguera – does that name mean anything to you?'

'Siguera?' said Uri Zander, scratching the place where his hair used to be. 'No, I don't know anybody of that name – unless you mean Figuera, of course. I think that was her name.'

'Figuera?'

'Yes.'

'And who's Ewa Figuera, then?'

Zander shrugged.

'I don't really know her,' he explained, 'but if I remember rightly that was the name of the woman Madeleine lived with for a while. She might have been a lesbian, but I don't know.'

'When was that?'

Zander thought it over.

'I can't really remember,' he said. 'It was Janis who

mentioned it. A few years ago, I reckon. We happened to bump into them. Down by the river.'

'Is she still living in Stamberg?' Van Veeteren asked.

'How the hell would I know?' said Zander. 'Why not look her up in the telephone directory?'

Not a bad idea, the chief inspector thought as he took leave of his melancholy host.

Another glimpse into an interesting life, he decided as he emerged into the sunlight again. And it occurred to him that he hadn't even bothered to find out what Uri Zander did for a living nowadays. Always assuming he did anything at all, of course.

Perhaps he could glean that information from the telephone directory as well, if the desire to know should get the better of him.

Figuera? he muttered to himself as he inserted a new menthol-impregnated toothpick into his front teeth, as a counterbalance to Zander's prejudices. What if it turned out that this whole case depended on a stupid misspelling?

F instead of S.

There was no evidence to suggest that this was the case, but it wouldn't surprise him.

Not one bit, dammit. Stranger things had been known to happen.

31

Since Inspector Jung turned up early, as usual, he had to sit down and wait a while for Ulriche Fischer.

It was no big deal, in fact. He declined politely but firmly the offer of Constable Matthorst's company, and instead sat down at a table under one of the chestnut trees that surrounded the big lawn (where one or two residents and one or two carers were wandering around, evidently aimlessly) – and this gave him an excellent opportunity to plan and polish his tactics for the impending conversation.

The only problem was that he couldn't concentrate. Not for more than three seconds at a time, that is. No matter how he tried to tame and channel his thoughts, they seemed to sleepwalk stubbornly back to the same topic.

His holiday.

The forthcoming holiday and the trip with Maureen and Sophie. That's the root of the matter! he thought vaguely. Something he'd read, presumably.

Maureen. Apart from a few short breaks, they had been

together for four years now, but during all that time they had never decided to live together – properly, as it were. Naturally, everything depended on a series of different factors and circumstances, but above all – there could be virtually no doubt at all about this – it was due to his own cowardice and the ambivalence he displayed.

Always assuming you could display an ambivalence?

If so, I'd be the one to do it, Jung thought.

But there wasn't long to go now, he knew that. Making a decision, that is. There comes a point when you have to either push ahead with things, or walk away; even a newly promoted detective inspector knew that. And this joint holiday – three weeks touring England and Scotland by car with Maureen and her fifteen-year-old daughter – well, this was one of those points. No doubt about it, none at all. Needless to say it was as unspoken as many other things in their relationship, but nevertheless it was as clear as . . . crystal. Yes, it was crystal clear.

He sighed and took a sip of the juice he'd just been served by a blonde nurse.

He liked them, of course. Both of them. Perhaps he was even in love with Maureen, sometimes at least, and probably he would never – never ever – feel stronger emotions for any other human being. He didn't think so, anyway. So why hesitate? Why?

But even if he'd been able to grasp why he hesitated, would that have made things any easier?

Perhaps not, he thought. And when he tried to imagine a future – as middle age approached – without Maureen or Sophie, the images he could conjure up in his bachelor mind's eye were not especially cheerful.

Football. Beer. One-night stands, as Rooth used to call them. Lonely evenings in front of the television, and depressing piles of dirty laundry he could never bring himself to wash. And annoying telephone calls from his senile mother, wondering why she never had any grandchildren to knit scarves for at Christmas.

Get knitting, he used to tell her. It won't be long now. (She never remembered anything they'd said.)

The same kind of images he used to conjure up before he met Maureen, in other words. Just slightly older and greyer in tone.

So why hesitate?

Maureen's strength? Her calm determination? Would that be a threat? Sophie's dissatisfaction with school, and her periods of unreasonable moping?

The fear of being dominated?

None of them were good reasons.

Giving up something although he no longer knew what it was? Was that what it was all about?

Disappearing? Your life is a footprint in the water, Reinhart used to say. So why did anything matter?

Oh bugger it! Jung thought and emptied his glass of juice. I can toss a coin. Or maybe ask her and rely on her judgement being better than mine. Yes, that would be a neat solution.

It would be just as well to sort it out before we go away, he decided just as Matthorst came out to announce that Ulriche Fischer was ready to receive him.

So, now it would be good if he could concentrate for a while. What had Reinhart said? Reinhart, who was even going to become a father . . .

Diffidence?

Let's go, then.

'I'm sorry,' he said, dropping his notebook on the floor. 'I'm sorry if I'm intruding on you, but the others have sent me here.'

She didn't respond. It's possible that the two wrinkles between the sides of her nose and the sides of her mouth narrowed slightly, but that was a highly doubtful observation.

'I have a few questions, but, obviously, you don't have to answer if you don't want to.'

He held his pen sideways in his mouth while leafing through his notebook.

'I used to be a member of a church when I was younger, but then my mother forbade me to go there any more.'

'Forbade you?'

'Yes. My name's Jung, by the way.'

She stared doubtfully at him, but then her eyes glazed over again.

The first verse, Jung thought. How the hell can she look so pale in weather like this?

'What I liked most about it was the feeling of liberation,' he explained. 'I was only about fifteen or sixteen at the time, so I didn't really understand the essence of the faith, but I liked the atmosphere. The light, as it were. But that's not what we're supposed to be talking about . . .'

'Are you winding me up?' said Ulriche Fischer.

Jung blushed. That was a trick he had developed over the years, and now he could produce one in less than a second.

'Excuse me,' he said. 'That wasn't the intention. I'll ask you my questions now.'

Ulriche Fischer muttered something he couldn't make out.

'They're probably the same questions as you've been asked before, I'm afraid. Some of them, at least. I've only just been put on this case – but I know quite a bit about it, of course. It's awful, absolutely awful; I really do hope we can catch whoever did it before he strikes again. You don't have any children yourself, do you, Miss Fisch? I mean Fischer.'

She started to answer, but it got no further than her throat.

'Nor do I,' said Jung. 'But it would be fun to have some eventually. What they want to know this time is when – exactly when – during that Sunday night your priest went missing. Or was it on Monday morning?'

She swallowed again. And raised her eyes slightly.

'And if he told you what his plan was.'

'. . .'

'For the moment they're inclined to think that you don't know where he is. That he somehow kept it secret in order to protect you. That would be quite a noble thing to do, in a way.'

'. . .'

'Let's face it, it's not all that odd for him to hide away. Maybe they'd be willing to give him some sort of amnesty . . .'

'What's that?' asked Ulriche Fischer.

'I don't really know,' said Jung. 'I'm just trying to inter-pret the mood. Nobody's said that straight out.'

He waited. Avoided looking at her while he scratched his wrists a little nervously. She's not going to say a word, he thought. Why the hell should she decide to talk to me when she's been sitting here and saying nothing for . . . how long is it now?

A week?

No, more. It must be about ten days by now.

Waste of time. He sighed.

'It was in the evening,' she said suddenly.

He gave a start and didn't dare to say anything else. Five seconds passed.

'It was in the evening,' she repeated. 'We didn't see him after that.'

'Really?' said Jung.

'He's got nothing to do with the death of the girls,' she said after a further pause that lasted so long Jung thought she had already put the lid on any continuation.

'Nothing at all?' he asked.

'No.'

Silence again. He wondered if he ought to drop his notebook once more, have a coughing fit, or merely repeat his blush; but none of those possibilities seemed adequate, and his repertoire was somewhat limited after all.

'About what time was it?' he asked in the end. 'When you last saw him, I mean.'

She made a strange gesture with her arms. Or rather her shoulders. As if she were rustling her wings, Jung thought, and almost smiled. Practising to be an angel.

'About half past nine.'

'But how can you be sure that the other two sisters didn't meet him later than that?'

'Because we are one spirit and one flesh.'

'Eh?' said Jung.

She's mad, he thought. How the hell could I forget that she's mad?

'I think I understand,' he said. 'You're referring to the Trinity.'

Her mouth suddenly formed a smile, and he responded with a blush of the first order.

'Ah well,' he said. 'I don't understand all this. It's so long since I was a member of that church.'

The smile withered and died.

'But Good Lord,' he said. 'That means that nobody has a clue about where he is? Or have you heard from him at all?'

It was clear that she had said all she was going to say. That reference to the spirit and the flesh was intended to be the punchline, he guessed. The smile she had produced was clearly no more than an expression of lunacy in general.

He thought for a moment, then gave up and began to reel off the questions in his notebook – all eighteen of them – but none of them received an answer.

Not a single answer, and not even a puckered brow.

Presumably she was feeling sorry for herself. Regretting having opened her mouth at all.

All the time he maintained the same irreproachable care and correctness, even though he was thoroughly fed up by the end. As a counter to her silence, every time she ignored one of his questions he drew a clear and very audible line in his notebook, and there was something in these short, sharp sounds – repeated over and over again and as inexorable as a razor blade – that he found very attractive.

Like the cuts made by a surgeon, he thought.

Ten minutes later he left Wolgershuus. The whole visit, including his private thoughts under the chestnut tree, had taken less than an hour, and it was hard to predict how much the fragments of information he had squeezed out of Ulriche Fischer were actually worth.

But of course there were others better qualified than himself to judge that.

Thought Inspector Jung with his usual becoming modesty, and began to walk back through the forest. There was a smell of warm resin among the pine trees, and before he had even caught a glimpse of the town of Sorbinowo, he could feel his shirt clinging to his back and his fluid balance declining.

If Reinhart hasn't come back yet, I'll go for a swim in the lake, he decided.

And I'll have a beer.

32

After the conversation with Uri Zander, Chief Inspector Van Veeteren drove back to town and had lunch at the Stamberger Hof. It was nearly half past one when he started eating, and as he decided he needed at least three courses – pâté, sole and figs in cognac – it was turned three by the time he'd finished.

After some hesitation (but the casting vote was dictated by considerations of the digestive process), he returned to his car and left Stamberg again. Drove in an easterly direction for fifteen minutes and then found, without a lot of effort, an attractive and shady slope covered in beech trees down to the River Czarna. With the aid of a blanket and a pillow he made a rudimentary bed, took off his shoes and lay down for a postprandial nap.

Once again he dreamed of a peaceful little antiquarian bookshop, a chestnut-haired woman and a sparkling blue sea, and when he woke up forty minutes later he recalled that he actually had a ticket for a flight due to leave Maardam in less than two days' time. He sat up.

It was all very promising, both the dream and the future prospects. Especially in view of the fact that right now he was sitting by an unfamiliar sluggish river, watching a herd of similarly unfamiliar and sluggish cows gaping at him from the high grass on the other side.

What the hell am I doing? he asked himself, well aware that this was a very old and frequently asked question. Still unanswered.

Over a hundred kilometres away were an investigation team and a hundred reporters waiting for the outline of a double murderer to become clearer.

Or perhaps they were waiting for him – the notorious Chief Inspector Van Veeteren with only one unsolved case to his name – to winkle him out.

Or her?

He moved a couple of metres to one side, leaned against a beech trunk and suddenly remembered one of Mahler's favourite quotations:

To live your life is not as simple as to cross a field.

Probably Russian, he thought. It had that sort of ring about it.

Then he lit a cigarette and tried to sort out his thoughts.

*

Two girls.

Aged twelve and thirteen. Raped and murdered.

About a week between them. First Katarina Schwartz. Then Clarissa Heerenmacht. But found in reverse order.

Both residents of Stamberg. Both members of the obscure sect the Pure Life and attending the sect's summer camp at Sorbinowo.

Pretty, slightly wild Sorbinowo.

And then the priest.

Shortly before the discovery of the younger girl's dead body, the alleged man of God, the church's spiritual leader, Oscar Yellinek, goes up in smoke. The rest of those involved, the sect that is, seal their lips. The younger generation – about a dozen girls around the age of puberty – slowly start to thaw out, but what they have to say is not of much relevance to the murder mysteries.

Or is it? Van Veeteren wondered, watching one of the cows that had just turned its back on him and demonstrated how remarkably efficiently its digestive processes were functioning.

And she probably hasn't even had figs in cognac for lunch, the chief inspector assumed before returning to his train of thought.

Had they missed something crucial in the tearful outpourings of the girls? Was there something more – something more deeply hidden – in all these testimonies about purity and self-deprivation and nudity? Apart from their dubious nature per se, that is?

He didn't know. The images of the girls' stylized behaviour as they bathed at the water's edge that first day came back to his mind's eye, and he wondered if there were images like that in the murderer's baggage as well.

In the actual motive. In so far as it was meaningful to talk about a motive in a case like this. Perhaps, perhaps not; in any case, it was hardly something that could be developed usefully.

What about the women? The priestesses who kept an eye on everything, and presumably had a lot of information they could share but had chosen to remain silent. Was it possible that one of them was the killer? It was a possibility he had been keeping in reserve from the very beginning. Oh yes. A blank card hidden up his sleeve. A woman murderess?

Could one assume that it was one of them who had contacted the police and tipped them off?

Perhaps.

But in any case, surely to God it was obvious that they shared in the guilt?

Most probably, he decided.

The only question was: what? Guilty of what?

'Oh hell!' muttered Chief Inspector Van Veeteren. 'I'm getting nowhere!'

For one bitter self-critical moment he realized that the cows on the other side of the river were probably not only a symbol of inaccessible wisdom – demiurges and all that sort of thing – but also a symbol of his own unrelieved inertia.

He lit a cigarette and changed track.

What about Figuera? he wondered.

Ewa Figuera? Hmm, he would have to track her down and find out why she was with the other three women in Przebuda's photograph. What had she been doing in Waldingen the previous summer?

In view of the fact that he had solved the problem caused by the misspelling of her name – and the fact that he had obeyed his celebrated intuition and come to Stamberg – his efforts so far certainly hadn't come to much.

Or was there a grain of gold dust hidden away inside the last couple of days' conversations as well? Had these confused members of the congregation contributed something after all that he wasn't in a position to notice?

Oh hell, Van Veeteren thought again. What a brilliant analyst I am! First I say A, then I say A can't be right. All the time.

He sighed. For the moment he was unable to think about anything other than this dialectic, and the dark river that separated him from the cows.

Ergo? he thought gloomily. Could there be a clearer

indication of the fact that it was time to hand in his police ID? Hardly.

He stood up and decided to go for a half-hour drive accompanied by Fauré rather than this fruitless vegetating.

Then he would have to search through the telephone directory.

Okay. All in good time.

The half-hour became a whole one, and Fauré received some assistance from Pergolesi. When the chief inspector parked behind Glossman's it was seven o'clock already, and the worst of the day's heat was over. There was a fax waiting for him in reception, from Reinhart, but it only contained a bad joke along the lines that members of the investigation team who didn't have a wooden leg seemed to have a wooden head instead. Van Veeteren threw it into the waste bin and asked for a telephone directory he could take up to his room. Plus the two obligatory beers.

'You'll find a directory in the desk drawer,' explained the receptionist, who was as sleepy as ever. 'In every room. Light or dark?'

'The usual,' said Van Veeteren, and was given one of each.

When he got to his room he lay down on the bed with the first bottle, the light one, and the local telephone directory – sure enough, he had found it in the desk drawer, underneath the Bible and some sheets of writing paper with the hotel's logo.

He took a swig and started searching. It was not a thick directory. Stamberg probably had a population of about – what? Fifty thousand inhabitants? – and he found what he was looking for almost immediately. Evidently he still knew the alphabet.

As he scanned the rows of names, it came to him.

Nothing more than a tiny nudge, in fact. A brief little twitch in some lugubrious corner of his old, tired brain: but enough to tell him that something was falling into place at last.

Or rather, being set in motion.

And about time, for Christ's sake, he thought.

He stared at the information for a few seconds. Then closed his eyes and leaned back against the pillows, trying to clear the junk and rubbish from his brain. Cows, priests and things like that. Lay there for quite a while without thinking a single thought.

And then they emerged from the slough of forgetfulness – two random comments he had heard one afternoon getting on for two weeks earlier.

Or was it in fact two different afternoons?

He couldn't remember, and of course, it didn't matter.

He allowed another few minutes to pass, but nothing

else happened. Just the information given in the telephone directory and those two comments – and when he opened his eyes again, he was aware that it was barely more than a mere suspicion.

He drank the remains of both bottles of beer. Then started ringing round and arranging meetings for the next day.

When he had finished, he read two more chapters of Klimke, took a shower and went to bed.

The telephone rang at two minutes past seven the next morning.

It was Reinhart, but before the chief inspector had time to tell him to go to hell he had taken command.

'Have you a television set in your room?'

'Yes . . .'

'Switch it on then! Channel 4.'

Then he hung up. Van Veeteren fumbled for the remote control, and managed to press the right button. Three seconds later he was wide awake.

As far as he could judge it was the routine morning news bulletin. An excited newscaster. Flickering pictures of a building on fire. Firefighters and sirens. Very realistic interviews with soot-covered senior officers.

He recognized it immediately. The camera even paused

for a few seconds on the abusive graffiti he had seen with his own eyes only the other day.

Murdering bastards and so on.

Practically everything was in flames, and the chief officer of the fire brigade thought there was little chance of saving anything of the building. So they were concentrating on stopping the blaze from spreading to adjacent buildings. There was quite a strong wind blowing. It was *finito* as far as the church was concerned, he reckoned.

But apart from that, everything was under control.

Arson?

Of course it was arson. The alarm had been raised at four in the morning, the fire brigade had arrived twenty minutes later, and by then the whole building was ablaze.

No doubt at all that it was arson. Perhaps that was understandable, in the circumstances . . .

Van Veeteren switched off. Remained in bed for half a minute more, thinking. Then put on a shirt and some trousers, took the elevator down to reception and sent a fax to Wicker's Travel Agency in Maardam.

Cancelled his package holiday due to begin on the first of August.

Then he went back up to his room and took the longest shower of his life.

33

From a purely physical point of view, acting Chief of Police Kluuge was a wreck by this morning.

When he got off his bicycle outside the police station in the fresh morning air, he was puffing and panting, his heart was pounding wildly, and unfortunately things were just as bad as far as his mind was concerned. He recognized that this was hardly surprising: the last three nights he had slept for less than ten hours all told, and obviously one was always bound to come up against a limit eventually. Or a brick wall.

We must bring this case to a conclusion pretty soon, he decided. Two more days like these and I'll have to take sick leave.

But then again, there were only five more days to go before Malijsen came back on duty, so perhaps it would be best to stick it out, no matter what.

Incidentally, Kluuge thought as he fiddled with the various locks, it's odd that he hasn't been in touch at all. No matter how isolated it is at the lake where he's fishing, it's surely impossible to imagine that he hasn't heard anything about what's been going on? There can't be a single person in the whole country who doesn't know what's been happening in Sorbinowo during these hot summer weeks. Very strange.

And odder still, of course, if you happen to be the real chief of police for the area.

But of course, Malijsen was Malijsen. He's probably dug himself in and is waiting for the Japanese hordes to arrive, Kluuge guessed, wiping the sweat from his brow.

He met Suijderbeck in the entrance, on his way out.

'Aren't you going to attend the run-through meeting?'

'Ciggy break,' muttered Suijderbeck, and spat into the flower bed. 'I'm just nipping to the news stand and I'll be back before you've even had time for a pee.'

Nice guy, Kluuge thought. Good camaraderie and a good atmosphere, just like they said it should be at police college. He entered his office, which had recently undergone several changes as far as the furniture was concerned, in an effort to keep up with the requirements of the investigation. But his desk was still there, and he flopped down behind it after greeting the others.

Servinus was in his usual place, as were Tolltse and Lauremaa, plus one of the latest newcomers – Detective Inspector Jung from the Maardam police. The other newcomer, the somewhat strange Inspector Reinhart, was smoking his pipe through the open window, and Chief Inspector Van Veeteren's chair was empty, as usual.

Ah well, Kluuge thought when Suijderbeck reappeared. We'd better get going, then.

'We'd better get going, then,' he said, logically enough.

'Not a bad idea,' said Reinhart.

'I have to say,' Servinus admitted, 'that I feel pretty disgusted when people start burning down churches. Despite my deep-rooted atheism.'

'Yes, they're going too far now,' Kluuge agreed.

'The mob's taking over,' said Lauremaa. 'We really must get this case solved PDQ – you all heard what the psychologist said on the television, I take it? This kind of thing always inspires copycat actions . . . And we know how pyromaniacs operate, don't we?'

'Yes indeed,' said Reinhart. 'But bollocks to what's happening in Stamberg. They have their own police force there, we can assume.'

'Yes, I think so,' said Suijderbeck. 'And this means that we'll probably lose about fifty reporters, so perhaps we don't need to spend all day weeping.'

'Anyway,' said Reinhart, 'I'd like to be informed about what's been happening. Let's get the gen first.'

'Okay,' said Kluuge, stretching himself. 'I suppose it could be summed up by saying that all our guesses have been confirmed. Katarina Schwartz had been dead for nearly two weeks when she was found – round about 16 July, they reckon. As I understand it, that fits in well with other information we have. Tolltse?'

Inspector Tolltse leafed through her notebook.

'That's right,' she said. 'We – Inspector Lauremaa and I, that is – have spoken again to five of the girls, and it seems that Katarina Schwartz went missing round about then. Probably a day or so earlier, the 14th or 15th, but they are all pretty bad at dates. None of them has been keeping a diary, and there doesn't even seem to have been a calendar out there. Not where the girls lived, at least.'

'Beyond time and space,' muttered Servinus.

'What about the circumstances?' wondered Reinhart impatiently. 'We can assume that she disappeared at a certain time of day, surely. Or did she just dissolve bit by bit?'

'Yes, there were various circumstances,' Lauremaa confirmed. 'In the first place they wanted everybody to forget that she'd ever been at the camp. It must have been her disappearance that the anonymous woman phoned about the first time, but right from the start the organizers and the girls denied that there had ever been more than twelve girls at the camp. It's not easy to understand the motive or the logic in that – personally I reckon it shows more than anything else that Yellinek is as mad as a hatter – but when the girls finally started to admit that there had in fact been a Katarina Schwartz among them until, let's say 15 July, a few more facts began to emerge as well.'

'What, for example?' Reinhart asked.

'Times, to start with,' said Tolltse. 'She vanished during the night. Went to bed as usual in the evening, but wasn't there the next morning.'

'Is that definite?' Suijderbeck wondered.

'Definite,' said Lauremaa.

'For Christ's sake!' said Suijderbeck. 'That must mean that whoever did it must have dragged her out of bed, more or less. Doesn't that narrow the possible candidates down pretty drastically?'

'Yes,' said Lauremaa. 'Unless she went out of her own accord, of course.'

'Went out?' said Suijderbeck. 'Why the hell would she want to go out?'

Lauremaa shrugged.

'Don't ask me. It's not impossible, but it does seem a bit improbable.'

'There's not a lot in this case that has any connection with probability,' said Servinus. 'Carry on.'

Tolltse turned a page.

'There's another little thing,' she said. 'It may be of no importance, but you never know. There had evidently been some sort of controversy that Katarina was involved in. Marieke Bergson indicated something of the sort, by the way – the first girl that Chief Inspector Van Veeteren interrogated.'

'Controversy?' said Reinhart. 'What sort of controversy?'

'Something between her and Yellinek,' said Lauremaa. 'She had misbehaved somehow or other. Said something to him; it's not clear what, we haven't managed to get the details out of any of the girls.'

'They're obviously a bit scared that they might get picked on as well,' explained Tolltse.

'Aha,' said Reinhart. 'A little rebel in Paradise, eh?'

'Could be,' said Lauremaa. 'Thinking for yourself – critical thinking – wasn't exactly something encouraged as part of their spiritual education. In any case, Yellinek evidently had a private meeting with her the evening before she went missing.'

Nobody spoke for a few seconds. Then Suijderbeck cleared his throat and leaned forward with his elbows on the table.

'So both of them . . . I mean both these poor little girls had strayed slightly from the straight and narrow, is that it?' he said. 'Clarissa had said something she shouldn't have done to the chief inspector, right?'

'Yes,' said Kluuge. 'There's some common ground there.'

Silence for a few seconds. Then Servinus slammed his fist down on the table.

'Yellinek!' he groaned. 'If I had that fucking creeping Jesus in here I swear I'd have poured boiling lead into his arsehole by now!'

'Harrumph,' said Kluuge. 'Perhaps we'd better move on. Or do Tolltse and Lauremaa have anything more to add?'

'No,' said Lauremaa. 'Except that we think we saw Chief Inspector Van Veeteren in a restaurant. When we were in Stamberg, talking to the girls, that is.'

'Really?' said Suijderbeck. 'Did you see what he was gobbling?'

He didn't get an answer, so he lit a cigarette instead.

'As for bodily injuries and that kind of thing,' Kluuge resumed, 'we've already been through that. Nothing new has cropped up. What happened seems to have been more or less the same in both cases. Still, I don't suppose anybody thinks we're looking for two killers?'

'No, nobody,' Servinus assured him.

'Then perhaps we should concentrate on the Sunday evening,' Kluuge suggested. 'We seem to have got a bit of new information, I gather. Which of you . . . ?'

He looked at Reinhart and Jung.

'Let Jung do it,' Reinhart proposed. 'Otherwise he'll drop off to sleep.'

'Thank you,' said Jung. 'Well, if we combine my results and Reinhart's, we can probably draw several conclusions. It looks like Oscar Yellinek went missing from Waldingen quite early on Sunday night. If the information is correct – the stuff we got from that Moulder girl and Ulriche Fischer – it seems most likely that he left the camp shortly before ten o'clock. He talked to the girls for a few minutes after evening prayers, and then left, presumably heading for those rocks where Belle Moulder had left Clarissa Heerenmacht four hours earlier, or thereabouts. After that, nobody seems to have seen him.'

'What you say seems to contain quite a high proportion of guesses, doesn't it?' said Servinus, looking doubtful.

'Of course,' said Reinhart, 'but we usually guess right. Everything depends on how much credibility we give to Miss Fischer's performance, but if we combine that with what the chief inspector managed to get out of that other woman – what's her name?'

'Mathilde Ulbrecht,' said Kluuge.

'Yes, that's right. If we add the two lots of fragments together, they do point in a certain direction: they don't seem to know where the hell he is.'

'So all that about him meeting God and being given a

mission, and that he was on probation, was just cobbled together by the women?'

Reinhart shrugged.

'Why not?' he said. 'The main aim was probably to keep the girls quiet, I presume. Yes, I think this makes sense.'

Silence again.

'What about the third woman?' Tolltse asked. 'Madeleine Zander. Maybe we shouldn't forget that there are three of them. It seems a bit presumptuous to lump them together all the time. Of course they give the impression of sticking together, but there's nothing to say that there aren't cracks behind the united front. Loads of cracks, perhaps.'

'And deep ones,' said Servinus. 'Personally I think it goes against nature to believe that three women can stick together like this. And keep silent as well.'

'Sauna philosophy,' said Lauremaa.

'Men's sauna,' added Tolltse.

'Except when they're trying to trample all over a man, of course,' said Servinus.

Kluuge began to look worried.

'Anyway,' he said, trying to change the subject, 'I think I'm inclined to agree with Reinhart in this case. It does make sense. The question is simply: where does it get us – the women not knowing anything about where he is? What do you think?'

Nobody thought anything, for at that moment the door opened and Miss Miller came in.

'Sorry to interrupt,' she said. 'There's a telephone call for the chief of police.'

'Not now,' Kluuge began. 'I said that—'

'I think this is important,' said Miss Miller.

'All right,' Kluuge sighed. 'I'll take it in your office then.'

He apologized and left the room.

'Well,' said Suijderbeck when Kluuge returned. 'Was that the murderer calling to give himself up?'

'Not quite,' said Kluuge.

'Why are you so white in the face?' Servinus asked. 'Are you not feeling well?'

'Green,' said Suijderbeck. 'I'd say it was more of a green shade.'

Kluuge sat down.

'That was Mrs Kuijpers out at Waldingen,' he explained. 'She says they've discovered another body. Or rather, her dog has.'

'Oh my God,' said Tolltse.

'Another one?' said Reinhart. 'What the hell . . . ?'

'Those fucking lap dogs?' said Suijderbeck.

'That's not all,' said Kluuge. 'She seemed pretty sure whose body it was as well.'

'Who?' said Lauremaa.

'Oscar Yellinek,' said Kluuge with a sigh. 'I assume the name is familiar to you.'

SIX

31 JULY TO 1 AUGUST

34

The fourth person to lose his life as a result of the Pure Life camp in the Sorbinowo forests this summer was a certain Gerald deGrooit.

DeGrooit was fifty-seven years old and for more than twenty years had been news editor on the *Telegraaf* – the last three years as editor-in-chief. He had a wife and two children, and the reputation of being a good husband and father, experienced and competent at his job, albeit a bit irascible when things grew too stressful in the office. The heart attack that put an end to his journalistic career and his life was no real surprise to his close circle of workmates. Being responsible for coverage, despite being short-staffed on account of people being on holiday, of two explosive events like the burning down of the church in Stamberg and the discovery of the murdered priest in Sorbinowo – on the very same day, dammit! – well, it was the straw that broke the camel's back.

The *Telegraaf* was probably the only newspaper in the

country that didn't have a reporter present at Waldingen that scorching-hot Wednesday.

Inspector Reinhart claimed that he had never seen so many bloody hacks gathered together in one place before. While the crime scene team was still crawling around in the taped-off area in the lunchtime heat, searching for clues, he estimated the comparative strength between the forces of law and order on the one hand, and the fourth estate on the other, to be about 25 to 75.

In percentage terms, that is. In actual numbers it was around double those figures. Twenty officers from the uniformed police in Oostwerdingen, Rembork and Haaldam had been hastily called in; the less than successful investigative patrol was on duty again, and together with the senior officers, doctors and technicians, they made a pretty good fist of justifying claims made by all the extra television and radio broadcasts that the police had turned out in full force. If it really had been a hallmark of the Pure Life (ever since the court proceedings against the sect) to keep a low profile, such aspirations were shattered on an almost parodic scale. In one news bulletin after another throughout the afternoon and evening, reporters trumpeted the latest developments in Waldingen, Sorbinowo and Stamberg. Half a dozen psychologists and behavioural scientists of various schools of thought pronounced sagely on this and that – as did also a handful of criminologists, a bunch of sect members (not necessarily linked with the Pure Life), two bearded religious scientists, an ex-pyromaniac and a bishop on holiday.

It wasn't much worse at Waldingen itself. At a comfortable walking distance from the place where the body had been discovered (some five hundred metres west of discovery point number one and about six hundred metres from the so-called bathing rock), various temporary installations were set up for the convenience of all concerned: two practical portable toilets (one for each sex), a stall selling beer and soft drinks, a sandwich bar and two hot dog vans. Sorbinowo had flexible and well-practised routines for dealing with sudden influxes of tourists.

An initial press conference (later re-broadcast in a hundred and eleven other media outlets, somebody worked out) was held between two o'clock and half past on the terrace of the manor house at Waldingen, and was anything but a success. On several occasions such unvarnished criticisms were made of the investigation team that Inspector Suijderbeck felt obliged to give a thorough dressing-down to a radio reporter of overblown proportions, both mentally and physically – in such terms that he was later reprimanded by no less a person than the Minister of Justice himself.

Oh yes, it was one hell of a Wednesday.

*

At about six in the evening the hard-pressed investigation team decided to leave Waldingen in the hands of the sentries provided by the Oostwerdingen force, plus any reporters still hanging around, and every other Tom, Dick and Harry with no home to go to. Any clues they had found were fully documented. Any leads had been followed up, interviews had taken place with families living nearby (Finghers and Kuijpers) – the first round, at least – and the earthly remains of pastor Yellinek had been placed in a body bag and transported to Sorbinowo as a part of the caravan which they themselves also joined. On Reinhart's advice, Kluuge had announced a rest period of two hours before convening once more for continued and intensified discussions – a decision that was received with restrained acclaim.

Reinhart retired to his hotel room during the truce. Jung dined with Suijderbeck and Servinus at Florian's, while Tolltse and Lauremaa were rumoured to have collected a packed meal and gone swimming in the lake.

As for the acting chief of police, he drove back home to his Deborah, declared that he loved her, and that he intended to start studying in order to transfer to an entirely different profession as soon as he had the time. Firefighter, monk, any damned thing but a police officer.

When Reinhart spoke to the receptionist at Glossman's hotel in Stamberg for the third time – and was given the same negative report with regard to Mr Van Veeteren (a travelling salesman specializing in woodwind instruments and libretti) – he gave up and called Winnifred Lynch instead. They spoke for twenty minutes about love, obstetrics, attractive names for children, and whether or not it was advisable to drink red wine during pregnancy. When he replaced the receiver, he experienced two seconds of utter oblivion, during which he had no idea where he was.

Or why.

But then he remembered.

'Okay, now I'm going to sum up where we've got to,' said Suijderbeck. 'Sorry, but I don't have the strength to listen to anybody else. And don't try to correct me if I say anything wrong.'

'We're all as deaf as a post,' said Reinhart, but Suijderbeck took no notice.

'Oscar Augustinus Yellinek has been lying dead out at Waldingen for about ten days. There is nothing to suggest that he didn't die that same Sunday evening when all the other things happened – 21 July, in other words. Why he should have first run away and hidden himself, and then come back to get murdered – well, I don't understand why he should do that. Mind you, I have to admit that there are a lot of things in this messy business that I don't understand.'

'You're in good company there,' said Lauremaa.

'Unlike the dead girls,' Suijderbeck continued, 'Pastor Yellinek displays no signs of having been raped, to borrow Servinus's elegantly worded statement on the television.'

'Kiss my arse,' said Servinus.

'Another difference from the girls is that he was killed by blows to the head. What does the latest missive from the post-mortem say?'

Kluuge fished it out.

'"Several violent blows with a sharp instrument",' he quoted. 'It still hasn't been established what that can have been. Something pretty heavy with sharp edges. Or a sharp edge, perhaps.'

'How many blows?' asked Jung.

'More than necessary,' said Reinhart. 'Ten or eleven. Presumably the killer carried on hitting him for a while after Yellinek was already dead. He might have finished him off with the first blow, but wanted to make sure.'

'Not a very professional job, in other words,' said Suijderbeck. 'It seems he panicked. Anyway, if we believe what the experts tell us, there were several blows to the chest and shoulders as well. He was evidently a bit desperate.'

'And no resistance,' said Jung.

'Apparently not,' said Servinus. 'But it'll be another three days before the analysis is finished.'

'What are they looking for?' asked Kluuge. 'Fragments under the fingernails and so on?'

'Yes,' said Reinhart. 'And strands of hair and dandruff and fingerprints.'

'After ten days?' wondered Tolltse. 'Is there any point?'

'It's almost impossible to get rid of dandruff,' said Jung, scratching his head.

'And we had that pouring rain of course,' said Kluuge. 'Whenever that was . . .'

'Now I'll take over again,' said Suijderbeck. 'He probably wasn't killed at the spot where he was found either, our pastor friend. But this time the murderer was probably trying to hide the body. It was a bloody good piece of luck that the pooches found him. A big pile of twigs and pine needles, we saw that with our own eyes. But it ought to have been possible to hide him more efficiently.'

'If there was time,' Servinus pointed out.

'Time, yes,' said Suijderbeck, looking thoughtful.

'Wasn't Miss Miller supposed to fix coffee and sandwiches?' wondered Reinhart, fiddling restlessly with his pipe and tobacco pouch.

'She'll be serving them up at ten o'clock,' Kluuge promised. Half an hour to go. 'Anyway, anything else? What do you think?'

Suijderbeck seemed to have got tired of summing up. Instead he stood up and began wandering around the room.

'My artificial leg is itching,' he explained. 'This always happens when my brain stops working.'

'What about the Kuijpers?' said Servinus. 'They seem a pretty odd couple, don't you think?'

'I've seen odder,' said Tolltse. 'I don't think the Finghers seem much better.'

Nobody spoke for a few seconds.

'You don't think they are involved somehow, do you?' asked Lauremaa, frowning.

Suijderbeck paused.

'Hardly,' he said. 'But then, whichever way you look at it, somebody must have done it.'

'Good thinking,' said Lauremaa.

'Can't anybody draw any other . . . any sensible conclusions?' Tolltse wondered, looking round the table. 'Because if not, I shall.'

'Please do,' said Reinhart, lighting his pipe.

'It wasn't Yellinek who murdered the girls,' said Tolltse.

'Really?' said Jung. 'Are you sure of that? He presumably didn't kill himself, I can grant you that, but as I understand it he could still have murdered the girls.'

Tolltse thought for a moment.

'Okay,' she said. 'I take it back. But who killed him, then? Isn't that what we're trying to discover?'

'Good question,' said Servinus. 'How do you women do it?'

Reinhart blew a diversionary cloud of smoke over the battlefield.

'I don't know who killed Yellinek,' he said. 'But what I do know is that it's time to present him to his fancy women at Wolgershuus. The fact that he's dead, I mean. The sooner, the better. If we don't have anything more sensible to do, I suggest we attend to that detail right away.'

Kluuge looked around for signs of any views on that proposal, but when he didn't detect any, he cleared his throat and made up his mind on the hoof.

'Exactly,' he said. 'Let's do that. Reinhart and Jung can drive out there, that should be enough. It might be best to take them one at a time, or what do you think?'

'What else could we do, for Christ's sake?' snorted Reinhart. 'We'll wait for a bit before showing them the actual corpse. It should be sufficient to show them a video of the news and a few newspapers – in case they don't believe us.'

'Do we have any video recordings of new bulletins?' asked Jung.

Kluuge shook his head and looked worried.

'It could be arranged, but it would take some time, I assume.'

'It doesn't matter,' said Reinhart. 'A radio will do – they're broadcasting news bulletins eight times an hour. We'll be able to convince them that the Prince of Light is dead.'

'The Prince of Light,' said Suijderbeck. 'Fucking hell!'

'Hang on a minute,' said Servinus. 'Can we be sure that they don't know about it already?'

'They're isolated,' said Kluuge. 'I phoned Schenck and gave him strict orders before we set off this morning.'

'Good,' said Reinhart.

'Who's Schenck?' said Servinus.

'He relieves Matthorst now and then. It's necessary – Matthorst says he's beginning to feel peculiar.'

'I can well believe it,' said Tolltse. 'He's been hanging around up there for as long as the women.'

'There are some people who've been in there for fifteen years,' Suijderbeck pointed out.

'Anyway,' said Lauremaa, 'I reckon that if those three ladies know anything about Yellinek's death, it means that they've known all along. Right?'

'Correct,' said Reinhart. 'That would put the cat among the pigeons. Come on, Jung, let's get going.'

'Leave a few sandwiches for us,' said Jung, getting to his feet.

*

'Has anybody heard anything from the chief inspector?' wondered Lauremaa when Reinhart and Jung had left.

'Not a dicky bird,' said Suijderbeck. 'I have to say he made a good impression on me, but now he seems to be like any old deserter. What the hell's he up to?'

'Hmm, I don't know,' sighed Kluuge. 'Let's try to make some headway even so. It would be good if we could make a bit of a better impression at tomorrow's press conference.'

'I'm going to give it a miss,' said Suijderbeck.

'I'd thought of suggesting that you should,' said Lauremaa, and smiled for the first time all day.

35

Van Veeteren met Marie-Louise Schwartz in a terraced house in the southernmost suburb of Stamberg. The visit lasted for an hour, and fifty of those sixty minutes were spent slumped in a cretonne armchair, observing his weeping hostess in the cretonne armchair opposite.

She occasionally managed to pull herself together to some extent, but as soon as he asked her a question, she started crying again. Eventually he tired of even making an effort; simply sat there and let her despair speak for itself.

Perhaps there was a sort of point in doing that, he thought; and when he stood up to leave she grasped hold of both his hands and looked at him with tear-stained eyes. As if he had really achieved something – exhibited great warmth and fellow-feeling, or whatever it was she had been looking for. Maybe she hadn't even realized that he was a police officer. In any case she succeeded in explaining that she was very grateful for his visit, and she would now go upstairs to the bedroom and look after her husband, who was finding it difficult to handle his sorrow.

Oh my God, Van Veeteren thought.

He took his leave, got into his car and drove around aimlessly for half an hour, accompanied by Pergolesi and Handel. When he parked again behind Glossman's in order to collect his case, he happened to switch on the car radio and heard that Oscar Yellinek had been found murdered in Waldingen.

For a brief moment he didn't know if he was dreaming or awake.

Then he realized that it didn't matter which.

His next meeting was fixed for seven o'clock that evening (appointments had to be attended, children needed to be collected, a piano tuner needed to be told what to do), and so he spent the whole of the afternoon sitting in various cafes, leafing through Klimke, and listening to radio and television broadcasts. Eventually the first of the evening newspapers turned up, and as usual they didn't improve matters.

He called the police station in Sorbinowo several times, but all Miss Miller could tell him was that the others were out in the forest, and he didn't leave a message.

After all, he had nothing to tell them.

Apart from a suspicion that had not yet been confirmed.

And which didn't fit in specially well with the latest development. The murder of Oscar Yellinek. Or did it?

Might as well leave them in peace to get on with their work, he thought.

Might as well keep out of the way and let others take over. Wasn't that what he'd already decided he was going to do?

She was sitting waiting for him in the cafe they'd agreed on, and he wondered again why she had preferred to meet him here rather than in her own home.

To protect her privacy? he thought as he sat down opposite her. To keep something sacrosanct despite everything? That would be perfectly understandable.

He introduced himself, and she reached out a hand over the table to greet him, somewhat nervously.

'So, here we are,' she said. 'I'm sorry I couldn't get away earlier. A lot has happened today.'

He nodded and dug out a toothpick. The thought suddenly struck him: I'm right. I can see it in her appearance and behaviour. How the devil could I have known that?

'You understand what I want to talk to you about, I take it?'

He was taking a big risk, but he'd decided on that opening gambit. There weren't really any other possibilities. No alternative moves.

She hesitated for a moment.

'I think so.'

He could see that there was no point in rushing her. It was more important to give her plenty of time, and let things come out in whatever order seemed most natural to her. Or rather, least unpleasant.

'We'd been together for eight years before I caught on,' she began. 'Eight years, and married for five.'

'It can be something that suddenly strikes,' he said. 'It might not have been there all the time.'

She nodded.

'I've tried to convince myself of that as well, but I don't know if it would be much consolation. It's so . . . well, so damned incomprehensible. It's simply not possible to understand it, that's the only conclusion I can reach. I just can't get over it, I have to forget it and bury it. I thought that was my only chance – but now I realize that was also wrong, of course.'

She paused and rummaged in her bag. A waiter appeared, and without even asking Van Veeteren ordered coffee and cognac for them both.

'Tell me about it,' he said when she had lit a cigarette.

She scraped with her fingernail at a speck of candle wax

on the tablecloth, and blinked several times. The chief inspector was holding his breath; it was his very presence that was digging up these old horrors, but he hoped to reduce the awfulness to a minimum.

'It went too far,' she said. 'What I can never forgive myself for is that I allowed it to go on for so long, instead of reacting to the signs immediately. Over six months . . . I just couldn't believe it was true. It's the kind of thing you read about, and . . . Well, you know what I mean.'

Van Veeteren nodded.

'It was in the bath that I caught him at it. Judith was only five, but old enough to understand what was going on. And to be ashamed. What was hardest to understand was that he could be so unconcerned about it.'

'Did he admit it?'

She inhaled and took a sip of cognac before replying.

'No,' she said. 'Or maybe yes and no. He pretended that he didn't know what I was talking about, but on the other hand he agreed to an immediate divorce. He moved out – I made him move out the very same day.'

'And you no longer meet?'

'No. When I'd got over the shock I hired a lawyer, of course. Prepared myself for a fight, but there was no fight. He gave up everything and left us without saying a word. That's what I regard as proof that he admitted what he'd done.'

Another pause. Van Veeteren snapped the toothpick and took a cigarette instead.

'How far had it gone?' he asked.

'A long way,' was all she said.

'Did you have her examined?'

She nodded.

'Yes, I wanted to know. Oh yes, he'd gone all the way. There was no doubt about it.'

The chief inspector felt a surge of disgust rising within him, and he emptied his glass of cognac as an antidote.

'When exactly was this?' he asked.

'Four years ago,' she said. 'Four years and two months.'

'You didn't report him?'

'No,' she said, sighing deeply. 'I didn't.'

Van Veeteren observed her hands clamped round her glass. He could have reproached her now. Turned up the heat and asked how the hell she could have failed to follow up something as horrendous as that – but of course, there was no need.

No need to torture her any longer. The whole conversation had taken less than ten minutes, and it had turned out exactly as he'd expected.

Or dreaded, rather.

Knew it would?

'I'll try to make sure that you are not involved in what

happens next,' he said. 'But it's not easy to see how it will—'

She interrupted him.

'I'll say my piece,' she assured him. 'You don't need to worry. I don't want to make the same mistake twice.'

'Okay,' said Van Veeteren. 'I'll be in touch when the time comes.'

They shook hands again, and he took his leave. When he emerged into the street, he was shivering. It was a chill that had nothing to do with the warm, pleasant summer evening. Nothing at all.

He found a public telephone and called Sorbinowo again, but all he got was a recording of Miss Miller's voice informing him that the police station was now closed for the day, and providing two numbers to call if he had relevant information to provide regarding the Waldingen affair.

Oh yes, Van Veeteren thought. I have relevant information all right.

But he didn't make any further calls. There were still several question marks – with regard to Yellinek's death, for instance – and what he would most like to do was to serve up the solution to his colleagues on a plate. All done and dusted.

That had a whiff of vanity, of course; but if this really was to be his last case, perhaps he could be forgiven that.

And needless to say there was nothing – nothing at all – better able to eliminate any further question marks than a car journey. A long, calm drive through the night.

He pondered for a while. Then made up his mind: together with Penderecki.

Yet again Penderecki.

36

'It's five to twelve,' said Reinhart. 'We might as well go straight to the hotel. I wouldn't have thought they'd still be sitting around deliberating.'

'We can always phone and check,' said Jung. 'Mind you, I don't know what we can say about these ladies.'

'Good God, no,' groaned Reinhart. 'Although Lauremaa had a point when she talked about them having their differences.'

'She certainly did,' said Jung, suppressing a yawn. 'But surely there was something distinctly unchristian about them, don't you reckon?'

The visit to Wolgershuus was over and done with, and perhaps the word 'unchristian' was not the most appropriate in the context. But when Jung tried to sum up his impressions, he couldn't think of anything better off the top of his head. All he knew was that he'd never experienced anything like it. Never ever.

★

So unchristian. Even so, they had followed the agreed tactic to the letter. Discretion. Professional approach; no more fuss than necessity and the law required. Without too much effort they had found a neutral room, away from the main corridors, and summoned the women in order to pass on the news without further ado.

The news of Oscar Yellinek's death.

One at a time. First Madeleine Zander.

Reaction: none at all. She listened to them for half a minute, then turned on her heel and left the room. Jung thought he had noticed a few twitches at one side of her mouth, but that was all. There was no denying the fact that both he and Reinhart had felt somewhat uncomfortable after that first round – and when Mathilde Ubrecht was ushered in and presented with the same unvarnished facts as her friend, Jung at least was worried that they were going to be faced with the same silent reaction all three times. The same rigid autism.

But that was not what happened. Instead, in the case of Miss Ubrecht, it was a dam bursting. Before they had the chance to take in what was happening, she had already lashed out with several blows and kicks (Jung's head, Reinhart's shin, Jung's back), hurled a chair and a vase across the room and run screaming straight into a wall. The latter – they assumed, at least – was a desperate attempt to knock herself senseless. They eventually forced her down to the floor, and by the time the significantly more hardened medical orderlies arrived, her bellowing had begun to sound more like a sort of epileptic gurgling. The older of the two orderlies produced a syringe and without any hesitation stuck it into her stomach, whereupon she lost consciousness after about ten seconds.

To be on the safe side, the orderlies stayed in an adjoining room when it was time for the third confrontation – with Ulriche Fischer, to whom Jung had already spoken. But when Reinhart delivered the news to her face, this time very cautiously and on his guard, she reacted at first as silently as Madeleine Zander. But then she slumped down over the table, her arms clasped round her head, and burst out crying.

'I expected this!' she whimpered, rubbing her fists back and forth over her face and the top of her head. 'There was no other explanation! He would never have abandoned us like that! He just couldn't!'

Not much more was said, and Inspector Jung at least was so shattered by now that he felt nothing more than extreme and genuine gratitude to the doctor who had been summoned in connection with Miss Ubrecht's outburst, who hurried into the room and wondered what the hell was going on.

'Routine investigation,' Reinhart explained. 'But we've finished now.'

Jung felt ready to drop when he clambered out of the car in the car park outside Grimm's Hotel. So much so that he firmly declined Reinhart's offer of a nightcap, and instead went straight to his room and collapsed onto the bed without having taken off anything but his jacket and shoes.

A hell of a Wednesday, as somebody had said.

There was something about Penderecki.

Something about this pain-filled Polish requiem that was quite unlike anything else he knew, and which almost without exception made him feel liberated. Cleansed, and as tall as a cathedral.

Touched by the divine, as Mahler would have said. His good friend the poet, that is. Not the composer.

And of course it was also to do with suspense. Suspense loosening its grip, and suspense building up; a sort of acupuncture of the soul, and an escape route away from the torments of the flesh. Probably also Mahler's words, he assumed . . . Something that applied to all music, in fact; but nowhere else was it so clear and so painfully beautiful as in Penderecki.

And it was in this space, under this dome of cruel clarity, that he drove the two hundred kilometres from Stamberg back to Sorbinowo.

And in that space that he solved the remaining questions in the Waldingen case.

This case that had been going on for two weeks now. No matter how he calculated this never-ending period, filled with evil, it was no more than fourteen days since he had stood in the car park and gazed out over the idyllic summer vista and the dark, glittering water.

Two weeks.

Two raped and murdered young girls. A priest beaten to death.

A burned-down church and a sect in meltdown.

That was the gist of it.

The yield of his final case. A pretty good conclusion, he thought. No doubt about that.

And the solution, what could you say about that? It had come to him via a mundane telephone directory. Thanks to an extremely trivial misspelling. The familiar old thought about lines and patterns and tuning in to existential processes felt so straightforward that he didn't even bother to keep it in mind.

Don't look a gift horse in the mouth, he thought. At least one difference between real life and a game of chess.

No, better to try to anticipate what would happen in a few hours' time, and to concentrate on what remained to be done. The conclusion. Confronting the guilty people with what they were accused of. Making them give in and confess. Make them face up to the overwhelming proof, and watch them break down.

The last verse. The checkmate manoeuvre.

In the lowest possible number of moves.

Needless to say he was tempted to leave this to the others, but it was his duty, he knew that. That as well.

Patterns as patterns.

He allowed himself only a five-minute stop on the way back to Sorbinowo, and when he finally walked through the door into Grimm's Hotel after an absence of four days, it was no more than half past midnight. He asked to check the hotel ledger, and five minutes later he knocked on the door of Reinhart's room with two beers in each hand.

Two light and two dark.

For the first time since that afternoon in the boat he felt the stimulus. That tingling feeling in his groin and thighs, and he knew that the time had come once more. Time to come to terms with it.

After watching a rather insipid action thriller on the television, he went to bed around midnight, tried to masturbate himself to sleep, but wasn't up to it. Lay awake for a few hours, waiting while the urge grew stronger and stronger and eventually dominated more or less every nook and cranny of his being. The compulsion. That evil instinct.

In the end he got out of bed. It was only just starting to get light, and he hesitated for a moment. Stared out of the window at the narrow bands of red over the forest to the east. Thought about the girls. About their outspread legs and fluffy cunts. Their naked helplessness. Then he dressed, checked to make sure he had the condoms in his breast pocket – the little extra pleasure he derived from rolling them into place was not to be scoffed at. He smiled at his indistinct reflection in the mirror, tiptoed down the stairs and out through the kitchen door.

Fetched his bicycle from the shed. Checked the tyre pressure and secured the rubber baton to the luggage carrier. Set off.

It took him twenty minutes to get to the main road. The regular pedalling sparked off an impulse that aroused images in his mind's eye of what was in store, overpowering and with no room for mercy.

No room for mercy. The black rubber baton that forced its way in and opened up the way. Their smoothly resilient skin. So smooth and so magnificently resilient. The hole, that hole. The pleasure that passeth all understanding. The wild terror in their eyes before he extinguished the sparkle. Extinguished it for ever.

Powerful images. Irresistible images. He checked his

watch. Only half past three. He would have to lie down in the forest and wait for a few hours, but that didn't seem much of a problem. The main point was that the time had come once more. That before long – before the day that was just breaking had come to a close – he would meet another one . . . Fair hair: he hoped that she would have long, fair hair this time. Yes indeed, if circumstances dictated that he would have a choice, that's the one he would select.

He pedalled away, and listened to the rhythm that welled up inside him.

37

There were three cars.

Van Veeteren, Reinhart and Kluuge were in the first one. Then came Tolltse and Lauremaa, with Jung and Servinus bringing up the rear. At his own request Suijderbeck stayed behind in the police station; obviously it was not a bad idea to have some back-up there. In case something went wrong – it had happened before.

They set off at exactly a quarter to four, when the first signs of dawn were no more than a faint hint over the string of lakes and the sleeping forests. Waking everybody up, assembling and bringing them all up to date had taken a fair amount of time; the chief inspector had reported, elaborated and explained at a leisurely pace, but once the truth had sunk in everybody agreed that there was no real reason to wait until a new day had dawned.

Better to strike while the iron is hot – both Reinhart and Van Veeteren were well aware what a few extra hours presented unnecessarily to a murderer might lead to. In the worst-case scenario.

And there were indications that this was a worst-case scenario.

They arrived at twenty minutes past four. A grey mist was slowly lifting over the lake, and the forest was filled with the sound of birds. They parked in a row on the narrow dirt road, and approached the house in close formation; the chief inspector belted twice on the door, but there was no sign of life.

He tried the handle. The door wasn't locked, and as quietly as possible the whole group crept in and assembled in the pitch-black living room. Jung found a switch and turned on the light. The chief inspector nodded to Kluuge, and they set off together up the stairs.

They paused halfway up. A door opened on the upper floor and Mrs Fingher came towards them.

She was wearing slippers and a worn blue dressing gown, but displayed no obvious signs of having been woken up.

Van Veeteren nodded again at Kluuge.

'Mrs Fingher,' said Kluuge. 'I'd like to arrest you on suspicion of having murdered Oscar Yellinek, and for . . .'

He lost the thread. Would like to? Reinhart thought.

'. . . And for complicity in the murders of Clarissa Heerenmacht and Katarina Schwarz. You have the right to remain silent, but anything you say may be used in evidence against you.'

Mrs Fingher stood still and hung on to the banister. A shudder passed over her roughly chiselled face, then she sank down onto the stair and buried her face in her hands. Five seconds passed.

'It's all over now,' said Van Veeteren, holding out his hand.

She grasped it and he led her down to the living room. Sat her down on one of the upright armchairs and waited for a few more seconds. He took out a handkerchief and blew his nose.

'Yes,' she said eventually. 'It's all over now.'

'Where's your son?' Reinhart asked.

She gestured with her head towards the upper floor. Reinhart and Jung set off up the stairs and vanished into the darkness.

'Why did you kill Oscar Yellinek?' the chief inspector asked.

She took a deep breath.

'I had to,' she said.

'Really?' said the chief inspector.

'He turned up.'

'Turned up?'

She shuddered once again, but it didn't seem to affect her adversely. The chief inspector realized that the border between her body and her mind was sealed off for the time being.

'Yes, on the road. He turned up.'

'Just after you had left Clarissa's body by the aspen tree?'

She nodded.

'Yes. I saw . . . I saw that he understood. He said as much. What else could I do?'

'How did you go about it?'

'The spade,' she said. 'I hit him with the spade. I'm sorry . . . I had . . . It was . . .'

But there was no follow-up. Instead, Reinhart appeared on the landing.

'He's not in his bed,' he explained. 'Where's your son, Mrs Fingher?'

She looked up in surprise.

'I don't understand . . .'

'What the hell's going on?'

Mathias Fingher's powerful bulk – in pale blue washed-out pyjamas – elbowed its way past Reinhart, with Jung in tow.

'What the devil do you think—'

'Sit down and shut up!' said Van Veeteren, cutting him short. 'We have come to arrest your son for the murder of two little girls, and your wife for the murder of Oscar Yellinek!'

'What?'

'Are you claiming that you knew nothing about it?' snapped Reinhart. 'You are also under suspicion of complicity and withholding information.'

For a moment it looked as if Mathias Fingher was about to faint. He swayed, but recovered his balance. Walked down the remaining stairs, looked round in confusion, and was then pushed down onto the striped sofa by Servinus.

'What the hell . . . ?' he stammered. 'There must be . . .'

'I'm sorry,' said Mrs Fingher without looking at her husband. 'It's . . . There just wasn't any other way.'

'Go to hell!' bellowed Reinhart. 'What have you done with your son?'

'Well?' said the chief inspector.

'He must be asleep . . .' said Mrs Fingher. 'Why . . . ?'

'Are you saying you don't know where he is?'

'No, how . . .'

It didn't take Van Veeteren many seconds to realize that her surprise was genuine.

'Jung and Servinus!' he said. 'Search the upstairs rooms! Lauremaa and Tolltse, take Mrs Fingher to the car!'

'But . . .' said Mathias Fingher.

'Let her get dressed first.'

The chief inspector shoved Servinus out of the way and sat down opposite Mr Fingher. Stared into his eyes from half a metre away.

'Mr Fingher,' he said. 'It's possible that you know

nothing at all about any of this, in which case you're in a goddamned awful situation. But the fact is that your son is a murderer and a rapist.'

Fingher opened and closed his mouth several times, and once again looked as if he were about to lose consciousness. His face was drained of colour, and his hands were shaking on his knee.

'We have to get him. Where is he?'

'I . . . I don't know.'

'When did you last see him?'

'It . . . Yesterday evening.'

'He was watching a film on the telly,' interrupted Mrs Fingher. 'We went to bed earlier.'

'And why isn't he in his bed now?'

Mathias Fingher shook his enormous head.

'He's probably gone out,' said Mrs Fingher and went to get dressed. Tolltse and Lauremaa followed close behind her. A few seconds of silence followed.

'Gentlemen,' burst out Mathias Fingher to break it. 'Tell me you're only joking! For Christ's sake tell me you're only joking!'

'I'm afraid not,' said the chief inspector.

'The missing bike!' said Reinhart. 'The bastard has gone off on his bike!'

The caravan was on its way back to base through the forest. In slightly different formation – the chief inspector, Reinhart and Jung in the first car. Tolltse, Lauremaa and Mrs Fingher in the second. Kluuge, Servinus and Mr Fingher in the third.

'What should we do now?' said Jung.

'Issue a Wanted notice, of course!' snorted Reinhart. 'Get every damned police officer for miles around out of bed and set 'em on the bastard's tail! On his bike!'

Van Veeteren nodded.

'Phone Suijderbeck immediately,' he said. 'It's not five o'clock yet, but we can't lose any more time. Yes, get that Wanted notice out in every single branch of the media that exists!'

Reinhart followed the chief inspector's instructions, then stepped on the gas.

'I feel awful,' he said. 'Fucking hell, I hate every second of this! We're up the creek without a paddle again.'

Van Veeteren said nothing.

'Do we have a picture?' wondered Jung.

'Hell's bells,' said Reinhart. 'Of course we ought to . . .'

'Przebuda,' said Van Veeteren.

'Eh?' said Jung.

'The local newspaper,' the chief inspector explained. 'They must have one. I'll phone the editor and wake him up when we get to the station.'

Reinhart cleared his throat.

'Do you think . . . ?' he began. 'I mean, do you think he's at it again?'

'What do you think?' said Van Veeteren.

For the rest of the journey all three of them remained immersed in their own silence.

38

Van Veeteren carried the tray in himself and placed it in front of Mirjan Fingher.

Tea. Juice. Sandwiches with cheese and cold sausage. He stepped back to close the door, then sat down on the other bunk.

'Help yourself,' he said. 'I have a few questions. I take it for granted that you will cooperate – there's no point in making things even more difficult for yourself.'

She nodded and took a sip of tea. He watched her closely. Her powerfully built body seemed to have shrunk during the journey to Sorbinowo. It was noticeably smaller. As if her outer features were being eaten up from inside, he thought.

'Where do you think he is?'

She tried to shrug, but it remained no more than an attempt.

'I don't know.'

Her voice was on the very edge of breaking down.

'We must catch him before he does it again,' said the chief inspector. 'The way we look at it there's quite a big risk that he's gone off for that very reason. Or do you have any other suggestion?'

She shook her head.

'No.'

'He surely can't have known that we were on our way?'

'No . . . No, certainly not. I think . . .'

'Well?'

'I think it could well be like you say.'

Not much more than a whisper. How much longer can she keep going? he asked himself. We must make sure she holds herself together.

'Have a sandwich,' he said. 'Let's see if we can sort this out now.'

She looked at him. Stroked back a wisp of her pale brown hair and straightened her back slightly. Took another sip of tea but didn't touch anything else.

'Yes,' she said. 'That's probably it. A longer time has passed than between the other two.'

Van Veeteren nodded and changed his toothpick for a new one.

'How much did you know about it?'

'A fair amount.'

'Were you the one who phoned?'

'Yes.'

'How did you know when he'd done it?'

'I could tell by looking at him. I'm his mother, after all.'

'Why did you make that call?'

'To put a stop to it.'

'Make sure the girls moved out?'

'I don't know . . . Yes, I suppose so.'

'You found the bodies and then moved them so that we would find them?'

'Only one of them.'

'You didn't find the first one?'

'Not to start with, no. But . . .'

'Yes?'

'I thought . . . No, I don't know what I thought. I daren't go after the first one, but then I was forced . . . Yes.'

He hesitated for a moment. Saw that she was starting to tremble now. Her hands were shaking, her face twitching.

'His daughter?' he said eventually.

'Yes.' She cleared her throat and braced herself. 'She . . . My daughter-in-law told me about it when they divorced. It was . . . Well, I refused to believe her of course, but I understood eventually. If it's possible to understand. I thought it was all over and done with, you have to believe that. Nothing had happened all those years since he moved back home. Not until that sect, those damned young girls . . .'

'Last summer?' asked the chief inspector.

She shook her head.

'No. Wim was working in Groenstadt for a few months then. For my brother. He has a market garden. I found some magazines he'd hidden away, and so . . .'

She dried up.

'I understand,' said Van Veeteren. 'But let's get back to the most important thing. Where do you think he is right now? You must try and help us with this.'

She gazed out of the window and appeared to be thinking.

'In the forest,' she said in due course. 'That's where he feels safe, as it were, he might well be there – oh God!'

She suddenly seemed to fall to pieces. She flung herself down onto the floor on her knees next to the bunk, wrapped her arms around her head and began swaying from side to side.

'Help him, please! Please help him!'

Van Veeteren stooped down and stroked her back rather awkwardly. Then he opened the door and shouted for Inspector Tolltse.

No, he thought. I can't take any more of this.

'We haven't forgotten anything, I hope?' said Reinhart.

'The Wanted messages are all seen to,' said Kluuge.

'All over the country!' snorted Suijderbeck. 'This is

where the bastard's lying in wait. He's riding a bike, have you forgotten that?'

'We have twenty-five officers in place here,' continued Kluuge, not to be deterred. 'And twenty more on their way. Two helicopters have already scrambled.'

'And the summer camps warned,' said Lauremaa.

'How many of those are there?' wondered Jung.

'Far too many,' said Kluuge with a sigh. 'At the moment we have between three and four hundred girls of about the right age in various camps.'

'Good God!' said Reinhart.

'But they've been given strict instructions,' said Lauremaa.

'That's no guarantee,' said Servinus.

'No,' said Reinhart. 'There are never any guarantees in our line of business, dammit.'

Inspector Lauremaa stood up in irritation and walked over to the window.

'Anyway,' she said, 'if he turns up on the streets of this town, he's had it. Every man jack will recognize him. We'll catch him all right, it's just a matter of time.'

'There's something else that's just a matter of time,' said Reinhart.

'I know,' said Lauremaa. 'I don't need reminding.'

The door opened and Van Veeteren came in, a toothpick sticking out of each side of his mouth. He flopped down onto Lauremaa's empty chair and looked around.

'The forest,' he said. 'His mother thinks he's in the forest.'

Nobody spoke for a few seconds.

'Okay,' said Suijderbeck. 'That sounds plausible. We can tell the helicopters to do a sweep over the forest. Around the lake first and foremost, that's probably where he thinks he'll get a bite.'

'Most probably,' said Jung. 'What kind of communications set-up do we have access to?'

'The cars parked outside,' said Suijderbeck, pointing. 'Servinus and I will see to that right away. What are the twenty-five officers who've already arrived doing?'

'Waiting for orders,' said Kluuge.

'Right, out into the forest with them,' said Suijderbeck. 'Long lines of them scouring the other side of the lake, or what do you think?'

'Yes,' said Kluuge. 'That's probably the best plan.'

'Oh hell!' said Jung. 'Do you know what? Something's just occurred to me. I saw a guy with a bike when we were driving to Waldingen. Last night, that is. He was having a pee against a tree trunk, his bicycle on the ground beside him. I only saw his back, but it could well have been him . . .'

'Oh my God!' groaned Reinhart. 'And they've made you an inspector?'

Jung shook his head and muttered something.

'Weren't you driving along the same road as well?' asked Van Veeteren.

'Enough of that,' said Lauremaa. 'If it was him, at least it shows that we're searching in the right place.'

'It's a quarter to eight,' said Suijderbeck. 'Let's get out there and catch this bastard!'

He woke up and looked at his watch.

Five minutes to eight.

He'd managed to snatch a few hours' sleep. It felt good, and he'd needed it.

Not a bad place either. Protected and warmed up by the sun. He could just see the lake beyond the fir trees, and in the distance he could hear the voices of young girls playing away merrily. Presumably he'd been able to hear them while he was asleep – his insides were in tumult already, and his erection was as hard as his baton.

He realized he was holding the baton in his hand. Gave a laugh, took hold of his own with his other hand and compared them.

A blonde, he thought. Ten points for a blonde.

But anything else would also be okay, of course.

He raised himself up on his elbows and gazed down the slope towards the water.

★

'I lost it yesterday,' explained Helene Klausner. 'When we were up there.'

She pointed into the trees.

'It must be still there. Are you coming with me?'

Ruth Najda shook her head.

'It's breakfast in ten minutes. And they told us not to go anywhere. Something's happened. They're having a meeting now.'

'It'll only take five minutes.'

'I don't want to.'

'You can borrow my diving mask.'

'I've already said, I don't want to.'

'Will you wait here then while I go and look myself?'

Ruth Najda clambered down from the rock.

'I think we should go to the dining room now. The rest are there already. You can fetch it later. It's only a hairslide, for goodness sake!'

Helene Klausner shook her long, fair hair.

'Maybe, but I need it now. I'm going anyway. Will you wait for me?'

'Okay,' said Ruth Najda with a sigh. 'But you'd better hurry up. I'm hungry.'

'Five minutes!' shouted Helene as she hurried into the trees.

39

Jung settled down behind Suijderbeck and Servinus in the radio patrol car. Felt how exhaustion was slowly taking possession of him as he stared at the red digital figures, slowly ticking out the ponderous minutes of morning.

08.16

08.17

How many more minutes? he thought. Before something happens. A hundred? A thousand?

Was there really anything to suggest that Wim Fingher really was still here in Sorbinowo? And not somewhere else? Anywhere else in the world?

If he'd happened to hear the radio for just one minute that morning, he must have known that they were on his trail. That he was a hunted quarry – and even if he was a mad murderer, he must have had enough sense to get the hell out of there.

By bike or on foot.

Through the forests.

Surely even a lunatic like him must have a certain kind of logic?

'What do you think?' he asked.

'Hmm, I'm damned if I know,' said Servinus. 'What do you think?'

'Hard to say. Obviously it would be most convenient if—'

'Shut up!' roared Suijderbeck, adjusting his earphones. 'What did you say? . . . Okay! . . . Good! . . . Where exactly? . . . After the bridge? Which fucking bridge? . . . Yes, I understand. I'll inform the others. Over and out.'

'Ha!' he said as he slid down his earphones so that they hung round his neck. 'They've found his bike. The bastard can't be far away now!'

'Where?' said Jung.

'The main road where the bridge crosses over between the lakes. Just on the other side.'

'Okay,' said Jung. 'I'm on my way there, to help out.'

'What the hell . . . ?' said Reinhart, adjusting the focus.

'What have you seen?' asked the chief inspector.

He eased back the throttle and the engine spluttered to a halt.

'There's a young girl sitting all by herself on a rock on the other side over there. Look!'

Reinhart handed over his binoculars and pointed at the bathing beach. Van Veeteren scanned the water and the forest several times before he found the right spot.

'My God, yes . . .' he said. 'There's a summer camp round about there, I'm pretty sure.'

'Start the engine again,' said Reinhart. 'She can't sit there, for Christ's sake!'

After several failed attempts, Van Veeteren eventually coaxed the outboard motor back to life and they headed straight across the lake. Reinhart was crouching in the bows with the binoculars, Van Veeteren in the stern, huddled up in an attempt to avoid the worst of the wind and the spray.

I prefer canoes, the chief inspector thought. God knows how much I prefer them. But I haven't escaped from this treadmill yet, of course.

'Hi there,' said the man, standing up.

She paused. Brushed her long hair from out of her eyes and squinted at him.

'Hi,' she said.

'What are you doing here?' he asked.

'What are you doing here yourself?'

He burst out laughing.

'I like people like you,' he said. 'I'm not doing anything special. Just looking for mushrooms – if there are any yet.'

'Oh, there are,' she said. 'We picked a whole bagful the other day. But we had to throw most of them away. Our teachers said they weren't edible, but I think they only said that because they couldn't be bothered to trim and clean them. Why haven't you got anything to put your mushrooms in? What's that thing?'

She pointed at the rubber thing he was holding in his hand.

'This?' he said, with a smile. 'Would you like me to show you how to use it?'

She checked her watch.

'Sorry, I don't have time,' she said. 'I'm just looking for my hairslide. I lost it up here yesterday.'

'Your hair?' he said, and gulped.

'Yes, it was somewhere near here.'

She made a sweeping gesture.

'Let me help you to find it.'

She smiled at him.

'Thank you! How nice of you. This way!'

'What are you doing here?' said Reinhart.

The girl slithered down from the rock.

'What do you mean?'

They got out of the boat and pulled it up a few metres onto the narrow beach.

'We're looking for somebody,' explained the chief inspector. 'Haven't you been told not to go off on your own today?'

'No . . . Well, yes, but I'm waiting for a friend.'

'A friend?' said Reinhart.

'Yes, she was just going to fetch something.'

'What exactly?'

'A hairslide.'

'And where had she left it?' asked Van Veeteren impatiently.

'She'd lost it up there in the woods yesterday.'

She gestured up the slope.

'What's your name?' asked Reinhart.

'Ruth Najda. And who are you?'

'We're police officers,' said Reinhart. 'So you're saying that your friend has gone up into the woods to look for her hairband, is that right?'

'Hairslide,' said Ruth Najda. 'Not hairband.'

'Okay. When did she set off?'

The girl checked her watch then shrugged her shoulders.

'A quarter of an hour ago, more or less. She said she'd be back in five minutes, but that was thirteen and a half minutes ago.'

'Hell and damnation!' said Reinhart. 'Show us exactly which way she took!'

'Why are you so—' Ruth Najda began, but the chief inspector interrupted her.

'Get on with it!' he bellowed. 'We're in a hurry and this isn't a game!'

'Okay,' said the girl, and set off through the alders.

'How's it going?' yelled Suijderbeck into the microphone. 'Can't you switch off that damned engine so that we can hear what you say?'

'It's not easy to fly a helicopter without an engine,' explained the voice. 'But we caught a glimpse of somebody down below a couple of minutes ago. It might have been him. And the guys down there are hot on his heels.'

'Well done!' roared Suijderbeck. 'Make sure he doesn't get away, because if he does I'll be up there with you before you know what's hit you, and kick you all out one after another. Is that clear?'

There was a crackling noise over and over again. Then:

'Your name's Suijderbeck, is that right?'

'Yes. Why?'

'I thought I recognized your style, that's all.'

'Over and out,' said Suijderbeck.

*

It was Reinhart who saw them first.

He glimpsed the girl's long, fair hair flashing past some tree trunks, then Wim Fingher's back appeared briefly. Then they came into full view as they emerged from between two large, moss-covered boulders – first the girl and then, ever so close behind, the murderer, clutching a black baton in his hand.

Van Veeteren stopped dead. Reinhart stumbled, recovered his balance and reached for his gun – but it wasn't necessary: at that very moment there was a commotion in the thicket and two uniformed police officers came racing out. One threw himself at Wim Fingher in a flying tackle that wouldn't have been out of place in any American B-movie you could think of, the chief inspector thought. It sent him crashing to the ground, and the other officer stood with his legs wide apart, his pistol aimed at the murderer's head from a metre away.

'If you move just one centimetre, you fucking monster, I'll blow your brains out,' he explained patiently.

All in all a very professional operation, and the chief inspector suddenly felt utterly exhausted.

Bottomless exhaustion, and he realized that he hadn't slept a wink for over twenty-four hours.

*

'Why did you do that?' asked Helene Klausner.

'It was necessary,' Reinhart explained. 'He's sick.'

'Sick?'

'Yes,' said Reinhart. 'Did he touch you?'

'Touch me? No, he was just helping me to find my hair-slide. This.'

She waved something sky-blue. The chief inspector nodded.

'Good,' he said. 'But shouldn't you be having breakfast now? Off you go!'

'All right. Bye-bye!'

They watched the girls slowly ambling towards the red building a little further along the shore.

'Can I borrow your diving mask now?' they heard the dark-haired girl ask. 'I was waiting all the time, and you promised . . .'

'Yes, of course,' said the blonde cheerfully, setting up her hair with a well-practised movement. 'Let's have breakfast first, though.'

The chief inspector cleared his throat and went to sit down in the boat.

'That's that, then,' he said. 'Would you be so kind as to cast off.'

*

Kluuge tried to glare into the telephone receiver.

It was three in the afternoon, he was in bed and Deborah was massaging his shoulders and chest. She was sitting astride him, and he could feel the baby pressing up against his own stomach. It was a divinely inspired moment, in both a spiritual and physical sense, no doubt about that. And then Chief of Police Malijsen interrupted it with a telephone call!

'Why the hell didn't you let me know?' he screeched. 'You ought to have known that you couldn't handle a situation like this on your own. It was just an amazing stroke of luck that it didn't end in chaos! I shall make sure personally that you get . . .'

Kluuge placed the receiver under the pillow and thought for three seconds. Then he took it out again.

'Shut your trap, you stupid bugger!' he said, and hung up.

'Well done,' said Deborah.

40

As far as he could recall, those present were the same as last time, and it was a while before he was alone with the editor.

'Well, what do you think?' asked Przebuda. 'I expect you've seen it before?'

Van Veeteren nodded.

'Yes, of course,' said Van Veeteren. 'I can't say that Mazursky is one of my favourites, but *The Tempest* is one of his best.'

'I agree entirely,' said Przebuda. 'Three cheers for *The Tempest*. There's something special about Crete as well.'

'There certainly is,' said Van Veeteren. 'Can I buy you a drink?'

Przebuda shook his head demonstratively. Then he smiled.

'No chance,' he said. 'But I have a decent meal up

my sleeve, and a few good wines. A Margaux '71 and a Mersault.'

'Why are we hanging around here, then?' wondered the chief inspector.

'Case closed, I take it?' assumed Przebuda after the mushroom pasty, veal medallions in a lemon sauce, watercress salad and one and a half bottles of wine.

'Yes,' said Van Veeteren. 'Case closed. A very nasty business. There are no extenuating circumstances when children are attacked. And heaven remains silent.'

'And heaven remains silent,' echoed Przebuda. 'Yes, it tends to do that. How did you work it out? That he was the one, I mean?'

The chief inspector leaned back and paused for a few moments before answering.

'It was in the telephone directory,' he said eventually.

'The telephone directory?'

'Yes. Do you remember Ewa Siguera?'

The editor hesitated.

'Er, that woman in the photograph?'

'Yes. Her name wasn't Siguera. It was Figuera. You'd heard wrongly. Or written it down wrongly.'

'Good God,' said Przebuda and froze, his glass halfway to his mouth. 'You surely don't mean that if . . .'

The chief inspector shook his head.

'No. Don't worry. The dead were already dead. It's just that things might have gone a bit faster.'

Mind you, on second thoughts he realized that this wasn't actually the case. The reverse was more likely, in fact. If he'd had the right name from the start, he might well never have caught on to the realities. Not in time, anyway – in time to prevent that girl with the blonde hair and the hairslide from . . . No, he preferred not to imagine what might have happened.

Przebuda was sitting there in silence, and seemed to be meditating.

'I don't understand this,' he said. 'What the devil had Ewa Siguera – sorry, Figuera – to do with Wim Fingher?'

'Nothing,' said the chief inspector. 'Nothing at all. This really is an excellent wine. It's so rare to find this very dry aftertaste penetrating even under the tongue . . .'

'I have another bottle,' said Przebuda. 'Cheers!'

They drank.

'Well?'

'Nothing at all, as I said,' the chief inspector resumed. 'But when I was preparing to call Figuera, I came across the name Fingher on the same page. The same column, in fact, just a couple of lines further down. It's not exactly a common name . . .'

Przebuda tried to nod and shake his head at the same time.

'Anyway, then I remembered the two comments I'd heard when I called on them the second time, on the Thursday. It must have been Mathias Fingher – the father, that is – who said both of them. He said that they only had one son, and he mentioned that his wife was going to visit a grandchild. Or it could have been her who said that.'

Przebuda said nothing, but toyed with his glass.

'Nevertheless . . . ?' he said eventually. 'It can't have been a very convincing indication, surely? Why should he be a murderer, just because he'd been married and had a daughter?'

The chief inspector shrugged.

'I seem to recall that the last time we met, my editor friend spoke warmly about something called intuition. His wife had retained his name – she didn't know why, but it acquired a significance in the end.'

'Well I'll be damned!' said Przebuda after another pause. 'It gives the impression of having been stage-managed. Who was this Ewa Figuera, then?'

Van Veeteren lit a cigarette.

'She was a friend of one of the three women out at the camp,' he said. 'She has nothing at all to do with the Pure Life. She just happened to be visiting them for one day only last summer, and . . .'

'And that was when I was there and took the picture,' said Przebuda. 'It's absolutely amazing, because if . . .'

He fell silent and stared up at the ceiling, as if searching for an answer among the dark recesses.

'. . . If I hadn't shown you that picture, and all the rest of it. What an amazing coincidence!'

'There's no such thing as coincidence,' said the chief inspector. 'This was merely one of the threads leading us to the goal. There are hundreds of other possible threads. If life is a tree, it shouldn't make all that much of a difference if you happen to land up on one particular branch or any other – if you're looking for the root, that is. Or whatever else it is you're looking for.'

Przebuda thought that over for a while.

'I'll go and fetch that other bottle,' he said in due course.

'What about the women?' asked Przebuda a little later. 'Those tight-lipped priestesses – why the hell did they refuse to say anything?'

'They thought that was the party line,' said Van Veeteren. 'Presumably Yellinek gagged them in connection with the disappearance of the other girl, before he was murdered himself and vanished into thin air. And then I suppose it was just a question of following the prophet's word. As usual, you might say. Both Mohammed and

Christ have been dead for quite a long time, if I'm not much mistaken.'

Przebuda smiled.

'How are they now? The women, I mean.'

Van Veeteren hesitated for a moment.

'I don't really know,' he said. 'Two of them left Wolgers-huus together this afternoon. The third one, Madeleine Zander, has apparently asked to stay on.'

'Stay on?'

'Yes.'

'Ah well, perhaps that indicates that she suspects she's not right in the head,' muttered Przebuda as he squeezed the last drops out of the final bottle of Burgundy.

'What about Wim?' he asked. 'Wim Fingher?'

The chief inspector shrugged again.

'A case for the medics, I should think. It's odd that he can be more or less normal nearly all the time . . . As far as we know he's only attacked his own daughter, and then these two. I can't say if he'll end up in jail or in a loony bin. I'm not even sure what I think myself.'

'But it will be jail for Mirjan Fingher, I suppose?'

'Without a doubt. What she did was both rational and logical.'

'And defensible as well, perhaps,' said Przebuda. 'Obviously, you can't just wander around killing any priest you come across . . . But from a mother's point of view . . .'

'You may be right,' said Van Veeteren. 'One might also ask who was worst affected by this nasty business. The poor girls and their families, of course, but I don't think we should forget Mathias Fingher in this connection. Maybe you could call in on him if you happen to be in his neighbourhood.'

'Yes indeed,' said Andrej Przebuda, raising his glass. 'Poor devil! Anyway, let's finish this off.'

It was turned half past one when he crossed Kleinmarckt for the last time, on his way back to Grimm's. The bar next door to the town hall was still open, but there was not much sign of night life there. The reporters had evidently been summoned back home as soon as the case was solved; as soon as the final whistle blew. As usual. The priority now was to construct a psychological portrait of the murderer instead – childhood, injustices suffered at school, let-downs, and all the rest of it.

The dead are dead, Van Veeteren thought. But the killers are still alive and are newsworthy. Every dog has its day.

Reinhart, Jung and the rest of them had also left Sorbinowo that afternoon: he was the only one to stay on for an extra day.

As if that was what decency required of him, he

thought. As if all those involved needed to have a line drawn underneath what had happened. Guilty or innocent. Victim or perpetrator.

All these social castaways, he thought.

And all this evil. All this accursed, uncontrollable murkiness that had flooded the stage on which he'd been performing for the last thirty-five years now. Always lurking in the background and ready to strike the moment you turned your back or dropped your guard. This brooding enemy that cast a shadow over all happiness, and made all rest seem indecent.

Was it more than just an illness, this murkiness? It didn't matter, you only needed to look at the result, at the people affected – maybe this was the context in which the problem ought to be described. His own problem, and that weighing down on everybody else.

As the difference between the motives of actions, and their consequences. Was this the vital factor that created evil?

Not really. He could see that this was merely one angle of incidence. One of several hundred more possibilities. As he walked down the steps towards the lake, he began to wonder if the Pure Life would ever resurrect itself. But he soon realized that this was not the heart of the matter either.

Would all those people, all those misled members, be

able to resurrect themselves – that was the question. Resurrect themselves as – as people.

Then another concept occurred to him.

God's finger.

God's Fingher?

No, time to put a stop to all this. Time to stop theorizing simply in order not to have to think about the bodies of those dead girls. I shall never be able to forget them.

And as he entered Grimm's Hotel, it occurred to him that this was the very evening, the very night, when he ought to have been going to bed at Christos. A hundred metres from the Venetian harbour at Rethymnon.

By hook or by crook.

Too bad, he thought. I'll call her when she gets back home instead. Time and space are concepts for cretins.

Yes indeed, for cretins.

SEVEN

10 AUGUST

41

When he woke up. the dream was lingering on inside his head.

The image with the pale girls in the background, at the very edge of the water. Slim figures in groups of three or four – and a strange, shimmering light over the lake and over the outline of the forest to the east. Morning. Yes, definitely morning.

The two dead bodies in the foreground.

Naked and strangely twisted. Covered in wounds and swellings, and big black holes instead of eyes – but even so they seem to be staring at him, accusingly.

Girls' bodies. Dead and violated girls' bodies.

Then the fire. Tongues of flame spurting out of the water, and soon the whole image is consumed by flames. A sea of fire. He can feel the heat in his face. Then he turns his back on it all and hurries away.

The same short dream. No more than one sequence, or a tableau. The third night now.

And when the image of Wim Fingher crops up, he is already awake. Inexorably awake. The murderer. Throughout the whole of the investigation he has been a mere stone's throw away from the crime scene, and on two occasions Van Veeteren has been face to face with him without reacting.

Unforgivable.

The ultimate signal.

He got out of bed. Opened the balcony door: pale sky, a warm, barely noticeable breeze.

A few half-hearted back exercises in front of the mirror.

Then breakfast and the *Allgemejne*. That took an hour; the mate-in-three chess problem another half – it all depended on the knight, the most difficult of all the pieces to master.

He showered, dressed and went out. Another of those friction-free days, he noted. Blank and unspecified, and a temperature that ensured the air had no effect on the skin. Not many people about on the streets. Holiday time – more crowded in the centre, no doubt, around Keymer Plejn and Grote Square where the tourists generally gathered. But that wasn't where he was going.

Instead he headed down towards Zwille. Crossed over Langgraacht and turned into Kellnerstraat from the opposite direction this time. It was only eleven o'clock, and he indulged in a glass of beer at Yorrick's first.

Sat outside under one of the lime trees, and took his time. Observed what was happening around him. The few passers-by. The Art Nouveau facades. The green crowns of the trees and the pale sky. Listened out for any whispers and doubts inside himself, but there weren't any.

So, let it come to pass, he thought. Emptied his glass and crossed over the road.

Pressed down the handle and walked in. A bell over the door announced his arrival. An elderly man – almost white-haired and with a full beard in the same shade – had been studying a map with the aid of a magnifying glass. He looked up. Gave him a nod and seemed to be slightly drowsy.

'Good morning,' said Van Veeteren. 'I'm here in connection with that sign in the window.'

'Welcome,' said the man.

extracts reading groups
competitions books new
discounts extracts events
competitions reading groups discounts
books
new
reading groups events books
extracts extracts
new
title reading groups
new books
interviews
events extracts extracts
discounts events
new books events interviews
events new events books extracts
discounts extracts discounts
www.panmacmillan.com
extracts events reading groups
competitions books extracts new